CLARE SOLLY

Christmas
&
Cleats

CLARE SOLLY

For Erin, my Hetty.

And for Jess, Joe, Henry, and Jack who adopted an elf into their lives and gave me Christmas in Connecticut.

CHAPTER ONE

Dottie took out her irritation on the shopping cart as she yanked to release one from the others. The cart squealed from abuse and an auburn curl fell in her face. She sighed heavily moving the curl for an instant before it obstinately flopped back in her face. This had been one of the worst weeks of her life. Her beloved museum, The East Haddam Historical Society was floundering. It had little money because of the late decline of visitors and several much-needed repairs. Dottie loved the place and didn't want it to close forever. She had put her life blood into it ever since her father had his stroke and her mother had to stop overseeing the curation of the museum. Dottie felt like she had grown up in those halls, taking in all of the town's history. But now it was failing. How would she ever pull the museum out of debt?

Meeting earlier today with the board, it truly seemed like there was no hope. If she didn't get some sort of profitable change by the end of December, the museum would have no choice but to close. This magnificent building held items that chronicled the history of the whole town. How could they close it? Over the years, the number of visitors had sadly declined. It was reduced to school groups and the ladies quilting society that met every Tuesday. Shaking off the thought of closure Dottie squared her shoulders and started down the first aisle. For now, she would ignore it all. She would at least take it back to its former glory for the holiday. Her focus in this moment was on decorating. Christmas season was her favorite time of year, after all.

She had come to Frankincense and Myrrh Hardware to get decorations to cheer herself. The larger-than-normal small-town hardware store was owned by Frank and Murray. The quintessential curmudgeons had an age-old rivalry to see who could get their house biggest and brightest with Christmas Decorations. It was a town holiday tradition for the last forty years. Murray claimed Frank had turned his hair white.

Distantly related second cousins, the two men had taken over the hardware store together adding more intrigue to their yearly contest. When Hetty, Dottie's best friend, was little she suggested the store be named Frankincense and Myrrh Hardware. Murray was her grandfather and Frank her godfather. So as a young child, immersed with the Christmas story of the wise men, thought that at the time, two of the wisest men she knew were taking over the hardware store as a gift to the town. Why shouldn't they call it Frankincense and Myrrh Hardware?

Dottie smiled for the first time in what felt like

weeks as she recalled the story. Even though Hetty was still a little embarrassed every time the story was told she took it in stride. She even started telling the story herself to patrons of the diner—Hetty had bought the place seven years ago. The local beauty queen with dark shiny hair and long legs; Hetty had won many pageants. Her talent was the flute, and her smile shone like a lighthouse and her blue eyes sparkled like the ocean. Everyone knew that was what really earned her the twenty-two crowns that decorated the diner The Queen's Table. Food was her passion and she served homemade favorites with a foodie twist. She was quite the chef and enjoyed eating. The best part about no longer competing she could eat whatever she wanted. Hetty believed that happy people had curves. These days Hetty was very happy but still gorgeous and her smile never faded.

However, even that award winning smile couldn't seem to keep the museum alive. Hetty was on board for the museum, but even she couldn't seem to talk the other trustees into keeping it open past the new year.

"Here, you need to be cheered up. Go buy some Christmas decorations." Hetty handed Dottie a handful of dollar bills after the meeting. The handful of ones and fives were Hetty's tips from the previous week. Hetty liked to call it her "fun money" and used it for any number of things.

"I... I don't know..." Dottie said defeatedly, trying to hand Hetty back the money.

"Come on," Hetty took her friend by the elbows, both as a way to shake sense into her friend and to make sure she kept the cash, "You *love* Christmas. I can't believe you haven't started decorating yet. You *know* Thanksgiving was five whole days ago. These past few years you've given 'Frankincense' and 'Myrrh' a run for their money in putting up decorations, and you know they always have them up by December first, always," Hetty said referring to her grandfather and godfather by the nicknames she had given them at the age of six.

"Ah yes, the Lamb and Van Allen of East Haddam," Dottie quipped.

"Go over to their store," she said shaking Dottie a little, "and go crazy." She squatted so she could look Dottie in the eye. "You know you want to. Now go." Hetty turned and shoved Dottie toward the door.

As Dottie walked up and down the holiday aisle, she dazedly filled the cart with lights, garland, bows and Christmas ornaments. Dottie turned the corner to find wreaths showcased at the end of the aisle. With only one left on the shelf at her eye level, she looked around to see if there were more. There were a few dozen on the higher shelf. Dottie knew that if she stood on her tiptoes, she could just reach the bottom one. She was sure that she could just give it a quick yank and only the bottom one would come out, like a magician with a table cloth.

Dottie reached as far as she could, but her fingertips barely touched the plastic green fringe. She had to have two, there were two doors at the front of the museum, the front door that led into the small mudroom or foyer, and the door into the front room of the museum. It was a Victorian style house that had been converted into a museum when it was bequeathed to the town when Esther Dorothy Williams had passed away with no known relatives.

Dottie's grandmother, then her mother ran the museum. It had a special place in Dottie's heart because she always loved history and would spend hours at the historical society all her life. She was determined to keep the museum afloat, or at least send it out with the best Christmas ever.

With no one nearby to help she put a food on the lowest shelf to give herself a boost. Grasping the shelf by her chest, she held on with her left hand and reached her right arm up as she stood on her tip toes. Dottie almost had a hold of the wreath. She pushed herself up on her toes a little higher. If she could only just—

Swoosh. All of the wreaths came falling down.

"OOOOUCH!" the deep male voice exclaimed from the next aisle.

She looked down as he came around the corner wrestling wreaths off of himself. "What in Pete's sake do you think you are doing you idiot—" He stopped as he removed the wreath from his sight and made eye contact. Of all the people to run into. Today. Why him?

"Dottie—" he said as his breath left him. A tall, handsome man looked up at her as she climbed off of the shelf. A two-day old beard peeked out of his chiseled jaw. Sun bleached curls recklessly peeked out from under a sun bleached, sweat stained baseball cap. In dirty jeans and a heavy Carhart jacket, he looked like he belonged in a hardware store. Well, more like the catalogue of a hardware store. Or one of those fundraiser calendars with hunky men.

She froze. She couldn't believe he was standing in front of her in the flesh. She had watched him on TV many times, her boyfriend Harold was a big baseball fan. They had grown up together, but she hasn't seen him in years. But what was he doing in Connecticut again? And what was the sudden breathlessness and heart racing she was feeling? She chalked it up to worry that he might cause a scene or sue for toppling a display of wreaths on him.

"Joe…" she said in a breathless whisper, "what are you doing here?"

"Getting hit on the head with Christmas, apparently," he said as he lifted a wreath with his hand. He grinned at her and blushed a little. The flirtation only lasted a minute and then his temper flared, "What do you think you're doing, throwing a Christmas display on my customers?"

She sputtered as their pleasant reunion turned bitter. "I… I… well, I'm decorating the museum, if you must know. Not that you would care, walking out of town and never looking back." Dottie didn't know why she threw in the barb and regretted it immediately.

Lashing back at her, Joe raised his voice, "Well, some of us had the good sense to get out while the getting was good! I—"

"Can I help you two with something," Frank appeared out of nowhere and interrupted. Dottie and Joe shared a shamed look. "Or can you stop carrying on as not to scare the other customers?" Frank's tone changed noticed the wreaths all over the floor. "What did you do to my store?" he looked accusingly at Joe.

"Me? It was—she—Dottie was—" Joe sputtered.

"So sorry, Frank. I was trying to get to the ones on the top shelf, and I toppled the whole bunch," Dottie said sheepishly as she started to pick up the wreaths scattered about on the floor.

Joe bent over to help when they bumped heads.

"OW!" they both said at the same time.

Joe stood up and scowled. "You are a menace, woman! Always have been." Joe said accusingly.

"What?" She stood up quickly, accidentally bumping her shopping cart, sending it into Joe who fell onto his backside.

"See, you're proving my point!" He said shouting back at her.

"Here," Frank said offering him a hand and pulling him up. "Joe, what can I help you with?" Frank said a little too starry eyed. He then cleared his throat and his excitement of a star in his midst. It was, after all one of the town's own. And Joe was just a man.

As Joe stood up, with just a little of Frank's assistance, his athletic legs flexed and did most of the work. Why was she looking him over? His voice snapped her out of observing him when he said, "I was looking for new tools. There don't seem to be any out at my parent's house, and I have many repairs to make. I need a good screwdriver, and a hammer to start with. I also need some paint and will need all the supplies to go with that."

"Right. Sorry to hear about your parents passing. Glad they left you the house though," Frank said.

"The whole town was sad to hear it," she said in an awkwardly comforting manner. "I always loved your mother," Dottie added.

A momentary revenant silence fell over aisle seven.

"So...." Joe continued awkwardly. "I came here to get started."

"Great," said Frank leading him away from the

chaos, "they're over on aisle four, come with me," he led Joe away from Dottie. "Oh Dottie, don't worry about those," Frank said over his shoulder to Dottie resuming her wreath cleanup. "I'll come back to tidy them up in a few minutes."

Dottie watched as they walked away. Absentmindedly she stacked the wreaths in her hands. Joe looked good, she thought to herself. But then any man who had fifteen and a half million dollars a year for the last five years and played baseball professionally *would* look good. There was something sad in him as well. She didn't know why. He was supposedly at the top of his game, engaged to a reality television star who was recently a hit as a model. Maybe it was just the wash of memories because of his return home. His parents had been gone for eight years, but he hadn't been back for almost twenty years. There was something, and she couldn't put her finger on it.

Memories flooded her brain of building a fort, running after the ice cream truck, and spending hours together. She, Hetty and Joe had been "The Three Musketeers" growing up, but in high school things changed. Joe became distant. She assumed it was because he was so focused on becoming the best at his sport. He excelled at baseball. In fact, when the scouts started coming their Junior year to his baseball games, it was no surprise when he got offers. It was a surprise that he elected to defer the Major League until he finished high school. The day after graduation, he went right into the minors and stayed playing for the Spokane Indians until he was called up just a few years later to the Majors for the Los Angeles Rangers.

Dottie was pulled out of her fond memories when she realized she had picked up all of the wreaths. She did one more pass down the Christmas aisle to make sure she had everything she needed. However, it was more to avoid Joe who was probably checking out now. Dottie made her way to the register and made her purchases; all the while Joe was on her mind.

CHAPTER TWO

As he walked out of Frankincense and Myrrh Hardware, Joe shook off the feelings tingling through his heart. Dottie was always beautiful, but somehow today she looked more beautiful than ever. When they were kids, her frizzy red hair was everywhere, unruly like the girl underneath it. Today it was tamed and had a lovely bouncy curl. Taller than he remembered, she had grown into a womanly body with soft curves in the right places. In school she was always bean-stalk skinny and more angular. Her face had softened, too. She had on make up today, something she didn't do much when they were in high school. He appreciated her minimal amount. His girlfriend wasn't ever without makeup on, even at home. Dottie was simply beautiful. His heart ached at seeing her. She was the one that got away. Or that he had let get away. He always regretted not...

But that was years ago, he shook off the memory and reminded himself. A different life. A different time. A different him.

Maybe it was a mistake to come back here, back to this town? He had come because he thought he would find answers. His game was off, and Coach said he needed to get his head together to be more productive next season. Besides he always meant to come back to fix up his parents' house and sell it. But what was he doing back here in this sleepy beach town in Connecticut? There were too many memories. He needed to just fix up the house and get out of here. Back to Los Angeles for Christmas. Not that there was anyone there anymore. Not since Heather had left.

Heather was the girl that looked like she should be on a baseball player's arm: blonde, fit, and stunningly toned. She was perfection personified. They were supposed to be getting married, but the papers leaked the location and details, they postponed to plan something different. Something had felt wrong, and he had called it off. Heather had been telling the press that it was still indefinite, but he knew they were wrong together. She had different goals. Heather liked the crazy life of being famous. Joe just wanted to play ball and then come home and live like a normal person. Cook dinner together with a family. Heather made it quite clear she didn't want that. Joe broke it off and left. The press would find out eventually. He would give her all of the time she wanted before he would admit to it. He did care about her enough not to blast it all over the papers. But with last season ending so terribly, and with he and Heather being the couple all of the paparazzi were following, it was hard to hide.

Where was better to hide then his parent's home.

So here he was fixing up this old two-story farmhouse trying to hide. But the memories seemed to spill out of every room the moment he walked through the front door. Most of them good, they were a very happy family. A terrible car accident that took both his mother and father on the way home from one of his Major League games. At least he hasn't lost them growing up. The memory of his coach coming up to him after a post-game interview with the press, whispering in his ear that he had something important to tell Joe flooded his brain. It was a moment when the whole world stopped. Coach tried to get him to take some games off, but he just kept playing. Baseball seemed to make the pain go away.

This homecoming was bittersweet. It seemed like he was both running away from and running to something.

As he stepped into the living room Joe was hit with the memory of his junior year. His first offer from a Major League team. He and his dad sat in the living room discussing all of the pros and cons. They made a list of all of the reasons Joe should go to college. And another of all of the reasons he should pursue his dream. They finally agreed that he might not be at the top of his game yet, but as a catcher, his knees only had a good ten to twelve years in them. Joe might as well go right into the game. College, his father agreed, would wait. High school, however, should be finished.

Maybe it was time to think about going back into college. Joe clenched his chiseled jaw knowing that his mother's dream was for him to get a diploma. He sighed and rubbed the back of his neck with his hand, almost as if to massage away the painful memory.

A knock on the front door took him from the thought.

"Hello," an older, raspy male voice hollered from the front door, as the squeak of the front door's hinge punctuated his entrance. "It's Frank."

"Hey, Frank," Joe replied as he turned toward the front door and the memory faded.

"I was in the neighborhood and thought I'd stop by to drop off your paint. I've got it in the truck," Frank trailed off as he slowly wandered through the house, looking around. Frank whistled. "You have got a great house here. With a coat of paint and a few nails and screws, you will have a great home. That is, if you're staying?"

Joe smiled and rubbed his neck and looked at his feet. "I don't know, Frank. I have my life out in LA. I just came home to clean this place up and sell it."

"Ah, I see." He gave Joe an all-knowing look. "Too many memories." Frank sighed, but had a glimmer in his eye, as if he were up to something. "Too bad, the high school was looking for a new coach. We were hoping that we would find someone with experience," the older man-made eye contact with the younger. "Thought that maybe you might be up for the task, but that was getting our hopes up, 'specially if you're just leaving again."

Joe chuckled. No one would expect a frowning, gnarly, curmudgeon like Frank to be as meddling as a lady in the East Haddam Knitting Club. Little towns in Connecticut were not quite tiny enough that everyone knew everyone. But small enough that everyone knew enough of everyone's business. And the hardware store was where the people in this town seemed to get their gossip. Joe knew that shortly after his visit to Frankincense and Myrrh Hardware, everyone in town knew he was back. Especially after that run in with Dottie. Everyone seemed to infer he and Dottie were meant for each other. He clenched his jaw again.

"What's wrong, son?" Frank asked seeing Joe's laughter change to strain.

"It's nothing," Joe said as he shook off the feeling. "The paint and supplies are in your truck, you said?"

Joe started toward the front door.

"You know, son," Frank said, not moving, "The past always finds us, no matter how far we run from it."

"That's what I've been told, Frank." He sighed. "And that is true about this house, too," Joe replied matter-of-factly. "It's not going to fix itself."

"Right you are, my boy. Now where do we start?" Frank said as he followed Joe out to Frank's truck. As they began to unload, Joe started to feel his anxiety starting to lift.

CHAPTER THREE

"**Y**ou did WHAT to Joe Thomas?" shrieked Hetty as she burst through the museum doors wagging her dark pony tail side to side as she looked up. She didn't disguise her astonishment. No one could make a puffy vest look as good as Hetty did. Dressed in leggings, lambs fur boots and a waffle weave shirt, Hetty was curvy and stunning. Even if she was dressed comfortably.

"That," Dottie said as she was on a ladder hanging up the garland up by the cornice, "was totally an accident."

"You know I don't believe in accidents," Hetty briskly reminded Dottie. "I also don't believe you ran into Joe on his first day back in town."

"How did you—" Dottie climbed down from the ladder, "Oh! Frank and Murray can't keep a secret."

"You know those two, East Haddam's own grouchy gossips. Not a thing happens that they don't pick up the phone let everyone know right after it happens. I swear they must have a group text with the whole town on it," Hetty joked. She then turned serious. "I hear you aggressively dumped an entire display of wreaths on his head."

"It wasn't like that," Dottie protested putting her hands on her hips.

"Well that is the rumor around town," Hetty goaded.

"I was reaching up for a second wreath for the decorating, that you," she accused Hetty, "convinced me I needed to do to spruce the place up and to feel better!" Dottie got worked up as she moved around Hetty to the pecan finished staircase that was just inside the front door. Carefully she started to wrap garland around the bannister. "So, I was just doing what you told me, and whammo—the wreaths were too high, and they came tumbling down on Joe's head," she dismissively shrugged.

Hetty ran around to the other side of the bannister so she could face Dottie. "And what did you feel?"

"Nothing. Well, bad that I hit him over the head with wreaths," she chuckled at her own joke. Dottie looked at Hetty who now had her hands on her hips. "I don't know what you're implying Hetty."

"You mean to tell me you didn't feel anything? No butterflies or shortness of breath?"

"No," Dottie said unconvincingly. "Of course not. You know I've been dating Harold since we were juniors. Joe was always just a... buddy," Dottie said as she crossed the room to get away from Hetty's stares. "What?"

"'What' nothing!" Hetty not letting up started

picking up lights and pretending to untangle them but making them worse while waiting for her friend to finally admit her feelings. "You have liked Joe Thomas since we were ten. Since you realized you liked boys."

"Nooooo!" Dottie drew out the word too long. "There was never anything there." She turned away and walked down the hall to the kitchen to end the conversation. Harold was whom she should be concerned about, since they had been dating so long. Joe Thomas would only be in town for a short while and would be gone from her life. Again. Hopefully for good this time, she told herself.

The museum was inside the old house, and the ballroom was occasionally rented to host parties and events. Dottie had the kitchen redone a few years ago for occasional catering purposes. During the year for meetings and some special events they would offer coffee or cocoa. To get more into the holiday spirit after coming home from the hardware store Dottie set her special cinnamon cocoa to simmer. She needed some now to give her stamina for Hetty's interrogation.

"Where are you going?" Hetty hollered after her before finding her in the kitchen. "See, I knew you'd get into the Christmas spirit," Hetty said as she entered the kitchen and smelled Dottie's signature drink.

"Do you want some?" Dottie asked handing Hetty an already full mug of cocoa.

"No, I want the story of what happened between you and Joe."

Both women stood their ground and neither moved for what seemed like moments. The old friends were used to each other's unrelenting and fought stubborn with stubborn. Finally, Hetty gave in and took the mug.

"Fine. You didn't have feelings for him," she said in a false deep voice and rolled her eyes, making fun of her best friend. "But can you believe he's back? After all these years? I mean he would call and send emails those first years on the road but—"

"Wait, what?" Dottie suddenly snapped out of her cocoa malaise. "He wrote to you?"

"Yeah, didn't he talk to you? You were better friends with him anyway. I thought it was because you two lived closer, and I was always off doing my pageants."

"No. He didn't call or write emails to me. I got a few postcards from random places that had a general, 'you'd really like it here' generic sentiment. But I never heard from him after he left town. Come to think of it I didn't really hear much from him senior year. I always thought it was because he was focused on baseball. Trying to make himself the best possible player possible."

"Well, I..." Hetty stopped mid-sentence stunned. Which didn't happen often. In fact, it probably had only happened two other times in her life. Once when she won her first crown, and the second when Dottie said yes to dating Harold. Everyone had always known that Joe and Dottie would end up together. Hetty thought that Harold would be just a phase. But a decade later and they're still a couple.

The women sipped their cocoa in silence.

"Not changing the subject, because I'm not letting you off the hook Dorothy Emelia Henry. But why haven't you and Harold," Hetty winced at his name, "ever tied the knot?"

"We have been waiting. First there was college, and then he went to grad school. And he has been trying to land a serious marketing job in a large market. In fact, he has a big interview this week in New York. We've been waiting until he was established to settle down." Dottie had given this speech in different forms over the years. Hetty knew it by heart, however she kept asking. Hoping that her life-long friend would admit that she didn't really have feelings as deep as she wanted to for Harold.

Dottie always had big aspirations to travel to distant places. She wanted to go anywhere that wasn't East Haddam, Connecticut. She didn't want to move, per se. But she and Joe used to talk about all of the sites they wanted to see. The Eiffel Tower. The leaning tower of Pisa. The Great Wall of China.

But in college Dottie's father had a stroke. It was too much for her mother to take care of him and the museum. Dottie felt the pull of her roots more than the lift of her wings. She settled for Harold and East Haddam. True she still had dreams about moving. And now that her father and mother had moved to Florida, and the museum was closing, there was nothing holding her here. Until Joe reentered her life, Hetty hoped.

Hetty finished her mug of cocoa and rinsed it in the sink.

"Well, I'd better get back to the diner," she sighed as she dried her hands on the Christmas towel hanging from the bar on the cabinet below the sink. "If you're not going to give me any more gossip, I guess I'll have to go insinuate something for my customers." Hetty winked. She would never toss Dottie as fodder in the gossip mill of this town, in fact she would go out of her way to stop gossip about Dottie. However, she wanted to know for herself what was going on.

"Alright. I'll be by later for dinner," Dottie said as she followed her friend out.

"The wreaths look nice. Both of them together. I'm glad you went for it," Hetty said dripping with double meaning.

"I'm sure you are Hetty," Dottie said almost with a warning.

"See you later," Hetty said as she walked down the porch and front walkway to her car.

Dottie closed the front door after her friend then turned around to look at the house. Decorations were scattered everywhere, over half of them were still in packaging or boxes. Christmas had exploded in the front hallway. Dottie sighed a heavy sigh.

"Why did you have to come back home?" She wasn't sure if she was saying it to herself or to Joe.

Taking a deep breath, Dottie dived back into decorating.

CHAPTER FOUR

Frank stayed over an hour at Joe's. They made lists of the projects to tackle. Frank did a quick assessment of each room to let Joe know what he should fix as they went from room to room inspecting everything. When Frank left, he had a burgeoning list of items send over from the hardware store for Joe.

Almost like an aged photo losing its color, the house was smaller and less bright than Joe remembered. The house was still fully furnished, but had tarps over most of the furniture, and plastic over the lamps to keep off the dust. Joe looked at the long-handwritten list in his hand and sighed as he yanked the cover off of the sofa, scattering dust mites all over the living room. He sat on the sofa and put his feet up on the covered coffee table. In his mind, he heard his mother shout at him to remove his feet from the table and started to lift his feet out of habit. Joe set his feet back down rationalizing that this was no longer his mother's house, and the table was covered anyway.

Lost in his thoughts, he didn't realize how late it had gotten. He heard the screen door slam and heard, "Where are you," in a bossy female voice that seemed so much a part of his world, that he smiled when he heard it. It was the voice that launched hundreds of crazy schemes when they were kids and made them play board games on his porch until such late hours they couldn't see. It was a voice he knew almost as well as his own.

"Over here, Hetty. On the sofa," he smiled through his weariness.

"Well, well, well… if it isn't The Park Place Wielding, Home Run Hitting, Joe the Go Thomas. Thanks for coming by to say hello," her voice was full of sarcasm.

"Hetty," he said as he stood up and tossed the list on the table. "Good to see you," he said as he embraced her. "I'm so glad your skinny butt finally ate something," he spoke into her hair before releasing her. "It was painful to watch you only eating celery in high school."

"Tell me about it. I love an evening gown, but I love pizza more."

They both laughed.

"What are you doing here, Hetty?"

"First night in town and its past eight o'clock. Figured the big city boy was used to delivery."

He looked at her confused.

"Diner was closing, and I figured you probably didn't have anything in the fridge. I brought you some food."

"Hetty, you're the best." He said noticing the bags

she had dropped at her feet to hug him.

"I know. Now, is your fridge working? Because I brought a few things," she motioned to the bags at her feet.

"As a matter of fact, I just plugged it in. It's probably it's not quite cool yet, but it should be on its way," he said starting to walk to the kitchen.

Hetty, looked at him from the back. His muscles showed through his shirt and his pants. Joe's job as a catcher required him to squat all the time. This had made him seriously muscular. His jeans and tee shirt seemed to fit him perfectly. Hetty thought to herself that if Dottie wasn't so in love with him, and if her own husband were out of the picture, she would jump at the chance to take Joseph Thomas off of the market.

"It's getting there," he said with his head in the fridge, as she rounded the corner. He closed the door and noticed that the weight of the bags was quite a bit. Hetty was managing, but she had brought enough food for a party. Joe jumped and took both bags away from her. They seemed to be as light as feather pillows to him instead of six different meals with a couple of side salads, side vegetables, and a two liter of diet soda that Joe was a spokesperson for.

They both started unpacking the bags. Joe stopped holding a tin.

"You brought me lasagna?"

"Yes?" Hetty said as a question, even though she knew she brought lasagna, Joe's favorite growing up.

"I don't eat carbs in the off season—," he stopped when he looked at her, and saw that Hetty's smile started to fall. "But I can't believe you remembered my favorite."

"Duh," she said. "It was the thing you couldn't eat enough of when we were kids. Do you remember when you—"

"Ate the whole tray of lasagna," they both finished together.

"Hey, I don't back down from a bet. Or free lasagna," he said as they smiled at each other in reminiscence.

"Oh, that Dottie. She always did think of the craziest things for you to prove yourself," Hetty said as she finished unpacking and putting things in the fridge.

"Prove myself?" Joe asked as he started to get a plate from the cupboard.

"Yeah, she was always trying to cajole you to be bigger and better than everyone else." She folded up the bags and set a pile of paper plates and cups on the counter. "Fine china, just in case you didn't want to use your mom's old stuff," Hetty winked.

Not to be deterred, Joe asked, "What do you mean she wanted me to be bigger and better? How much bigger could I get than a pro baseball star? I could never be good enough for her," Joe slammed the lasagna into the microwave and punched at the buttons, taking his frustration out on the machine.

"Well, that's the funny thing with us women, we see potential and we just keep squeezing to get out every last drop," Hetty twisted her words.

Joe with his back to Hetty braced his hands on the counter making his back tense and his shoulders raise to his ears. Through gritted teeth he quietly said, "But I was never good enough for her."

"Oh Joe," Hetty said starting forward to put a

hand on his shoulder, "You don't understand—"

"What?"

Hetty jumped back.

"What don't I understand, Hetty?" He lashed out. There was a painful question underneath this aggression. The one about Dottie. She waited for him to ask it, but he didn't.

"Hey," she said standing up to him. At her full height she was just two inches shorter than him. "It's water under the bridge. And I hear from Frankincense that you're not staying long anyway. So, what does it matter?" Hetty tested Joe. She wanted him to confess.

Joe stepped back and shirked. "You're right. Hetty, I'm sorry. Old wounds, ya know?"

The microwave beeped.

"Well, if you can't throw a tantrum at one of your best friends that you haven't seen in almost twenty years, who can you, eh?"

Joe rubbed his neck.

"Oh, come here, you idiot," Hetty said as she held out her arms. Joe stepped in to her embrace and they hugged again for a good, long hug. "Now," she said as she pushed him away, "before I get the solid idea to leave my husband and convince you to run away with me, I'd better get home."

"Thanks, Hetty."

"You're welcome, and if you need any more, stop by the diner any time," she said walking toward the front door. She opened it and turned back, "Well, anytime we're open. This isn't the big city, and we don't do delivery." She shook her finger at him then turned to leave.

"I wasn't only thanking you for the food."

Turning back to make eye contact with him, Hetty said, "I know, kiddo. Good to have you home. No matter how long you're actually planning to stay," she tossed over her shoulder as the screen door slammed.

He walked to the door and waved as she drove off. The microwave beeped again, reminding him of the food he was warming. He smiled and walked back to the kitchen and heaved a big sigh. This wasn't going to be as easy as he'd hoped.

CHAPTER FIVE

Recalling his post season checkup, Joe tried to focus on why he had come back to this town. His main focus was to fix up and sell his parents' place. But there was also another reason. Joe had to get his head right. At least that was what his coach said at his end of season checkup.

"Your knees give out before anything else will, and they're in good shape for a guy your age," his trainer said at the end of the season.

"Yeah, but your head isn't right these days, Thomas," said Coach said using Joe's last name. It's like Coach could see inside his head, Joe thought. "I'm not a meddling man," continued Coach as he smacked his gum, "but if I didn't know any better, I'd say you've got some sort of unfinished business that is bouncing around in that brain of yours. Its making all of your other processes slow down." Coach put his hands on his waist that seemed to be hidden by his stomach and shook his head. He started out the door, and turned back to Joe, "You've gotta get your head right if you wanna come back next year. If you walk into my spring training and you're still like this," he looked Joe right in the eye with his steely grays, "I don't care what your contract says, you're gonna be benched for the season." He snapped his gum to emphasize the point.

It was now ten weeks before catchers and pitchers reported. If he even wanted to go back. There was so much to think about. Joe wasn't quite sure what he wanted anymore. This whole thing with Heather and the press hunting them both down about their upcoming wedding and his role in losing his last game. His head was a mess.

What was unresolved in his life? Confused, Joe thought back. It was almost a month after they lost the pennant when he remembered. Earlier in the season he got a letter from the bank in East Haddam about paperwork for his parent's property. He had set it the letter aside and forgotten it. Like he had forgotten about this town, because his life had moved on. It wasn't until he started packing up boxes to move in with Heather that he found the bank's letter.

An alarm went off in his head, or maybe something clicked into place. Since it was off season, he suggested that he and Heather come here for the holidays to get away from the spotlight and fix up the house together.

"I'm not going to go all Chip and Joanna with you in the country for a couple of months," she had told him as she filed her nails and changed the channel on the television to some reality show chronicling her life with a bunch of strangers. He must have looked completely disappointed because moments later her tone changed, and Heather snuggled up to him.

"Look, baby. Go back to your quaint little town and work on your house. Maybe that's what your coach was talking about. Get rid of your parent's house and let go of the past. That will get your head on your future." He looked at her but said nothing. Maybe she really did understand him he thought pushing aside a distant warning in his head. "You get it all fixed up," she snuggled in closer and whispered in his ear, "and I'll even come out for Christmas if you want." This was what he wanted. Closeness.

When her phone buzzed from the coffee table thirty seconds later, she pushed herself off of him and the moment was broken. That phone always got her attention first. Sighing heavily, he got up and went into the home gym.

"You know I have to keep up with my social media. My fans need me," she hollered after him. Great, he thought, I'm in a relationship where I have to compete with two million other people for her attention. He dialed up the treadmill, cranked up his music and started running to nowhere. A few weeks later he decided to break off his relationship with Heather. They decided to make it an amicable break but would wait to break it to the press.

* * *

Maybe that was what he was doing in his parent's house: running to nowhere.

He didn't want to think about it. So, he threw himself into fixing the house. He needed to finish and leave all of this behind him. Joe had everything he wanted back in Los Angeles. Didn't he?

Joe hurt inside and out. Even with his daily off-season workout regimen, painting still made feel muscles he didn't know he had.

Working his way room by room, Joe was now updating the formal sitting room with the big picture window that looked out over the big front yard. He had been avoiding being in here. Memories flooded his brain every time he walked into this room. Long discussions about his future were had in here. Joe had broken at least three vases in this room from playing in the house. In this room, he signed his first baseball contract. And he would never admit this to anyone, but he came home the terrible day that Harold asked Dottie out and cried in this room. It wasn't a long cry, and no one was witness. Two or three heart wrenching sobs. He hadn't cried since. Not even at the news of hearing about his parent's deaths.

Joe needed a break. He got himself a cup of coffee and went and sat on the porch. Looking out over the five acres his family owned. Like much of the area it was densely wooded all around. The gravel driveway sloped down from the road in a semicircle that ran in front of the house. There were big azalea bushes that grew and a few evergreens to liven up the middle of the yard. It wasn't a place to play.

However, his father had cleared away much of the back yard so there was plenty of room to practice; the remains of a baseball diamond were still barely outlined, almost two decades later. Just down the back section of the wrap around porch there was a fire pit past the small, now overgrown, herb garden. And farther back there was a large barn that was more for storage. Joe's father wanted to retire and work on cars, but he just didn't get there. A couple of horseshoe pits were inside, and some stale hay, but that was it. Brush and trees looked like they were sneaking up on the house but hid a pond just beyond their border. In the summers he, Hetty and Dottie would sneak off to the pond and fish. Well, pretend to fish. It was idyllic. A recognized Community Wildlife Habitat, deer and other wild animals wandered freely through the front yard. The wrap around porch his father always claimed that his mother required, was glassed in. Even though it wasn't as warm as the house, anyone sitting on the porch was protected from the elements. There was a wooden swing and two overstuffed chairs, that had claimed their share of dust. Being outside year-round and the remodel wasn't allowing them to stay clean. Other chairs and two benches, all a light yellow to match the traditional exterior were scattered about as if they were having their own individual meetings.

Excited voices squealing at every roll of the epic Monopoly games he, Hetty and Dottie played years ago. Sometimes leaving the board set up for days, they kept going around and around and around until one of the three had money left. She was always bending the world see things her way. Joe was surprised Hetty wasn't in politics or broadcast news with how much she always convinced them of her thoughts on things.

Dottie was always the optimist and urged them to keep playing. She was always sure "just one more roll" would get her back in the game. And they stayed with her. Hetty because she was always supportive of her best friend. And Joe, because his heart belonged to her. Dottie's voice echoed through his head beautiful as a bell. He could almost hear it now...

"What are you grinning at?" Dottie's inquisition broke through his reverie.

Joe looked up to find Dottie standing in front of him with a large plastic container with a red lid filled with something, and a smaller one sitting on top.

Slightly embarrassed, he smiled at the vision. "Remember when we would sit out here until the sun went down, or later playing Monopoly?"

"That dumb game," she said coming to sit next to him, setting the dishes down on the table in front of them and kicking her feet up, crossing her ankles. "I don't know why I always let you two talk me into playing that game. I always lost. Hetty almost always won. I still say she cheated," she said somberly, and then cracked a smile.

Oh, how that smile made him ache to touch her. Instead, he smiled back woodenly as to not give away his feelings. "Yeah, well, she certainly changed the rules. Did you know you're only supposed to go around twice, auctioning off the properties as you go?"

"No! Really?" Dottie looked shocked.

"Yeah," he continued awkwardly. "I actually sat down and read the directions a few years ago. One of my favorite bars has a boardgame corner. I picked up the directions and read them cover to cover. In fact, I could tell you anything you want to know about Monopoly," his face filled with braggadocio.

"Huh," she sighed and sat back.

"I know, right?" He shrugged, "But that's what you get taking the rules from Hetty!" he relented, laughing.

With her beside him, he relaxed. Then as if the swing were on fire, he jumped up. "What are you doing here, Dottie?"

"I, uh…" she stood up and held up the containers. "Hetty said I should bring you food to apologize for throwing Christmas decorations on you."

"You didn't have to—"

"It's chili. And gingerbread cookies," she smiled standing up and playfully shaking the containers at him. "I think chili is still your favorite," then her smile faded as she mentioned matter-of-factly, "I don't know much about you these days, but I know you always liked my mom's recipe. You could never get enough when we had it at my house when we were kids. Always sitting next to me and asking for more."

He could feel the heat of embarrassment rising in his face. Joe did like the chili, but he liked being close to Dottie more. That was why he was always staying for dinner, especially on chili night. Turning away so she couldn't see his face turning red, he started inside, "Thanks, uh, let's put them in the kitchen." He went to the door and she hopped up and started after him. "And the wreaths, well, I've been hit by enough wild pitches, a pile of wreaths is nothing." He held the door for her, still trying to hide his face. It would give everything away, and neither of them was in a place to rehash their feelings. Especially if she was with someone. He noticed there was no ring on his finger, but last he heard. Dottie was still with Harold.

"Harold says to say hello," she said bringing up his arch nemesis as if on cue.

"Oh really? That's nice," he feigned cheerfulness.

"So how is old Harold these days?"

"He's fine," she weightily sighed. "Working for a small marketing company, and he's applying for a few firms in New York," she reported woodenly.

"Ah, he always was good at selling," Joe said making a joke to himself. "So, have you two.... tied the knot, yet?" He turned back to her and motioned for her to enter the house as he held the door for her.

"No," Dottie found herself replying much too quickly. "Timing just hasn't ever been right. And with my parents in Florida after my father's stroke, and me at the museum, we just... haven't," Dottie found herself trying to explain everything to Joe and she didn't know why.

"Watch your step," he said as they walked past where he had been painting. "I've just started in here. I did the hallway and the dining room earlier, but I need to tackle the front room."

"Wow, Joe Thomas, big time baseball star is now his own labor force," she said slightly teasing as she walked past him and put the chili in the fridge.

"Someone has to do it, and 'labor is good for the soul' my father always used to say," he said walking to the counter and getting another coffee mug, "Coffee?" he asked holding up the cup indicating like an idiot. "it's not your signature cocoa, but—."

"Sure," she said taking the lid off the cookies on the counter and feeling the bridge between them rebuilding. "Cookie?" she held out the container, but quickly pulled it away. "Or are you 'not doing carbs in the off season,' she said lowering her voice trying to sound like him.

"Ha," he said filling both cups, "You've been

talking to Hetty," he said handing her the cup. "Are those your mom's recipe, too?" he asked peeking over the top of the container.

"Sort of. It's my grandmother's recipe that was passed down through the family. The tradition is that you're supposed to learn the recipe, then experiment and then adapt the recipe in your own way. I've added crystalized ginger chunks to these. I also bake them a little shorter time, making it so they're extra chewy," she said and then bit into a cookie.

"Then I will definitely try one," he said reaching in and grabbing one that looked like a professionally iced gingerbread man. "Wow, these are beautiful."

"Thanks," she said with her mouth full. And then she smiled and chewed, taking the coffee from him and grabbing milk from the fridge. She looked at the carton in her hand then eyed him skeptically. "Really? All you have is Almond Milk?"

"Yeah, because—"

"No carbs in the off season," they said together.

Smiling they both looked up and their eyes locked.

"Well, I guess it's enough like regular milk," Dottie finally said pouring a dollop in her coffee and quickly putting it back in the fridge. She took a sip of her chalky coffee and tried not to make a face at how disgusting she thought it was. Trying to distract herself from both the disgusting coffee and the awkwardness of this situation, Dottie walked back into the living room to look at Joe's progress.

"You should," Dottie tried to say breezily, "come up to the museum, sometime."

"I'm trying to keep a low profile," Joe responded a little too quickly. Then seeing a bit of disappointment on Dottie's face, he cleared his throat and added, "It's just I want to get this house fixed up, and I only have so much time before I have to get back. For the holiday. And before pitchers and catchers report." He hoped these were answers that would satisfy her.

"So, what is the plan in here?" she changed the subject.

"Well, I'm hitting the whole house with a fresh coat of paint. Then I'll go through the furniture to see what needs to be tossed, and what can stay to stage the house," he said motioning at the furniture with his half cookie he had left. Then took a bite. "These are really good."

"Thanks," she said and blushed a little. Quickly she changed the subject. "Can I help at all?"

"You wanna paint?" he asked a little sarcastically.

"Sure, why not?" She said popping the rest of the cookie in her mouth and setting her cup down. Thank goodness. She was glad to be rid of that terribly tasting beverage. Dottie picked up a paint brush that was resting on the tray and started painting near the trim on the wall.

Standing back, he watched her paint for a few moments. Joe had always admired how Dottie just jumped into things. There was a great amount of courage she had always possessed. Before he started anything, he always thought out everything. Joe assessed and picked through all possible outcomes. He would always strategically plan out everything.

"Well, are you going to let me paint this room by myself," she said sassily.

"You're doing such a great job, I would hate to get in the way," he countered.

Twisting around, Dottie took her finger and poked him in the stomach.

"Hey! What was that for?" He laughed and pulled away.

"You are still ticklish!" Dottie delighted.

"No!" he said as he twisted away, protecting his ticklish spot and sloshing his coffee.

Instinct made her reach out to help steady the cup and the paintbrush snapped back and paint flew on her face.

Joe laughed.

"What?"

"You have paint on your—Here let me get it." He reached up and softly touched her cheek with his thumb. His hand lingered on her face for a moment before he quickly realized it had been there too long and quickly wiped his hand off on his already paint stained jeans. They remained only inches apart as the tension sizzled between them. Joe had the urge to kiss her. He wasn't sure, but he thought she was leaning in, too. Before he could stop himself, he leaned in closer as she closed her eyes, and took in the fresh smell of her just before leaning close enough to feel her breath on his face. This was a moment he had been waiting for—

Loudly, Dottie's cell phone bleated. They both jumped back. She fumbled in her jeans pocket and pulled out the phone.

"Harold," she said to Joe before swiping the screen and answering, "Hi… Harold. How are—Oh, you're at the museum waiting for—Oh, well I'm at—"

Joe took the paintbrush from her hand and started backing out of the room.

He mouthed, "Go if you need to!"

"I'm sorry," she mouthed and wrinkled her brow. Into the phone she said, "Harold, I'll be right there. I'm just—" She waved goodbye to Joe and walked out of the house.

Joe shook his head and muttered to himself, "And once again Harold comes in and sweeps her away from me," he grumbled. Painting could wait. Joe deposited his cup in the kitchen and grabbed his jacket before going outside to the woodpile where he could take out some frustration on splitting logs.

CHAPTER SIX

"**Y**ou *almost* kissed him?" Hetty said loud enough for the entire diner to hear as she was refilling Dottie's coffee mug.

"Shhhh!!!" Dottie warned as she gazed around the diner. Apparently Hetty wasn't as loud as she thought, or everyone was used to it because no one was looking over. Still, Dottie's face blazed crimson. "That isn't what I said," Dottie said emphatically in a low volume. "I said I *think* we were close to kissing."

"Well that's good, isn't it?" Hetty prodded as she turned to put the coffee pot back on the warmer. "NO! It's NOT good," Dottie exclaimed. Then returning to her low volume and speaking pointedly, "We both have fiancées!"

"Well, technically, you don't unless Harold suddenly proposed."

"He didn't. You know I would tell you if that happened," Dottie replied.

"Hmm, I don't know," Hetty thought aloud. "I know the tabloids say he's with that reality star turned model, Heather Smolen." Hetty's thought drifted. She then snapped her fingers and said knowingly, "But she doesn't seem Joe's type. Besides, why would Joe have tried to kiss you if he was with someone? And you also said the other night after you left Joe's house and went to the museum, Harold said he had a big question he was going to ask you soon." Hetty's voice raised to an excited squeal.

"I know," Dottie said downtrodden not echoing Hetty's excitement. Why was she not as excited as Hetty was about what Harold wanted to ask? Wasn't this what she wanted? "I guess I'm just more focused on keeping the museum alive," Dottie said answering her own question. But that didn't seem right to her either.

"Well," Hetty said as she leaned over and took a cookie from the tin that Dottie brought and took a bite, "it seems to me like there is something brewing, and I'm not the only one that thinks so. Those two gossips," she nodded her head over to the table where Frank and Murray were chatting with their heads close together. Every once in a while, they would look up and over at Dottie. "They're planning something, and I don't think it's the year they're planning to do matching Christmas displays on their houses."

Dottie looked over at them. "Maybe they're hatching a plan to save the museum," Dottie said feigning hope.

"I don't think so. Those two are worse than two little old ladies when it comes to matchmaking in this town. You know how they got me and Don together? They convinced him to come and help fix my kitchen plumbing. My husband had never touched a wrench before setting foot in my house to help Frankincense and Myrrh fix my plumbing. Next thing you know, we're walking down the aisle," Hetty said taking another cookie. "These are fantastic. What did you do differently this year?"

"Crystallized ginger. It's really tiny but it gives a little extra chewiness and punches of the spice here and there," Dottie said absently. "If only they could help the museum."

"Hey, that's an idea!" Hetty exclaimed. "Why don't you make some or give me the recipe and we will make a bunch here. You could sell them at the museum, and I'll sell them here, and give you the proceeds."

Frank walked up and handed Hetty his bill with cash. "Thanks for lunch Hetty," he said then he spied the tin of cookies. "Dottie, are those your gingerbread? What did you do to doctor them up this year?"

"It's a secret, and if you want to know, they're two bucks a cookie. Proceeds go to the museum," Hetty said, tossing a wink at Dottie.

Frank pulled five dollars out of his pocket and slapped it down on the counter next to Dottie. "Even if you put cod liver oil in them, they'd still be the best cookies this side of the river." Hetty took three cookies and wrapped them up in a plastic container for Frank.

"I threw in in extra one," she said handing them over.

Dottie stood up and placed a kiss on his cheek. She loudly whispered to him, "The secret this year is crystalized ginger." Then in a normal voice she said as she sat back down, "Let me know if you like them.

We'll be selling them here and at the museum," she said loud enough for the entire diner to hear, even though only two of the twenty tables were occupied.

"Will do," Frank said as he headed toward the door.

The ladies giggled to each other.

The bell to the diner door rang twice, and Dottie could hear Frank exchanging pleasantries with someone.

"Be right back," Hetty said and she walked away.

"Hey, Dottie," said a strong masculine voice that she knew all too well. She turned to see Joe Thomas standing right beside her.

"Hey, Joe," she said and immediately regretted not saying something more profound. But what do you say when you accidentally, almost kiss one of your best friends who disappeared so many years ago that you hit with Christmas wreaths, especially when you both are almost allegedly engaged?

"Hey, Joe," Hetty echoed saving Dottie from her mental crisis. "Here is your dinner, grilled chicken, broccoli, spinach, sauce on the side."

"Thanks, Hetty," he said taking the bag and handing her a twenty-dollar bill.
"I'll go get your change," said Hetty looking back and forth from Joe who was looking at Dottie, to Dottie who was making bug eyes at her.

"Thanks," Joe said. As Hetty walked away, he said quietly, "Hey, Dottie. Um, so what happened at the house earlier, I—"

"You don't have to say a thing, Joe," Dottie whipped around feigning courage. "We are two grown-ups who knew each other as kids, and I just stopped by and left you food, and we painted. That's all that happened," she said emphasizing her last few words.

Joe looked at her with confusion. Almost as if he wasn't going to apologize for almost kissing her.

"Oh. Ok. Right," he said trying to wrap his head around what Dottie was saying. Or not saying.

"Here's your change," Hetty said handing Joe back his money. "Hey, do you need a dessert? Dottie is selling her specialty gingerbread cookies to raise money for the museum."

"Really?" Joe asked.

"You don't have to—" Dottie started.

"They're two dollars each and they're delicious," Hetty cut her off.

Joe looked in the tin and made a face.

"I know that you don't eat carbs—" Dottie started.

"I'll take the rest of them, there look to be fourteen in there?"

"I think so," Hetty said, putting the lid on the container and picking it up to hand to Joe.

He pulled out a ten and a twenty and held them out to Dottie. "Here. It's for a good cause. I know how much you love that place." Dottie took the bills after a moment of hesitation. Joe took the cookie tin with his free hand.

"See you ladies later," Joe said smiling. He turned to go and started to whistle as he walked out of the diner. After the door closed behind him, Hetty looked at Dottie.

"Why do you look stunned?" Hetty puzzled.

"Hetty, I brought him a whole container of those cookies a few hours ago."

"Well, he either likes the cookies or you. And my money is on you." Hetty said and she walked away leaving Dottie dumbfounded at the counter. "I guess it's time to figure out how you feel."

CHAPTER SEVEN

As he walked into the hardware store, Joe found Frank and Murray bickering.

"I'm telling you when you have a sturdy siding, you don't have to have a thick cementation!" Murray exclaimed.

"Well, soft is great until you have to use it as a foundation for the house. For that you need sturdier," Frank countered.

The two men were fighting about consistency and hard versus soft. For a moment Joe thought they must be discussing cement.

Then Murray said, "If you're gonna put icing on it and decorations, you need harder."

Joe had reached the counter, and got looped into the conversation, "Yes, but softer is better for the overall aesthetic. What do you think, kid?" Murray said turning toward Joe.

"Well," said Joe trying to catch signs from both men as to what they were talking about and rubbing his neck with his hand, "I think if you need a firm foundation, hard is always better," he stated firmly. "But, isn't this the wrong time of year to be pouring cement? Isn't the ground too cold and wet?"

The proprietors looked at each other and then burst out laughing. "Oh kid," Murray said, "We're talking about gingerbread houses. That Dottie has me with gingerbread on the brain with those cookies she's selling at the diner."

"Oh," Joe said chuckling. "Yeah, her cookies always were the best."

"Myrrh here is trying to take the stand that you don't need a thick icing to keep the walls together. I say, if you have a good sturdy gingerbread, you don't need to worry about the icing," Frank turned to Joe. "So, what do you think?"

"Well, uh, I don't do much building. I've mostly just done eating. And for that I prefer Dottie's, because they're soft. This year's batch is particularly tasty," Joe said trying to remain neutral. But the way the men looked at him, it was if they already knew. To deflect he sputtered, "I have more in my car, if you'd like them."

"We wouldn't want to take your cookies—" Frank started.

"But we will happily take the delicious things off your hands, as I hear you don't do carbs in the off season," Murray finished his sentence as he stood up and batted away at Frank.

"Sure, sure. I'll go grab them," Joe said laughing. "While I'm out, could one of you grab some more painter's tape and an edging brush for me? I ran out and I want to get the painting finished tonight, if possible," Joe said as he walked toward the door.

A few moments later Joe returned with the cookie tin. A paintbrush and a roll of blue tape were on the counter. Frank was nowhere to be seen, but Murray was sitting behind the counter, reading a paper that he had folded into quarters.

"Ya know," Murray started as if he and Joe were in mid conversation, "The museum has been a part of this town for over a hundred years. Maybe longer."

"Uh huh. Dottie's mom ran the place and we would hang out there after school sometimes. Doing our homework and playing hide and seek in the rooms," Joe reminisced.

"Well, its closing," Murray said, looking over his reading glasses and paper.

"Really, Dottie didn't—," he stopped himself. "I didn't hear that. That is too bad," Joe cleared his throat. "How much do I owe you?"

Murray looked at Joe scrupulously, and then back down at his paper. "A tin of cookies," he said seriously.

"Murray," Joe said, "I can afford tape and a paintbrush. How much do I owe you?"

"Like I said," Murray said reaching for the tin, opening it and taking out a cookie, "A tin of cookies."

"Fine, then," Joe said picking up the tape and the brush. "Thanks, Murray," he said tapping the brush to his brow like a scout salute. "See you later," and Joe turned to walk back to his car.

"Those boards and shingles and such should be in tomorrow," Murray called out after him, mid chew of his cookie.

"Great, give me a call and I'll come down," Joe

hollered over his shoulder waving the brush just over his head as a wave goodbye. "Enjoy the cookies."

The moment the door closed behind Joe, Frank muttered, "Well, it looks like it's up to us, Murr."

"What are you talking about, you old coot?" Murray looked at his friend with a mixture of confusion and judgement.

"The way I see it, those two are meant for each other, and it's up to us to make it happen," Frank gave his friend a knowing look.

"But if we spend our time on this, it will delay our Christmas decorating. I don't know that I can meddle and plan out my big display on my house that will beat you to tarnation, again."

"What do you mean, *again*?" Frank sputtered. "You know I beat you last year. And the year before that."

Murray waved him off. "Pah!!"

"We'll have to get your gal involved, too. We won't let that boy," Frank indicated to the door meaning Joe, "leave this town without swinging for the fences to get those two together. I think they just need a little push."

"Alright, you meddler," Murray gave in. "I'll call Hetty and get her on board. 'Course, she won't be hard to convince. That one is always one for meddling to make a good love story."

* * *

The next day Dottie rolled over and slapped at her nightstand with one hand to find her phone, looked at the time on the screen. It was still early, and it was her day off. Soft pattering of rain outside her window made her curl back under the covers. She was just dozing off again when her phone bleated at her. It was Hetty.

"Why are you calling so early," Dottie yawned as her greeting.

"Why are you not up and moving yet? We have cookies to bake!" Hetty replied over the phone.

Not one to let a good idea cool, Hetty had ordered extra supplies to cover the ones she was taking from the diner for the first batch of cookies. Dottie had forgotten she agreed to today being baking day. "I have all of your ingredients, except your crystalized ginger. But knowing you, there is a five- or ten-pound bag sitting at your house, because that was the smallest quantity you could find, so you have plenty,"

"It's only 7:30. I'm hanging up now," Dottie groaned. She had every intention of rolling over and going back to sleep. The rain pattered on her window and coaxed her to nestle farther into the sheets. It was if she snugged in far enough there was no way to get out.

"There will be plenty of time to sleep in if you let the museum close," Hetty threatened.

Dottie's eyes flashed open. "I'm up, I'm up," Dottie unconvincingly moaned but still didn't move.

"Great. I'll be at the museum in twenty minutes, and you better not be far behind me, or I'll send the fire department to your apartment."

"Fine," Dottie replied muffled into her pillow.

"I'll bring the coffee. Goodbye." Hetty said, rolling her eyes.

"And cinnamon rolls!" Dottie hollered, hoping her

demands were heard before the call disconnected.

Dottie cursed herself for making her family's traditional cookies as she tossed the covers off of herself and rolled out of bed, wiggled into her favorite jeans, cozy socks and for a dash of festivity, threw on her shirt, a baseball raglan tee that had a broken cookie man on it that said "Oh, ginger snap!"

Yanking her hair back and tossing it into a bun, she didn't brush it. She washed her face and brushed her teeth while a single pod of coffee brewed.

Her small one-bedroom apartment that she had rented when she moved back from college suited her just fine. It was cozy and was new with updated appliances and heating. She had painted it a warm white color and accented the apartment in grays and greens. The furnishings were a mishmash of vintage, goodwill and new, and it looked a bit like a coffee shop on a hit TV show. She wished the kitchen was a little bigger, the stove wouldn't fit a turkey inside. The kitchen at the museum was much more spacious, and better for large baking projects. However, she could zoom back and forth in her apartment, walking between coffee maker and bathroom to get out of the house in a matter of seconds. Helpful to get out quickly.

Cracking the door, she saw the rain pelting down, but it was a warmish day for early December. She grabbed a lightweight cardigan and a puffer vest. Dottie jammed her feet into her brown and navy duck boots and grabbed the keys off the table. Looking back into her apartment, Dottie sighed. No Christmas tree yet, she just hadn't had the time or the desire. Grabbing her mug of coffee, she pulled the door closed behind her and walked the stairs from the second floor out to the parking lot. She didn't even bother locking her apartment door. Small town with a low crime rate.

The routine of falling out of bed and being out the door in ten minutes was something Dottie perfected. When pressed, she could even do hair and makeup and be out in twelve minutes. Hopping into her father's old burgundy sedan, she made her way from bed to museum in just eighteen minutes.

"I'm impressed," applauded Hetty as Dottie came over to her car as she pulled up.

"Well, it's not my first rodeo," Dottie joked as she grabbed for the canvas shopping bags that were sitting in Hetty's back seat. "Just these?" she asked of the four bags.

"Yeah, that should be enough to make a few dozen cookies to get us started," Hetty said as she climbed out of the driver's seat balancing a pink pastry box with cinnamon rolls inside, two ceramic mugs from the diner, and a thermos. "Be careful, there are eggs in one of those bags!" Hetty hollered as they both dodged raindrops and puddles to the museum. It was only a few feet, but they were both drenched when they reached the expansive porch.

The museum exterior looked as if it were made of gingerbread. The exterior was painted a deep brown color and the shutters and ornate lacy trim were a creamy white. It had a porch deep enough to hold a dinner table for twelve. It wrapped around to the side of the house, skirting two sides. The steps led up to the main entrance but, following the porch around to the side was a door right into the kitchen. Probably to allow the large porch meals to be served easily.

"You know, I've always loved how this place looks like it should be from a Victorian novel. It's dark and brooding from the outside, but with a pop of icing on the windows. The roof with its sloping wooden shingles and all of the windows on all three stories make me think of a mix of Nathaniel Hawthorne novels and *Anne of Green Gables*," Hetty commented as they shook the rain off and walked inside.

"Really? I always thought you hated coming here."

"Don't get me wrong, Dottie. When we were kids," Hetty said as they both unpacked the groceries, "I used to think it was creepy that you wanted to hang out here every day, with all of the old photos and pictures all over the walls, and the cold glass cases that show off books and jewelry so that you can look but not touch," Hetty shivered.

"Yeah, but you loved when we were allowed in the ballroom and held, *Grand Dances*," Dottie said the last words with a highbrow accent.

"That's right! I would make you and Joe dance!" Hetty exclaimed. "What crazy kids we were. Too bad we don't do anything like that anymore. It was so much fun to play pretend. To have no worries. To ride our bikes anywhere in town, and not come home until dark or dinnertime, whatever came first."

Dottie said nothing, just set out ingredients and grabbed a piece of paper.

"Maybe with Joe back in town, The Three Musketeers can reunite and get up to some trouble," Hetty slyly suggested.

Dottie glared at her. "Here's the recipe," she pointed at the paper that was translucent with butter and wrinkled from age that had blurry handwritten notes in several hands all over it. "I figure we do a batch at a time, and while they're cooking and cooling, we can keep mixing together the ingredients and refrigerating them."

"Great," Hetty said reaching for the flour.

"It works best to refrigerate the dough before rolling it out so we can use the cookie cutters. It will be a bit of a laborious process," Dottie mentioned.

Hetty dusted off her hands and grabbed her phone from her pocket. "I'll just text Don. He's managing the diner today. I'll have him bring lunch to us." Hetty tapped away at her phone. And then suddenly exclaimed in anger, "Autocorrect is out to destroy the world! We thought it was politicians and oil. Nope autocorrect! How could it think that the word hamburger was meant to be Hun Berets!?!"

Quickly texting again, Hetty corrected the error. Then she smiled. "My husband is sometimes irritating, but he's cute. Especially with texting," Hetty quietly sighed. Dottie smiled to herself knowing that her best friend was happy and still in love. Hetty looked up and reported, "He says he will bring us lunch. He's good like that." Then changing to a practical, almost bragging tone, Hetty continued, "He cleans my hair out of the drain and tells me every day that I'm beautiful. I think I'll keep him," she said tapping something else and then putting the phone back in her pocket.

Dottie had started to cream the butter with the mixer. "You can measure the dry ingredients, there," she pointed to a bowl indicating Hetty should start there. As Dottie mixed, she smirked, and said,

"Remember when we used to take the hanging red velvet ropes and poles from around the displays and make a runway for you to practice your 'queen walk?'"

Hetty laughed, "And you would be the announcer. And we would make Joe be the judge!"

Joining in the laughter Dottie said, "And that time he gave you a really low score and we ganged up on him?"

"He said that it was for my own good," Hetty started to laugh harder. "He said it was so I would know the feeling of defeat."

"And we chased him around the museum, and he got locked in a closet trying to hide from us!'

"Oh yeah, that creepy closet! He said that he thought there was a ghost in there because someone touched him." Hetty started to cry she was laughing so hard. "When it was just your dad's jacket arm that landed on his shoulder."

They both were cackling and laughing so hard that they started crying.

This was how life was supposed to be: two best friends spending time together. Laughing over shared memories while baking cookies, not caring that it rained outside. Dottie was glad that her best friend had made her get out of bed early today. Even though it was her day off. She wouldn't have wanted to miss this for the world.

As their laughter died down, Dottie wryly added, "Did you get cheese on my Hun Beret?" They both cackled again with laughter as they drank their coffee and continued to make cookies.

A few hours later, they had baked three dozen cookies. Two auxiliary batches of dough were in the refrigerator ready for the oven. Cookies were cooling on the counter waiting to be iced while they ate the lunch Don delivered.

Hetty kept sliding Joe in conversation trying to get an understanding for how Dottie felt about him. She knew there had to be something there, even after all these years. Dottie wouldn't have felt that they almost kissed, let alone bring it up to Hetty in the diner if she didn't feel something. Much to Hetty's chagrin, Dottie kept changing the subject. She wasn't sure if Dottie was avoiding the conversation on purpose. She was getting to the point where she was running out of ways to bring Joe up.

"I don't think these are cool enough yet to ice," Dottie said as she checked a couple of the cookies. "The icing will just melt if we try them now. Instead, let me show you what I've done in the library."

"You know, they say that Joe still reads a lot." Hetty took the opportunity and once again dropped Joe stealthily into their conversation. "They say he gets on the treadmill and while he is doing cardio, he is working his way through the classics. He read *Anna Karenina* this year, a magazine said," Hetty reported as they walked up stairs.

Nonplussed, Dottie said, "Well, it's about time he got around to actually reading it. He faked his way through a paper about it. I should know. I let him cheat off of me."

"Dottie!" Hetty chided. Then in a singsong way Hetty said, "Well, maybe someone is trying to get into the interests you have, so you can share them!"

Whipping around mid-staircase, Dottie leaned down over Hetty. Being a step above was the only way Dottie was taller. "Listen to me, Hetty. There is *nothing* going on between Joe and me. It was just one of those weird moments. He's probably feeling lonely and missing his fiancée and I was just in proximity," Dottie sputtered with explanation. "I read about those kinds of things all the time." She turned and started up the stairs again, "And that's probably more accurate than those gossip magazines."

"Well, you can't blame a romantic for hoping, can you?"

"No, but you can tell the romantic to stop meddling in a life that isn't hers. Besides what would your buddy Harold think if he knew you were trying to set me up with another man," Dottie teased. It wasn't a big secret that her best friend and her boyfriend weren't close. Why, Dottie didn't know. Neither of them ever had a distinct answer when asked.

"Fine," Hetty relented.

"Fine." Dottie replied and shook off her anger and entered the room to the left off the stairway.

The library, one of the larger rooms on the second floor, had two eight-foot-long and three-foot-wide glass cases sat parallel in the middle of the room. Dottie moved between the four-foot space between them. The bookshelf lined walls were packed from floor to ceiling and stretched from floorboard to crown molding and covered all wall space, only leaving room for a big bay window that looked over the side yard. Dottie walked over to the large oak desk near the window. Although this was one of the active museum rooms, it was barely used, except when historians or curious public wanted to stop in and find a book.

"I'm not as much of a reader as you are," Hetty's voice was reverent. "But it never stops me from being amazed to walk in this room."

Hundreds of books filled the room that had been donated or curated by those who worked for the museum. It was Dottie's favorite room even as a child. She loved to take down a book and sit on the massive multicolored braided rug that covered the original wooden floor. Moments after opening the book she would get lost in its pages.

"I know," said Dottie. "I love this room, because it was a true community effort to build it to such a great library," she said opening the drawer of the desk with a key and pulling out a laptop. "It's hard to believe that every book in here has something to do with this town, Connecticut or was written or published by a Nutmegger."

Hetty had been in this room at least a hundred times, but she still did a loop running her fingers along some of the spines. Amazement filled her and then she turned back to Dottie. "So, what did you want to show me."

"Well," Dottie said with a large sigh as she plopped herself down on the bay window seat. "I had an idea for a new installation in the Baker room," she motioned to the room across the hallway. The open door revealed a large open room that was two flat walls and then a circular wall of windows. Currently it held nothing but an assembly of about fifty chairs. It was a very open space, almost as large as the ballroom that was directly below it. It was used for larger meetings or lectures and was even outfitted with a flatscreen tv.

"What is it?" said Hetty sitting next to her friend.

"Well, I'd need your help, and your permission of course," she said holding tightly to the computer and then turning it around to face the screen toward Hetty, "But I wanted to make an exhibit about you."

"What?!?" Hetty exclaimed as she looked at Dottie instead of the screen. "Me? Why?"

"Well, just look at the screen," Dottie held up the laptop. "Use the touchpad and scroll down."

"This is just pictures of me in all of my pageants."

"Yes, and there is a rich history in that," Dottie said handing the lap to Hetty and walking into the center of the room. "Just picture it: a visitor walks into the room and at the windows are your dresses on forms lined up like contestants on a stage. Over on the wall to the left are the photos and pictures of you. I'll get some of the news article clippings too. On the wall to the right is a case of all of your crowns. On the television, we will run a loop video of all of your different talent moments and your big winning moments," Dottie paused for a moment to look at her friend whose mouth was gaping open like a fish. She hurried on before Hetty could say no, "Don told me that Murray has a lot of footage, since he was at almost every pageant you ever did, and I'm sure we can find someone to cut all of those together. It wouldn't take much time to set up, just a week or so. And it wouldn't cost much. I would just need to borrow your crowns, and dresses, and probably dress forms." Hetty still said nothing. "It would just be for a few weeks. But I think the town would get a kick out of seeing The Path of a Pageant Queen—that's what I want to call it. I'm hoping it will stir up business. Bring visitors in." Dottie clasped her hands together and stepped closer to Hetty. "So... what do you think?"

Hetty remained unmoving and blinked a few moments later. "What do I think? What do I think?" She jumped up and set the computer down on the bay window, "I think this is the greatest present you could ever give me!!" Hetty raced over and hugged Dottie. "You've really worked hard on this. I'm very impressed, I knew you were good, but I didn't know you were *this* good!" Hetty paced a few steps back and forth. "I'll only do it on one condition: you hold a ball here on Christmas Eve to celebrate the exhibit. I've always wanted to have a ball here, and this would be the perfect reason for there to be one: me!"

"Really?" Dottie asked.

"Really? Of course! I can't believe you were even nervous to ask." Hetty held her friend out at arm's length. "You know I would do anything for you!"

They hugged again and then started jumping up and down and squealing with happiness. "Hey if you charge for the ball, I'm sure that would help keep the museum open, at least for a few more months, anyway!"

"That is a great idea," Dottie replied, "I can't wait—"

Her thought was interrupted by a large crash that came from the direction of the Baker room. They looked at each other in terror.

Dottie ran toward the room, Hetty right behind her almost knocking her friend down, because she had stopped in the doorway.

"Oh no," Dottie said in almost a whisper with her hand over her mouth.

"We will fix this," Hetty said in her calmest voice as she pulled her phone out of her pocket and pulled up the number for help and hit connect. "Frank, come quick. The roof just fell in over at the museum."

CHAPTER EIGHT

"**M**urray, the roof at the museum just fell in," Frank said hustling over to his oldest friend, and distant cousin, as he was ringing up a customer at the register.

Murray stopped what he was doing and looked up.

"What happened? Was anyone hurt?" Joe, was at the counter being rung up, took the words out of Murray's mouth.

"Hetty called from the museum," Frank said as Murray moved from around the counter and started to grab his coat.

"Is she okay?" Murray asked.

"Fine. She's fine." Frank said putting both hands in the air and motioning to Murray to sit back down in hopes of calming his friend. Frank turned toward Joe said, "They're both fine. Apparently, the roof in the Baker Room is leaking," he said to relieve Joe's confusion. "It's the front one with the rounded front window. There wasn't anything in the room except for that new fancy television, but they say that the leak is not near it. I'm going to grab some tarping and head over there," he said starting back toward aisle three. "Unless, Murray, you want to climb up on that roof?"

Rubbing his knee, Murray shook his head. His knees weren't what they used to be, and to be honest he needed help putting up the Christmas decorations on his house these days. Being up on a ladder wasn't the easiest anymore. Frank his oldest friend, knew all of this, of course. He said it in his question without revealing it to anyone else. "Naw, you're right. Need one of us to stay here and watch the shop," he said shirking off his coat. "But if that gal of mine needs help, I'll close the store and be on my way in a flash."

Frank hollered from down the aisle as Murray slid out of his coat and resumed ringing Joe up. "Hetty is stronger than the both of us put together. I'm sure she's fine," Frank came around the corner putting his rain slicker on while carrying his toolbox. "Shoot, Marilyn has the car today. I rode in with you and I'm not sure how long you'll be," he muttered to himself.

"Joe, you headed home?" Murray asked.

"As a matter of fact, I am," Joe nodded. "Need a ride, Frank? I'd be happy to drop you."

"That'd be great. Let's get going, though. The rain isn't slowing, and that house is getting wetter by the minute," Frank grabbed one of Joe's bags and headed toward the door.

"I'll put it on your account," Murray said handing Joe his bag. "Better get going, or he'll likely drive your car off without you."

"Right. Thanks, Murray."

"Can you believe a major league baseball player is

my chauffeur!" Frank hollered as he followed Joe out the door.

"Frank's plan might just work yet," Murray muttered to himself. "That gal and that boy are meant to be together. And with Joe back in town, we just need to keep those two meeting and they'll take care of the rest themselves. Probably," he said as he sat down and picked up the folded newspaper beside the register with the half-finished crossword. Suddenly he looked up and out the front door. "He wouldn't have poked a hole in the roof." Murray shook the idea out of his head. "Nah, he's crafty, but not that crafty. Although..." Murray chuckled to himself and looked down at his crossword. "Ah ha! Six letter word for 'clever at achieving one's aims by indirect or deceitful methods' C-R-A-F-T-Y."

* * *

Ten minutes later Joe pulled up to the museum. A small hole, the size of an apple could be seen in the roof from the driveway. It looked like it had been stuffed with something, because a black shiny wad was sticking up out of the hole.

Letting out a long slow whistle, Frank leaned forward and craned his neck to get a better look out the windshield. The wiper blades squeaking back and forth clearing the unrelenting rain. "This is a job for more than one person." He looked at Joe. "Don't suppose you could spare a few minutes to help me climb up there and temporarily patch that?"

Joe leaned forward and cocked his head, mimicking Frank. He sighed deeply. Like his parents' house, the museum had many memories he wasn't quite ready to face. Many of which involved alone time with Dottie. Joe never realized how far back he had actually been in love with her. He realized as they arrived at the museum that he probably had feelings for Dottie from the day they met. Coach's voice echoed in his mind, "Get your head right..."

"Sure," Joe sighed. "I don't know that I'll get much work done on my place in this weather anyway."

Grabbing the tarps and the toolbox, Frank made a swift retreat to the porch. Joe turned off the engine and took the key out of the ignition and followed. Joe smiled to himself when he saw the wreaths hanging on the door. They walked through the first door and hung their jackets on the hooks just inside. Frank knocked as a courtesy, but then walked right in through the second door. A wall of laughter hit the men as soon as the second door opened.

"We're here," Frank walked to the stairway and hollered up from the bottom step.

"In the kitchen!" both ladies called back in unison. Then laughing continued.

Frank's head swung from up the stairs toward the kitchen. He marched into the kitchen to find Hetty and Dottie apron clad, and amess with icing all over their faces and clothes. Hetty had a streak of green and white on each cheek. Dottie had green frosting dripping from the back of her hand and a red slash of frosting that went from above her right eye to her left cheek.

"What are you two doing?" Frank asked in a stern voice.

"Icing cookies?" Dottie stifled a laugh and questioned

why he was asking what seemed obvious.

"Looks like you're finger-painting your faces," Frank said disapprovingly and trying not to smile. "Now let's—" he turned to talk to Joe behind him, to find he had disappeared. "Let's get this roof patched." And he walked out of the room.

"We shoved some trash bags up in it to keep the rain out," Hetty yelled after Frank.

Dottie put down her icing bag and while wiping her hands on a dishtowel, followed Frank who was already ascending the stairs.

"I've brought some tarps that we'll tack to the roof, for a temporary fix," Frank shouted as he went up the stairs, "but we'll—"

With her head down, she did a hairpin turn to follow up the stairs, and she ran straight into a tall, strong man also trying to get up the stairs.

"You." Dottie realized it was Joe.

"Yeah." He said staring back at her. "I… um… I was—"

"What are you—" Dottie spoke at the same time.

Nervously, they both laughed.

"I hope you don't mind. I was taking a quick look around. It's been so long since I've—"

"You coming? Or are you visiting?" Frank's head peered over the banister. "We don't have all day. Room is getting soggier by the minute!" He said as he walked back into the Baker room.

Taking the steps two at a time, Joe chased after Frank.

"You're welcome anytime," Dottie yelled after him. "Free of admission."

"Don't say that," Hetty's whisper chided. "We

need all the paying customers we can get!"

"Think we should help?" Dottie looking concerned.

"Nah," said Hetty as she chomped on a cookie. "Let them be manly and figure it out themselves," and she walked back into the kitchen. Dottie looked up for a few moments until she heard groans and an ouch, and she hastily tiptoed away in retreat. Walking back into the kitchen, she hoped that the museum's insurance policy still had good medical coverage.

Forty-five minutes later Frank and Joe walked into the kitchen.

"Well, you have a mighty good hole in your roof," Frank commented. "No telling how it will affect the ceiling more than it already has, but for now we've minimized the possibility of more. I'll need to come back after the rain is over and it dries out to patch the shingles and check the ceiling."

Dottie sighed. "Thank you, Frank. Would either of you like a coffee? Or a cookie?"

"Sure," he said taking a mug and the carafe, pouring a cup-full, and a cookie from the plate she motioned to. Joe did the same. "It's only a short-term solution, however. This place needs a new roof," Frank said.

Her face sank. "Cookies aren't going to be nearly enough then." She turned to Hetty, "Unless you think you can give up working at the diner for the next few weeks to help me bake?"

Putting a hand on her friend's shoulder, Hetty sighed. "I think even if I did, it wouldn't be enough." She hugged Dottie. "Listen, we will put on a great last exhibition, and have a ball and go out with a bang."

Dottie leaned out of the hug and sighed. "Yeah. It's not like this wasn't a possibility," she said turning and putting her elbows on the counter and resting her chin on her hands. She looked totally downtrodden.

"What do you mean, 'a great last exhibition'?" Joe asked.

Hetty chirped in, "Dottie has a great idea to put me on display. Well not me. But my dresses and crowns. Show what it was like to be a pageant queen." Then Hetty's face fell. "But it was going to be in the Baker Room, but now that it's a mess," she turned to Dottie, "will we still be able to do it?"

"Sure," Dottie said, her head still in her hands. "We will just put it in another room and close of The Baker. It will be fine. It won't be as grand as I had imagined," she chewed on her bottom lip. "But it will still be a fantastic show," Dottie said now trying to comfort her friend.

"No, I mean, why is it the last show?" Joe asked with confusion.

"Well," Dottie sighed as she stood up and grabbed another cookie, snapping a bite in her mouth and chewed. She couldn't look Joe in the eye. "The museum has lost its funding. My mom was great at raising money for the place and getting different groups of visitors in to keep it alive. I haven't been able to do the same thing. I keep asking Harold for help, but he says this place is a marketing disaster. So, the board voted we close the doors on December thirty-first. Permanently."

"So, you need advertising?" Joe asked. His eyes warmly looked into hers.

"We need everything. Something exciting to keep

people coming back. Money to help fix the roof. Advertising to remind people that this place exists and is good for events and meetings as well as just educating them on the area and Connecticut," Dottie said.

"Or at least a good rumor or ghost story, like the castle," Hetty said referring to the pile just down the road that used to belong to 'Sherlock Holmes,' popular with tourists.

Silence hung over the room.

"Well, I'd better get back and fill Murray in. Hetty, can you drive me?" Frank said, and Hetty's head snapped up as if she'd missed a cue.

"Um… sure," Hetty said as if she was trying to grasp what she was missing. Frank gave her a look and she suddenly caught on, responding with, "I… probably should… go check on Don at the diner," she seemed to come up with out of nowhere. "That is, if you'll be ok, Dottie?"

"Hmm? Oh, sure, sure. I'll be… fine," she said with distraction

"Alright. Bye then," Hetty called as she walked out of the kitchen.

Dottie was deep in thought about how to restructure the exhibit on Hetty. It wasn't until she heard the car engine start that she pushed herself off of leaning on the counter and looked up that she wasn't alone. She jumped when she saw Joe still standing there. "I thought you'd gone with Frank and Hetty," she said surprised.

Joe too seemed deep in contemplation. "No, I… I drove Frank over on my way home."

"Oh?" Dottie started to tidy up the kitchen.

"That... was very nice of you." She stopped wiping the counter to face him, "Thank you for helping today."

"It was nothing."

"No, but it was," Dottie corrected him. "You didn't have to give me the time of day, let alone come over and patch my roof."

"Sure, I did," he said smiling and handing her the dirty dishes from the safe distance of the other side of the counter. "What are neighbors for?"

She smiled when a memory popped into her mind. "Do you remember when we would pretend that the museum held an army, and we would charge up the hill from your house and creep through the bushes? We did it so much that we made holes in between them. Your mother was so mad when she found out," Dottie was laughing now.

"And you wouldn't let me take the blame," Joe said chuckling. "You said we were saving the bushes from the deer that were eating them."

"I don't think she believed me."

"Nope. She didn't," Joe said rubbing his neck. And then he sighed a deep sigh transitioning from a happy memory to sadness. "She was such a kind soul, and she loved you so much. She knew you were lying to protect me, and she let it go. I mean, I did have to vacuum every week for two months after that," he faked a frown to make her feel guilty. "But knowing you had my back was worth it," Joe said as he looked at her and warmly smiled. The silence between them turned from warm to awkward. "Well, I should be going," he said, feeling that his smile and his presence had lingered too long. "When Frank comes back to patch the roof, have him call me. If I'm not busy next door, I'll help out," he motioned toward his house.

"Thanks, Joe," Dottie said as she walked him out.

"Wreaths look nice," Joe said pointing to the one on the front door as he put on his rain jacket. "Almost worth getting hit on the head for," he smiled at her. "Almost." Joe gave her a stern look.

"I am so sorry for that. I really—"

"Dottie, I'm teasing you." He cut her off and broke into a chuckle. "My head, as my mother used to say, is thick as an oak. It's nothing that hasn't already healed," he reached for the door knob. "See you soon," he said giving her one more boyish grin as he left the museum.

"Bye," she said watching him leap to avoid puddles on the way to his truck only to step into one and make a giant splash just before he climbed in. He turned back and threw his arms in the air. "If it's not one thing, it's a puddle," he hollered.

She smiled and waved from the overhang of the porch. As he drove off, she hugged herself, feeling a bit cold and not realizing she was missing the warmth that Joe had brought inside.

CHAPTER NINE

Although the future for the museum seemed bleak, Dottie forged ahead anyway. Not one to take any problem lying down, she was determined to fight for the museum she loved and knew that the community had simply forgotten about. To go down swinging, as the baseball cliché goes. If she could only get the community involved again in some way Dottie knew the museum would thrive. She kept baking cookies every day. They were selling out at the diner. Hetty started telling people the only place to get the cookies was at the museum. Foot traffic at the museum doubled. Dottie even started getting holiday orders to ship outside of Connecticut. Baking was taking her time away from working on the new exhibit, but she knew it was guaranteed income. But would it be enough?

"Can you believe Harold thinks I should sell these, and go into the cookie business?" Dottie said flabbergasted to Hetty on the phone. "He says he will actually do the marketing for me. Why is it that he doesn't do a thing to help the museum, not even hang posters around town when we have a new exhibit? But the moment I start getting buzz with these cookies, he wants me to be the new Mrs. Fields?"

"I know honey. I don't understand men," Hetty commiserated. "Don convinced me I was a good cook, and that's how we ended up with the diner. And I hired a chef to cook here! Listen, not to change the subject," Hetty trod carefully, "but I think we should call an emergency board meeting. They should know we're making steps in the right direction. Maybe it will inspire some of them to help out a little more instead of just sitting at home, just making decisions on shutting down the history of this town," Hetty told Dottie over the phone while Dottie rolled out another batch of dough.

"Yes, I think that is a great idea," Dottie agreed. "We can also let them know about the new exhibit we're working on, and the ball."

"And maybe some of them will help with the roof," Hetty said.

"Not likely, but it's worth an ask," Dottie said.

There was a knock at the front door.

"Frank is here," Dottie told Hetty. "Why does he always knock? He only comes here during museum hours."

"Tell him just to walk in," Hetty suggested.

"Believe me, I have," Dottie said to Hetty then yelled toward the front door, "I'm in the kitchen!" Then she said into the phone, "Hetty, I'd better go so I can focus on Frank and these cookies."

"Sure, sure. Give me a call later."

"Will do!" Dottie said then hung up.

"Hey, Frank, do you—" She said as she walked out of the kitchen and right into Joe. Again.

"Hey, Dottie," Joe grinned sheepishly at her. "Frank headed upstairs with the supplies. He wanted me to ask you for the museum's ladder."

She stood motionless for a moment. Why did she continually freeze when Joe was in the room? It wasn't his fame. She had known him before he was famous. Maybe it was the distance of years. It was certainly not she protested to herself, as Hetty kept implying, that she had feelings for him. She loved Harold—even though these days he was gone more and more. But no matter, that would change once he got his job and they settled down. Shaking it off, she pushed past Joe, "Follow me," she said a little colder than she wanted to. Dottie walked into a closet just below the stairs. "Remember your old hiding spot? It's now the maintenance closet. Help yourself to anything in here," she said businesslike walking into the small, slanted ceiling room and pulling the string to turn on the free hanging lightbulb. Leaning against the wall were a folding ladder, a broom and a mop on the shelf parallel were boxes of what looked like craft supplies with wooden sticks, glue and pompom balls brimming over.

"Great, thanks," Joe said as he reached for the ladder. She swerved trying to anticipate his move, but he stepped the same direction. In trying to back up so he wouldn't step on her, Joe lost his balance but quickly caught himself putting his arms out flat against the wall. And around Dottie. She was caught. With his arms on the sides of her, they looked into each other's eyes for a moment. Feeling something rekindling. Suddenly, they both gave off a nervous laugh, and Joe drew his arms back suddenly.

She was stock-still for a moment, then went scurrying out of his way and walked out of the closet. "I'll go up and see if Frank needs anything else," she shouted as she rushed up the stairs. Running away from the weird wobbly feeling she had in her stomach. Again.

When she reached the top of the stairs, her stomach seemed to settle. With a calming deep breath, she took in the wonderful aged history aroma of the museum, and felt the sunlight washing in from the different rooms. She walked into the Baker room. It was a beautiful sunny day and the circular wall of windows doused the with light. Suddenly a beam of light burst in from the ceiling.

"Hey there, Dottie," Frank called as he peered in the hole from the roof. "I'm taking off these rotten shingles." Then as almost an afterthought he said, "Oh, and Joe volunteered to come with me."

"Volunteered?" she heard Joe ask from behind her. The hairs on Dottie's neck prickled.

Once again, she quickly moved out of his way while he set the ladder up directly under the hole.

"You told me you would teach me how to repair a roof, and next thing I know I'm driving you over here again," Joe said in a jokingly defensive tone. "I really need to find another hardware store," he said jokingly up the hole, then turning to Dottie and winking. Feeling the blush grow on her face, she pretended to check out the floor for damage as Joe looked back up at Frank.

"Well, no better way to learn how to repair a roof then to actually do it," wisdom spewed from Frank.

Dottie and Joe shared another look and did a simultaneous eye roll. This caused the both to laugh.

"I don't care what anyone says, you're a sneaky devil, Frank," Dottie teased and shook her finger up at the roof. She started to walk out of the room and said over her shoulder, "If either of you need anything, I'll be in the kitchen baking cookies. Oh, and we're having an emergency meeting of the museum board today, but we should be out of your way. Just wanted you to know they might want to come up and take a look at the hole."

"Why are they meeting?" Joe asked.

"Well, among other things, so we can chat about a new roof, and possibly have a ball here on Christmas Eve. And I'm doing one last big exhibit for the last weeks of the museum on Dottie and her pageant life. I want to present that to them. Hopefully one, if not all of these will be good fundraisers to keep the museum open."

"Oh," Joe said with more questions on his mind, "What—"

Dottie perked, and then dashed out of the room as she shouted, "I'll be back, the timer is going off..." her voice drifted away as she ran off into the kitchen.

"I hate to see her like this with the museum closing at the end of December. Dottie is so worried these days. But don't tell her I said that. If my whole life was invested in a place that meant as much to me as this place does to her, I'd be more frazzled than she." Frank had a distant look in his eye.

Joe pretended his intensity was focused on the roof and no concern for Dottie.

Frank continued, "They made that decision the day you came back to town. It's never been an economical project. And with the house getting older, the board just doesn't want to put the time or the money into helping it stay afloat," Frank started tossing things off of the roof. "Look to see if the drywall there looks like it dried, or if it's going to need a whole new piece."

Joe examined the area. "It looks like its swollen, and there are big rings on the ceiling," Jack answered.

"Yup. Figured. Alright, son. You'll have to cut out the drywall. Did you put down tarps around you on the floor to catch it all?" Frank directed.

"I'll do that now," Jack answered. He moved the ladder out of the way and spread the plastic tarps over the floor and taped them down on the corners so they wouldn't slip around. He put the ladder back in the middle, just under the hole and took a hammer up with him. "So, what's next?" he hollered back at Frank.

"Well, if they can raise the funds, I guess they could keep the museum open," Frank mused. "For a few more months anyway. But now with this roof needing replaced—"

Jack interrupted, "No, I meant what do I do with the ceiling."

"Oh, sure, sure. Take a hammer, flat side and start whacking away at the drywall. It will just fall off. Make sure you've got protective eyewear. Don't want any of this flying into those million-dollar eyes of yours," Frank teased.

"Fifteen million," Joe corrected him with a smug

grin.

As Joe started to bang away at the damaged drywall, he could hear Frank treading the boards above, and pulling out all of the immediate shingles that needed replacing.

"Too bad, this place has a lot of history. A little money pumped into it could do wonders," Frank muttered to no one in particular.

An hour later, Joe had cut away the damaged parts of the ceiling exposing the beams overhead. "Frank, I think I've cleared away all of the soaked drywall," he hollered up as he started to wrap all of the debris up in the plastic tarp. "What should I do next?"

"You afraid of heights?" Frank said sticking his face near the hole.

"Nope," Joe answered a little to boldly.

"Well then. Why don't you come outside and climb on up here with me, and I'll show you how to shingle?"

"Great. I'll be up in a minute," he said wrapping up the last of the tarps and starting downstairs. Joe had a great idea. "I'm just going to stop in the kitchen and … get a glass of water," he said over his shoulder toward Frank.

He was already walking down the stairs, so he didn't see Frank watching after him. Nor did he hear Frank mutter, "Mm, hmm. Take your time."

Joe walked the large bundle that rivaled Santa's sack in size out the front and put it in one of the trash cans. Joe walked around the porch, so he wouldn't track in more dust or dirt inside the museum and walked in through the kitchen door.

Music was playing loudly. He called out a hello to

Dottie, but she couldn't hear him over her own singing. He stood back and watched as she sang and wiggled her hips to the music. He smiled as he took in the sight of her. Joe started to feel guilty and reached out to get her attention.

"Oh, you scared me," Dottie jumped as Joe touched her gently on the shoulder. She reached toward her phone to turn down her music, but her hands were so covered with dough. Circling herself to find a towel or something to wipe her hands-on Dottie seemed scattered. Finding nothing she bent over to the phone. Stuck out her tongue to one side of her mouth as she closed one eye and squinted to focus with the other on the phone screen. Touched her nose to the screen and swiped left three times before the music was muted.

"I'm so sorry to frighten you," he said laughing now audibly at her actions.

"It's ok," she said and wiped a curl that fell into her face with her arm. Flour striped her face. "You have," with a single finger he made a wiping motion to his own left cheek indicating that she had flour there. She reached for her right cheek, missing the spot where the flour lay. "It's   still—"

"What?" she said wiping the clean cheek again. "Here, let me," Joe said taking the dishrag he found under the cookbook close to him. He raised it up to her face and gently wiping the flour off her cheek. They were so close he could almost touch her and could smell the vanilla of her skin. Dottie was even more beautiful than when they were kids. The curl fell back in her face again. Joe couldn't take his eyes off of her. He started to lean closer. She wasn't sure if he was going to kiss her. Joe stared relentingly deep into her eyes. He licked his lips and edged a millimeter closer. Dottie seemed to hold her breath, until she reminded herself that he had come into the kitchen for something specific.

"What was it you needed," she asked, and he jumped back, taken out of his trance.

"Oh, I uh..." Why did she keep getting stuff on her face? He needed to stop reaching out and touching her, Joe thought to himself.

"Water?" she guessed as she reached for a glass and started filling it from the new stainless tap. The kitchen had been completely redone a few years ago, Frank had mentioned. It was modern with white cabinets and countertops with silver appliances.

"Yes, I—No. I mean, I'll take the water. But that's not why I came down here. In here." He was usually so good with words. Why couldn't he speak. He took a breath to regain composure. "I mean. I came in to talk to you about the museum," he said finally able to put words together in the right thought. He took a drink of the cool water to center himself before beginning. "As I was up there, I started thinking about this place and what you need. My advisors and my accountant are always suggesting that I give to charity, and I think this museum would be a great cause to support and—"

"A great *charity*?" she said showing offense.

"No, I mean. I'm not saying it right, I—"

"If you're looking for a *charity*,' why don't you send a donation to underprivileged kids or puppies or something." Dottie spat defensively.

"I mean, I want to help you—"

"Joseph Thomas," she was suddenly formal, "that is very nice of you to offer your hard-earned money for this museum, but I'm fine," she said unconvincingly as she started to put on oven mitts and walked over to the oven.

"Frank says that you'll need a new roof and that the museum is closing. So maybe if I just get you a new roof until you can figure out what to do with all of this stuff—"

"This stuff? This *stuff*?!?" she repeated, her anger rising. "You mean the history of this town and this area?" She dropped the cookie sheet on the counter just a little too hard. "This is the whole problem. People like you who think they can swoop in and just fix things. When you well know that it's just a temporary patch. We need a long-term commitment."

He couldn't be sure if she was only talking about the museum.

As she reached deep in the oven she spoke with strain in her voice. He wasn't sure if it was from the weight of the cookies or the museum. "There are so many treasures here. So many things that have meant a lot to so many people over the years. They just don't remember. This community is always there for each other. They just need to be reminded of that," she said dejectedly with her back turned toward him. "As for moving it all out or leaving it all behind, I... I just don't want to think about it yet. I'd prefer to think that we will find an answer. Somewhere. Somehow."

"Okay... so how are things going with these cookies? Are you going to be marketing them to a bigger audience in order to make—?"

"Ugh! What is it with you men and the sale of

these cookies? Harold wants me to sell them en masse and turn a profit from my family tradition. It was all Hetty's silly idea to begin with. I'm not a baker. I mean just because I'm really good at the recipe that has been passed down for generations, doesn't make me a baker," she yelled. Dottie looked Joe in the eye. "Honestly, I don't know how to get over that something I love so much won't be a part of my life anymore. I don't know that I could take something else from my life just being... gone." She turned to him pointing a finger with accusation, "And you slapping a Band-Aid on it by tossing a donation my way isn't really going to fix this," she said motioning between she and him. "I just can't," she untied her apron and yanked it over her head slamming it on the counter. She looked him right in the eye. "Keep your money and your lousy suggestions. What I really need is a great idea how to keep this museum open," she said as she stormed past him and out onto the porch.

He watched her walk the length of the porch through the window, and out into the yard until she disappeared into the trees.

Joe was only trying to help, and thought it was a good idea. Confused and unsure of what he did or said that set her off, Joe walked to the front of the house and out the door. He sighed and shook his head. The best he could do was to keep helping fix the things he could in the short time he would be here. He climbed up the ladder to find Frank.

CHAPTER TEN

A walk in the woods always made Dottie feel better. The trees and birds calmed her and gave her clarity. Maybe it was walking at a fast pace mixed with the forest scents, but it cleared her head and calmed her. Extra emotional, even as a child, Dottie could run away to the woods and regain sensibility. Even as a child, she snapped quickly and said things she shouldn't.

As an adult she was better at it, except under times of extreme emotional stress. Dottie guessed she just couldn't deal with both Joe's return and losing the museum in the same moment. Both seemed wrong right now. Too many emotions were stoked, and she didn't know how to fix either one.

She found herself at the small cabin her father even built was still her respite. Cabin being a loose term. A sturdy yet small enclosed building that was no more than a six by eight-foot room with a couple of stools and blankets. Over the years she had stocked it with bottles of water, candles and books so that she could escape here. Today, though it didn't seem to help ease her frustration like it normally did.

His voice rang through her head the entire hike to the cabin. How dare Joe call it "charity" and just blatantly offer her money! Of course, a big baseball star would just come home and see a poor failing thing in his hometown, toss a little money at it as a heroic gesture to make himself feel better before just disappearing again. Probably never to come back. She'd seen this plot in movies and read it in books. He would offer a glimmer of hope only to disappear into his big life and never look back. And never help or care again. How *dare* he think he could be her friend again after all of these years. He just dropped out of their lives and...

Dottie stopped abruptly. Why was she upset? Dottie reasoned that he was doing what anyone in his position would do. She reasoned that she was really just upset that the museum, which seemed to run flawlessly under her mother's care, would be shutting down under hers. Once again failing her mother felt like a tragedy in Dottie's life. True, the museum was old and not really a tourist destination. It had so many memories she wanted to preserve. And although her mother talked of closing it when her father took ill, Dottie refused. The museum was a magical place to her, and she would do anything to keep it open.

Reasoning again with herself, she knew she shouldn't be mad. It would finally be a chance to leave this town behind and live in the big city like she always wanted to do. Harold was going to get one of these jobs and take her away from it all. And that is what she ultimately wanted. Right?

If she was honest, she had always felt like a failure, not living out her own dream. When her father had his stroke, her mother quit the museum to take care of him. Dottie took over for a supposed temporary stent. Then she and her mother decided the warmer Florida climate would do both parents good. And they were right. Her father now had a clean bill of health and there was no sign that he had a stroke. Her parents were thriving in Florida and sold their house in Connecticut. Dottie assumed the museum role full time. She would never admit it, but she was never sure what she actually wanted to do with her life. In taking the museum over Dottie always felt that she was running away *to* something.

"You hide in this museum," Hetty said once accusing her.

"I do not!" Stubbornly refusing to admit it, Dottie lashed out at her friend.

"Yes. Yes, you do. You hide in what you claim to be your responsibility to this museum. I think you also hide how much you love this town, no matter how much you say you want to see the world." Hetty's words stung deeply.

Dottie didn't speak to her for a while after that. Maybe Hetty had been right those years ago. Maybe Dottie was hiding. Question was, how deep did it go? Was she happy in anything she had including Harold?

With the time in her cabin in the woods not helping, and knowing she had more cookies to bake, Dottie started back to the museum. As she walked out of the clearing, she saw Joe on top of the museum. She tried to wave at him and get his attention, but he was kneeling and very focused below. As she got closer, she realized he wasn't kneeling, but actually almost waist deep in the roof.

"Oh no," she said out loud as she ran toward the house.

When she was closer, she saw the museum parking lot was full of cars. As she rounded the house, Dottie saw that all of the trustees were standing looking up at the roof. Could this get any worse? As if in answer, the whine of a firetruck got louder as it rounded the bend and turned up the driveway. This was becoming a full-on spectacle.

"What is happening?" she asked Mayor Santino who was standing out front of the pack.

"Hey, Dottie," Replied the tall, dark haired, well suited man with concern. "Well, it seems that Joe and Frank were on your roof fixing it. Joe went higher to see if there were other places that might need a quick patch, and he fell through up there. Luckily, he's landed in the attic of the house. He seems to be stuck and they're going to have to cut him out. Which means more repair for you," Mayor Santino sighed and patted Dottie on the shoulder. She had put her head in her hands and was shaking in frustration and worry. Her shoulders began heaving as the ladder from the firetruck started to raise to the roof.

"Is there anything I can do," Amanda Littleton, with her brown hair pulled tight in a French braid and her average height disguised with heels too high for the country said as she put her hand on Dottie's shoulder.

"No. Thank you, Amanda," Dottie said to the board member as she lifted her head. She seemed to be laughing.

Amanda removed her hand, "Well, I'll be right here. I suppose we will be starting the meeting soon?"

"Yeah. Yes. We... should," Dottie said remembering the meeting as she watched Aaron Kemper, one of their high school classmates, climb the fire ladder to her roof.

Gritting her teeth, Dottie watched Aaron, who's frame seemed too small for his muscles, edge his way down the slope of the roof to Joe. She thought she heard Joe say, "Do what you have to do," and she saw the axe go up in the air when a hand pulled at her elbow turning her away.

"Come on, honey," Hetty said, pulling Dottie toward the house. "You don't need to see this."

Sighing heavily, Dottie acquiesced and followed Hetty into the front room of the museum. Amanda, Mayor Santino, Robert Sampson, principal of Bacon High School, and Kathryn Taylor, another board member all entered the museum as well. Dottie set up a few chairs and just as they all sat, Hetty brought in some of the newly baked and decorated cookies with a pitcher of milk on a tray and walked around and handed everyone a cookie and a glass before setting the tray down and then filling each cup.

There was silence in the room and the ambient sounds of what was happening on the roof trickled down as they munched on their cookies.

"You're making these as a fundraiser," Kathryn asked.

"I don't know. We are making as many as the two of us can," Hetty interjected before Dottie could. "They're very popular, we're even getting advanced orders."

"They are tasty," Robert said. "But are they enough to save the museum?"

"Yes, but it won't be something I can keep up with making while I run the museum and Hetty her diner," Dottie said.

"Not to mention that the demand might lower after the holidays are over," Amanda said. Then quickly qualifying as Hetty gave her a death stare, "Not to be negative, just stating the facts."

"Well—" Dottie started but then was interrupted by a knock at the front door.

"That will be Frank," Hetty said as she started for the entrance of the museum. "Come on in, Frank," she said opening the door and letting him in. "We are all in here, she said motioning to the front room. Why don't you come on in and tell us what you were telling me before?"

"Well," Frank said has he walked in to the room, and then quickly removed his baseball cap to show manners, "Oh hey Mayor. Bob. Ladies," he said acknowledging everyone with a nod. "Well, the roof needs work."

Dottie let out a loud laugh. Everyone looked at her.

Frank continued, "but I don't think it's as bad as we previously thought. The whole north side looks like its sturdy and doesn't have any issues."

"But your man up there fell through and that hole isn't going to be inexpensive," Robert said.

"True. You're right. But we were able to find some—" Frank was cut off as Joe walked down the stairway. A tension fell over the group. The kind where a celebrity suddenly appears in an unexpected place.

Dottie unaffected by the sensation. She stood up and felt a wash of relief, then ran over throwing her arms around him in a huge bear hug. "You're loose! Are you hurt?" she pulled away and looked at him clinically.

As Hetty and Frank exchanged a look, Joe's face turned crimson as he realized the front room was full of people.

"Oh, hey folks," Joe waved at them. All of the board members stood stunned as they looked at Joe Thomas in the flesh.

Like a true politician, Mayor Santino crossed the room and shook Joe's hand as Dottie stood a little too closely to Joe still assessing him.

"Welcome home, dear boy. We are so happy to have you back home in East Haddam, and in our prestigious museum," the mayor oozed charm.

"I can't believe it," Robert said, and he ran across the room. "Mr. Thomas, I'm such a big fan. When you caught that high pop up in the sixth inning of the game with the Indians, I was holding my breath, but I knew you could—"

"My husband is a big fan—" Amanda chirped in.

"You are much more handsome in person," Kathryn gushed.

"Please ignore my hair, with this rain it's just a mess—" Amanda joined.

They all talked over each other, all trying to get Joe's attention. He looked at Frank asking for assistance. Frank put his fingers up to his lips and gave a loud whistle. Silence fell.

"Now, Joe, was there something you wanted to tell

us?" Frank asked.

"Um. Yeah. Sorry to interrupt your meeting," Joe cleared his throat. He didn't really like talking in front of a lot of people. He faked most of his post-game interviews. Most of the time everyone wanted to talk to the pitcher or the star hitter, so he ducked out of many. "When I got cut from the roof—"

A huge gasp filled the room, then all of the board members started speaking again at the same time.

"You were the one on the roof?"

"How long were you stuck?"

"Dottie, do you have the current insurance policy?"

"Son, you know the museum, nor the town have a lot of money. I hope you won't sue—"

Another loud whistle came from Frank.

Joe looked at Dottie. He took the opportunity and said to her, "I think there is something you need to see." He said taking her hand and pulled her up the stairs after him.

"Joe, we're having a meeting," Dottie protested as she gestured back to the faces below. Everyone watched them go, and Hetty and Frank shared another look and a smile.

"Joe, if the roof is that bad and we need to replace it, I just don't know what to say. We have the museum board in today to talk about getting them to pitch in for a new roof. But as you heard the mayor say, the museum nor the town has the money. And if we're closing at the end of this month, no one is going to want to pay to put a roof on the building—" Dottie stopped speaking when they reached the bottom of the pull-down ladder for the attic. She had always wanted to go up there when they were little. Hetty even dared her once. But her mother always told her never to go in the attic. When she was an adult and was here alone, she had pulled down the ladder a few times, climbed to the top of the steps and poked around the attic finding nothing. It was dark and was full of insulation.

"Want me to go first?" Joe asked, seeing the trepidation on Dottie's face.

"Sure, I—"

Joe started up. "What are we going up there for, Joe?" Dottie asked.

"Just follow me," he said excitedly.

When she reached the top, he held out his hands to help steady her the last few steps. "Only step on the beams or the boards laid out. I don't want you falling through the roof."

"Two of us doing that in one day doesn't seem the best way to keep the bills for the museum down," she said trying to make a joke. He gave her a short consolation laugh.

"Follow me," he said masterfully balancing himself, and keeping a hand out for her to take. At first, she refused, but after taking a few unsure steps and almost falling off to the left, she grabbed Joe's hand and let him safely lead her over to a far corner.

"I really don't need to see the hole—"

"Here," he said pointing a flashlight into the corner. She had to bend down as the slope of the roof became shorter.

"Did you have to knock this down to get through?" she asked pointing at remnants of a short wall that she hadn't noticed before.

"Yeah. I don't know a ton about insulation, but it looks like this was put up to block the elements. From over at the pull-down door, you wouldn't have noticed this, unless you got up really close," he pointed. "But these are what I wanted to show you," he said pointing his flashlight.

Leaning against the walls were a few dozen picture frames. They had been turned glass side to the wall. They didn't reflect and Dottie couldn't have seen them from only a glance around the attic. The first was covered with dust and she carefully turned it around to take a look at it. A man and a woman stood next to each other in a sepia toned photo. Dottie gasped as she took in the picture. She was in a drop waist dress that would be circa 1920s and held something in her hand. The man had his arm around her shoulders and was wearing a sweater vest with long socks and short pants that poofed like jodhpurs or old golf pants. Both were wearing school sweaters emblazoned with a large B on the chest. His arm was extended out to his side holding what looked like—

"A horseshoe?" Dottie asked the picture.

"Looks like it," Joe said as he had come up to her side and shined the light over the photo.

Dottie reached for the next picture and she found a few at Gillette Castle, a few of people at the river, and a few of several people playing horseshoes. It looked like there was snow on the ground.

"I don't remember hearing of winter horseshoes before," Dottie said as if she were thinking out loud.

"My dad built a couple of indoor pits out in our barn. He liked to play the game to clear his head," Joe said with a grunt as he picked up a box that was hidden under some of the frames. "There is also this," he said starting to unfold the flaps. "Wow," he said as he reached in. Dottie was still holding the snowy horseshoe photo, so she looked over her shoulder to see Joe holding up a paper bound book. He had cracked it and was carefully leafing through the pages. "It's a Bacon High School yearbook from 1944. This is amazing. Look they even had a baseball team back then."

Squatting down next to him, Dottie dug into the box. Picking up a few at a time, she glanced quickly and then set them gently on the floor before digging in again. "There must be forty or fifty of them in here. Hey, Joe," she said with a glimmer her eyes, "Do you think you can carry these downstairs for me?"

"Sure," he said replacing the book and picking up the box.

"I also want to take down these photographs. I can't believe I never knew they were up here," she marveled talking a look around the entire attic in case there were other treasures hidden.

"Nothing else up here. I already took a look around in the tight places. Just seems like these were put up here for storage and then forgotten about," he said walking to the stairs and setting the box down right next to the opening as he started down. Halfway he grabbed the box and descended. "Hand me some of those frames," he shouted up the ladder.

Gently she handed him two at a time. There were thirty-two pictures in total.

"Hetty, you'll never guess what Joe found." Dottie felt the surge of excitement like they were kids again. She hollered down the stairs forgetting that anyone else was in the museum. Hetty, Joe and her on an adventure in the museum just after closing hours, when they all were supposed to be working on their homework.

Hetty, followed by Frank and the rest of the board members made their way to the top of the main staircase. Joe lifted the ladder and pushed it up to the ceiling to give more room in the hallway they were all standing in.

"Robert, look at this," Kathryn said, standing over the box of books. "These are old yearbooks. How are they here?"

"Who knows," Dottie said, still transfixed by the first photo she had found of the couple holding the horseshoes. "People drop off what they think are helpful donations, but really it's just junk they wanted to get rid of but didn't really want to throw away. So, it's either here or the thrift store. I'm sure they did the same thing for my predecessors."

"People just leave their old junk on your porch?" Kathryn asked.

"Yup." Hettie answered. "A couple of boxes a week. I help look through it, so I can get first dibs on the rejects."

"She's joking, right?" Amanda asked.

"Not really," Frank said.

"It happens a couple of times a week, with surges around the spring and fall," Dottie continued.

"Spring cleaning," Joe and Hetty said at the same time. "Jinx!" They both shouted and then laughed together just like they did when they were kids.

"What is this photo that you're looking at," the mayor asked over her shoulder.

"I don't know," Dottie said mesmerized. "I want to do more research, but it looks like there was some sort of winter horseshoe tournament. I can't tell if it was through the high school, but the people in the pictures all look so young. Robert," Dottie said looking up for the first time since they came down from the attic, "Do you think I could come by the high school and take a look at the past yearbooks? All of the ones in the box didn't seem to be from around the same time as these photos."

"Sure," Robert said. "Joe, you're welcome to come visit your alma mater, too," he said hopefully.

With a pile of yearbooks at his side, Joe chuckled and said, "Maybe. Dottie is the one who is more interested. And I have so much work to do on my parent's house." He started packing the books back into the boxes, "In fact, I should leave you all to your meeting, since I've done enough damage here," he said abruptly. Joe started to climb around everyone and headed toward the stairs. "Dottie, I'll see ya," he waved.

Dottie didn't register that he had left until she heard the door close.

Quickly, but carefully, she set down the picture on the floor, ran down the stairs and out the front door. "Hey Joe!" Her voice caught in her throat. "Thanks!" she hollered after him. He had made it into his yard, their old way through the bushes so she only saw him from the waist up. He stopped and waved, then quickly turned and walked toward his house. There was something about watching him disappear that brought back a warmth of nostalgia. She walked back to the museum and hugged herself as the temperature seemed to drop. She pulled the door closed distractedly and leaned against it for a moment and smiled to herself.

"We're in here," Hetty called from the front room. Dottie walked in to find the board members standing. She hadn't realized she'd been outside that long.

Hetty continued. "While you were outside, I've told them about your plan for the ball and for the exhibit featuring my dresses and crowns."

Kathryn stepped forward. "We think it's a great idea."

"We also would like you to curate these new findings and make an exhibit of those," chimed in the mayor.

"And whatever you find at the high school that might shed more light on the history behind the photos," added Robert.

"Wow, I... that's amazing!" Dottie was ecstatic. Then her face dropped. "I... I can't. There is no way we can get all of this done in the three weeks left before Christmas. And you're closing the museum soon. I would in a heartbeat, and you all know that I always go down swinging, but it just seems like there is no point."

"Yes, but..." Hetty chimed in but seemed afraid to finish.

"I told you this might be a bad idea," Frank muttered.

"Hetty said that since Joe lives next door that you could probably get him to visit the museum occasionally," Amanda dug. "We could put it up on social media that there are Joe Thomas sightings here, and that would bring people in," Amanda chimed in.

"Speculation of where he disappeared too is hot in the media right now."

"And with refreshed exhibits we think that it might drive up excitement and interest about this place, creating a buzz," Kathryn said.

"The idea is that people will visit, chat about it or post about it on social media and encourage others to visit as well. Maybe with a brief tour of the space, they will also remember it for their events and book it for those types of things," the mayor chipped in.

"Ultimately, we need to get the community invested in this as a property, not just a museum. The Christmas ball is a great idea. We all love it," Henry said. "Especially if you can get Joe to attend. He will be a big draw."

They all jumped in voicing their ideas and they all were in agreement that Joe was the key. Dottie sighed. "Sure. Why not?" she replied to all of the expectant faces beaming at her. What else could she say? They were giving her and the museum a second chance. It would be a lot of work. But what else did she have to do? Convincing Joe... she wasn't quite sure how to do that. Squaring her shoulders, she added, "It will be no problem. I'm up for the task."

"Great," said the mayor. "Meeting adjourned. I'll see you all at the opening of the exhibits and the ball."

As they all said their goodbyes and left the museum, Dottie's face was dull. She tried to think of all of the ways she could get around it, finding no solution. Frank and Hetty stayed behind and came over to her.

"Dottie, I just wanted to let you know that I'm just going to finish a few things, so the elements don't get in, but I'll be back tomorrow to complete the patching," Frank said. If she didn't know better, he seemed to be wanting to tell her something.

"Was there something else, Frank?" she asked.

"Well..." he started but was cut off by Hetty coming back in the room eating another cookie.

"These are just so good," she said a little too overwhelmingly. "Here Frank, have another and then get going on that roof," Hetty said.

"I feel like you know something too," Dottie accused Hetty.

"What? What could I know?" Hetty said. "Oooh!" she said looking at her phone. "Dinner rush is about to begin. I've got to get back to the diner. Great meeting. Thanks for the cookies. See you later," Hetty made a hasty retreat for the door.

Now Dottie knew her friend was really up to something. But what could it be? Hetty couldn't keep secrets for very long. Dottie knew she would spill the beans eventually. She just hoped it didn't have to do with Joe Thomas.

CHAPTER ELEVEN

"So, the board is going to let you keep the museum open longer?"

"Yes. Well, no. Not exactly. I'm not quite sure on the terms of the agreement—" Dottie said to Harold. He had stopped by the museum about an hour after all of the board members had departed. She told him all that had happened that afternoon, leaving out the parts about her close moments with Joe, of course.

Harold was an average height and had hair that he always combed and gelled in place. It was shiny and didn't move. He had bright brown eyes and toothy grin filled with shiny white teeth that were so straight, everyone knew he still wore his retainer to bed. Almost always he was dressed in a suit. Dottie had not seen him in jeans and a tee-shirt outside of his house since high school.

"Well, that seems like a risky undertaking." Harold

stood in the kitchen with his hands on his hips. "Why would you put all of your time and effort into saving this place if it's not a sure thing?" Restlessly, he started fiddling with things on the counter and around the kitchen. Dottie was annoyed by his behavior, but stood with her arms crossed, sipping on cocoa. She made it because she needed the comfort. "And for that matter," Harold continued, "what if you're not even around to see the place stay open next year?"

Laughing at the thought of not being stuck in East Haddam, Dottie laughed. "Not be here, I think I'm stuck in this town for life."

Harold looked at her with a pained look. "No. No, you're better than this small-town life. We've always talked about the dream to live in a big city." He paused to let that sink in. "Dottie, I've been meaning to ask for a while now..." he paused as he walked around the counter to her. "But I was waiting for the right time..." he took the mug from her hands and set it down next to her on the counter and took her hands in his, "and now seems to be as right as any..."

Oh, no! Dottie's mind said. She wasn't ready for this, especially not after all that had just happened. Harold wasn't doing this today, of all days. The day that Joe fell through the roof and she found an amazing treasure trove in the attic. The day that the fate of the museum was put in her lap. Her heart raced, but anxiously and full of pressure. Not in the zippy romantic way. She made a face of confusion, and Harold took it as his cue to continue.

"Dottie," he said taking a deep breath. "Will you..." he paused making sure she was still looking at him, "... move to New York with me?"

Bursting with relief that moving was all he was proposing today, Dottie laughed.

Confused, Harold stepped back and dropped her hands. "I don't think this is a laughing matter, Dot. I have been working and trying to make this dream come true. You want to travel? New York is a great departure city with three international airports, plus all of that traveling takes money." He sighed as if she didn't understand, but then smiled as he continued excitedly. "My interviews went really well, and they've offered me the job in New York. I'm to start in two weeks, actually."

"Sorry, Harold. I'm really happy for you," she leapt forward and hugged him in congratulations. "Two weeks? Wow, that is really fast. That's the week before Christmas."

"They actually want me to start sooner," he said. "There is a big campaign launching in January they want me working on. I told them I needed a little time to talk to you and find a place up there."

"Harold, I think," she said stepping back from him and rationalizing, "I think if they want you sooner, you should go. As long as it's fine with Mrs. Hobbes." Harold had been freelancing with a temp agency and had been taking on assistant work. He hated it but was waiting for the right agency to hire him.

"Really?" His face lit up. "I know that it will be a quick move up to New York, but I've already scouted some places that you'll love——"

"Harold. I can't leave before Christmas," Dottie said shaking her head. "You go on without me and get started and I'll——"

"What do you mean? They're closing this place

anyway. Why not go right away and we can start a whole new life together," Harold was almost pleading. Dottie realized he did this a lot. He tried to make it seem like Dottie was holding them both back from living their dreams.

"I know it doesn't make the most sense, but it really means a lot to me to see this through. You should have seen how excited Hetty was about her exhibit. And I've never seen the board get so excited about the possibility of featuring anything as they were those photos," Dottie felt an energy and lightness soar through her. She hadn't felt this way in a very long time. It was exhilarating. "It feels like I have a genuine mystery on my hands, and I would really like to figure it all out."

"But I don't understand. Is all of this," he said pointing at the innocent cookies on the counter, "worth giving up a great dream with me?"

"Harold," she reasoned, "New York will still be there in a month or two. I just want—"

"It's Joe, isn't it? I've heard he's been skulking around here a lot lately," Harold surged with an anger that Dottie rarely saw.

"Are you... are you really competing with Joe Thomas?" Dottie was confounded. This was out of left field.

"No," Harold looked away as if he were hiding something. And then he looked back and said sternly as he looked out the kitchen window in the direction of Joe's house. "I just," he took a deep breath and his anger subsided. In a caring voice he said, "I just want you in New York. I'm no good without you. I've done all of this for you." Harold took her arms and wrapped them around his waist and kissed her forehead. She sighed as if Dottie were upset, and he was soothing her. In a calming voice he said, "Listen, I hear you want more time. I'll go on ahead and you can come up when your temporary assignment is done."

Dottie just smiled but was unconvinced. Not knowing how to voice what she was really feeling, she decided to just roll with it all for now. "Sounds good," she said with a false smile.

"Great!" he exclaimed. He started walking toward the kitchen door, pulling out his cell phone. "I'll call and accept. You go home and get dressed up; we're going out to celebrate!"

"I can't tonight, Harold," she frowned. "I..." she needed to think up something quickly. "I told Hetty, I'd help her out with—"

"Fine, fine. We'll go tomorrow. Hello. Mr. Abbott?" he said into the phone waving Dottie off as the call on his cell connected. "I'll see you later," he whispered to her, covering up the speaker, then pulling the door closed behind him. "I would like to officially accept your offer. Now, about company housing..." his voice drifted away as he walked to his car.

It all seemed reasonable. And the big city was a dream they always talked about. New York seemed exciting. But why did all of this make her skin crawl. Had he always done this, thrown out every tactic in the book? Dottie started thinking—when did she actually start dreaming of living in a big city? And why did it not seem to have such a pull now?

CHAPTER TWELVE

"So... you're telling me the 'big question' Harold had to ask you was *moving to New York?!?*. How rid—" Hetty said leaning on the diner counter in astonishment. She turned away to grab the coffee pot to refill Dottie's cup and changed her line of thought. "You know though, it really doesn't surprise me," she said a bit dumbfounded.

Dottie looked at her friend, waiting to talk until Hetty was done ranting. Honestly, Dottie still didn't quite know how she felt about the situation herself. Even now, a day later, Dottie didn't know what her answer was. She knew what it should be. She knew what Harold wanted to hear. Dottie was just now realizing they were no longer one and the same.

"Hetty, I have a question," she looked at her friend in the eye. "And I need you to give me a serious answer, as someone who cares about me deeply—"

"Loves you!" Hetty shouted and a few heads turned in the diner. "You all heard me, and you know it's true! I LOVE DOTTIE!"

"Stop it!" Dottie threw her napkin at Hetty in protest but gave way to laughter bubbling up inside. She needed that laugh. Everything was so serious lately with all of the plans for the museum; first closing, and now having the pressure to plan and execute two new exhibits and a ball.

After they stopped laughing, in a more subdued volume, Dottie said, "And I love you, too Hetty. But stop trying to change the subject." Dottie swallowed her fear and said, "I'm not blind, and I know you're not partial to Harold—"

"Pffft! I hardly tolerate that man. And its only because I love you so much."

"I know. I know. But in your honest observation, did I want to travel or live in a big city before we started dating."

Hetty looked puzzled. "I don't really remember... I know you and Harold started dating after I finally qualified for International Junior Miss, so I wasn't around a ton because I was getting ready for that one." Hetty drifted away into her memories.

With a brain that could take a dress apart and turn it into a pattern, Hetty's mind worked like a backwards assembly line.

"I remember when Joe, you and I used to sit in the woods or at the pond we would wonder what far off places were like. Joe promised he would send you postcards if he went."

"*That's* what all of those postcards were! He visited some of the places we talked about as kids," a light turned on inside of Dottie.

"Yeah, you said you wondered if they all were as impressive in person." Hetty drifted through more memories. Dottie could see the memories churning in her head like old film being rewound slowly. "Nope."

"Nope, what? Nope you don't remember?" Dottie asked.

"No. Nope you didn't really talk about living in a big city until Harold. I remember you and Joe wanting to see places. You would talk about The Taj Mahal and The Leaning Tower of Pisa. I know you wanted to see all of the big cities in America... but I don't think you were on the bandwagon to live the big city life until you got older."

"Huh." Dottie said, leaning her head on her hands on the counter.

"Now, that's not to say it wasn't a grownup fancy of yours. But, look at you," Hetty said pointing to Dottie in her clogs, comfy jeans and her shirt with "Future Mrs. Darcy" printed on it. "You were always getting adventure in books and that museum. You've always balked at coming with me on my pageant trips—"

"No, I haven't! I've gone with you several—"

Hetty cut her best friend off. "I didn't say you didn't go. I said you balked. In other words, you hesitated to go to a big city for a week." Hetty continued as she came around the counter and sat on a stool next to Dottie. "And think about college."

"I left town for college!' Dottie rebutted.

"Yeah, but you went to Yale for a very specific History degree," Hetty said like it needed no further explanation.

"Which is a very prestigious school!" Dottie said in wounded protest.

"New Haven is a sleepy college town. AND

history is not one of the sexier majors that leads into a career where you have to be outgoing and social," Hetty added.

"Well, I…"

"Listen, honey. We all have dreams. When we are kids, our dreams are big and grand. As we get older, they take more shape, or become redefined. Sometimes the dreams we have as kids fade away entirely as we realize other things like family and security become more important or easier to obtain. As adults we figure out ways to adapt the original dreams into our lives," she motioned to the walls of the diner. "It doesn't mean that the dream loses value. It is still a part of us, no matter what." Hetty looked around the diner. "When I was seven, I wanted to be a princess or a queen and rule a kingdom; to be worshiped and admired by all in the land." She sighed. "And now? I have twenty crowns to my name and have lines out the door to visit my place. Is it the exact same dream? No. But did I get what I wished for?" Hetty looked around again, a tear coming to her eye and a smile filled her face. "Yeah," she said almost breathlessly. "Yeah, I did."

Reaching across the tiny divide, Dottie wrapped her arms around a woman who knew her better than she knew herself and hugged her.

The bell rang from the kitchen and the cook shouted, "Order up!" Making them both sit back, and Hetty wiped her tears on the bottom of her apron.

"I'll get this one, Hetty. You sit for a moment."

Grabbing the plates from the small window, and checking the ticket for the table number, she walked over to the guests at one of the repurposed wooden tables.

"Hello, Aaron. Kitty," Dottie greeted the firefighter who was up on her roof and his daughter. "Now let me guess… Kitty you got the eggs over easy with sausage and rye toast."

"No!" the eight-year-old girl said in a delighted wail. "I got the chocolate chip pancakes!"

"Oh!" Dottie said. "It's a good thing I asked." she said giving Kitty a wink. "Here you go, guys. Aaron, do you need a warm up on that coffee?"

"No. Thank you though." Aaron said smiling up at her.

As Kitty dug into her pancakes, Dottie continued. "Thanks again for cutting Joe out of the roof."

"Just in a day's work," Aaron said giving a bit of a nod. "Besides, how many people can have the bragging rights that they cut a famous person out of a roof?"

"You and probably half of Los Angeles!'

They both laughed.

"Holler if you need anything," Dottie said looking first at Aaron then at the chocolate faced Kitty who was making a complete mess of her face and her plate."

"Will do, Dottie. Oh, and hey," Aaron had reached across and started cutting up smaller bites for Kitty, "Sorry about the museum closing."

"The museum is closing?" Kitty wailed again, this time she was not pleased. Her saucer eyes started to tear up as she looked back and forth between Aaron and Dottie. "But, but, but… if it closes, we won't get to take the field trip. Everyone knows that the bestest part of third grade is going to the museum in spring!" Kitty protested.

Kneeling down so she was eye level with Kitty, Dottie said, "Yeah, I'm sad too. I remember taking that trip when I was your age. But I'll tell you what," she looked conspiratorially at Aaron then back at his daughter, "Your daddy helped me this week, so why don't you two have your own trip over to the museum in a week, and I'll give you a sneak peek at the princess exhibit."

"You're going to have *real* princesses?" Kitty asked excitedly, her emotions switching as fast as the weather on the Connecticut River.

"Well," Dottie lowered her voice almost to a whisper, even though none of the surrounding tables were full, "We're going to highlight Hetty. She's a real live queen, you know!"

"Woah!" Kitty and Aaron both said together, Aaron being the wonderful parent and playing along.

"How do you think this diner got its name?" Dottie lowered her voice, "But you can't tell, *anyone*. Pinky swear." Dottie held her pinky out to the little girl.

Kitty linked pinkies then looked at her father, "You too, Daddy," she said sternly. Aaron laughed and wrapped his pinky around Kitty and Dottie's.

"I swear," he said.

They solemnly shook to seal the promise. Standing up, Dottie said, "Ok, I'll see you soon,"

"Ok," Kitty whispered loudly and tried to wink making both Dottie and Aaron laugh before she went back to massacring her pancakes.

"You are so good with kids," Hetty said.

"I only wish I was as good with adults," Dottie replied sitting back down on the stool and putting her hands on her face. Muffled, she said, "How am I going to talk Joe Thomas, who is obviously hiding out, to just 'pop up' on social media at my museum? It's hopeless." Dottie put her head down on the counter.

Stroking Dottie's hair, Hetty said, "Well, have you tried just asking him?"

"Oh sure," Dottie snapped her head up, "Hey, Joe! Sorry you fell through my roof! Could you do me a favor of putting out to the masses that you frequently visit our small museum so it can increase foot traffic, because people will hope for a chance sighting of you?"

"Well... when you put it that way..." Hetty shrugged her shoulders. Dottie put her head back down on the counter making a loud grunting sigh on her way back down.

"What if you made him some food? Maybe more cookies?" Hetty suggested.

Dottie gave a muffled response from her head buried in her arms on the counter, "No carbs in the off season, remember? And I already made him chili... and you bring him food all the time."

"Ok. Well. What else does he need? Could you help him clean up his place?"

"Hetty!" Dottie petulantly raised her head with her brow knitted, "I have two exhibits to set up, one which needs a lot of research, and a ball to plan! I will barely have time to sleep in the next ten days, let alone any free time to help Joe fix his house!" She threw her arms up in the air.

"Right. Well... what about something festive. A wreath?" Dottie snapped her head around only to see Hetty was grinning from ear to ear. It was a joke.

"Wait," Dottie said after a moment. "What could I do to spruce up his house? What doesn't he have that everyone needs this time of year?" Dottie's voice grew with excitement. "What am I going to get this afternoon for myself and the museum?!?"

They hollered together, "A Tree!" They both jumped up and hugged.

"Wait. Why are we hugging?" Hetty asked. "It's not like we cured a disease or solved world hunger."

"Yet." Dottie replied. "See you later," she replied full of hope. She grabbed her keys and bounded out of the diner.

"Go, get 'em kid." Hetty said. Then she mumbled to no one as she walked back behind the counter, "It's good to see she got her gumption back."

CHAPTER THIRTEEN

Taking a deep breath and attempting to discard her nerves in an exhale, Dottie wrapped on the front door. "Joe!" she called and knocked harder. She heard nothing, but lights on and his truck in the driveway made it obvious he was home. Maybe he was upstairs or had music playing or something and couldn't hear her. Taking another deep breath to steady her courage, Dottie walked in and hollered again, "Joe! It's Dot! Are you home?"

Dottie heard footsteps above her and then on the stairs. His staircase went straight up twelve stairs and hit a landing before turning and four stairs went up to the right to connect with the second floor. She knew it well. They used to taboggan down these very stairs, using towels to allow smoother sliding.

Standing above her on the landing was a dripping Joe Thomas clad in a towel.

"Everything ok?" he asked, looking concerned.

Dottie blushed and looked quickly away covering her eyes with her hand. "Don't you have any modesty?"

"No. No, I don't. I'm in a locker room with teammates, coaches, reporters and who knows what else," he replied. She could hear the grin in his voice when he continued, "and I look pretty good in a towel. Besides, you're the one walking into my house."

Dottie laughed. "I'm… sure." She cleared her throat. "I… I can come back if this isn't a good time."

"What's up?" he said trying to sound breezy, and not overly excited that Dottie was near him again. His happy tone quickly turned to concern. He asked, "nothing wrong at the museum, I hope? Not the roof again?"

"No! No," she said making the mistake and looking up at him again. Wow he was muscular. Diverting her gaze, she explained, "Frank and Myrrh said you were trying to get the place ready to sell," she looked around to see all of the hard work he had put in. The walls were freshly painted. Sparse furniture arrangement confirmed her observation. "They said you didn't have a Christmas tree, and I thought—"

"Oh, I won't be here for Christmas," Joe said a little too quickly and mentally scolded himself for being so sharp about it.

"Oh?" she said downtrodden. "Well," she sighed, then added with a persuasive tone, "I thought it might help prospective buyers get into the spirit, and so I bought an extra one for you, but I can—" she started to walk out the door.

"No!" Joe hollered and ran down half of the staircase. "I mean. If you bought it," he shrugged, "we might as well put it up."

"Great! I brought some colored lights and some tinsel for you—"

"I actually just found the boxes of my mom's decorations—" they spoke at the same time, and then laughed at cutting each other off.

Joe rubbed his neck and looked down at his bare toes.

"Why don't you... um... the boxes are actually in the living room if you want to start looking through. I'll go get dressed and then help you get the tree in here."

"Great," she said making a thumbs up sign and then feeling like an idiot.

Joe ran up the stairs. Dottie tried not to look at him, but she did. Then blushed. Unzipping her puffer vest and taking off her gloves, she walked into the living room and turned on the light. The giant front window was perfect a tree. People would be welcomed by it not only as they walked up the front walkway, but as they came down the driveway as well.

There were three boxes, and Dottie carefully opened the first. A collection of boxes and wrapped objects inhabited it. Gently picking up an object carefully wrapped in leftover red and white Santa paper, Dottie pulled back the edges of the crumpled paper to reveal a handmade snowflake of popsicle sticks covered with glitter. It had a light blue loop of tattered yarn at the top. It had a light blue loop of tattered yarn at the top. She remembered making a similar one in Mrs. Misse's first grade class.

Echoes of that day floated into her mind. Joe asked to borrow her scissors. She had loaned them to

Hetty after promising them to him. Not one to go back on her word, Dottie mustered courage and walked up to the teacher to ask for the coveted adult pair for Joe to use. She smiled at her own gumption. If only she had retained more of it as she got older. She audibly sighed.

Unwrapping a few more, reminders of past holidays flitted through her mind. Opening up a brown square box, Dottie gasped. It was a snowman holding a baseball bat, ready to swing.

"You gave me that one," Joe said from behind her.

Turning toward him, Dottie held up the ornament and smiled. "It was the third or fourth year you played baseball. You kept changing positions that year, and every year you changed numbers," she turned back and set the ornament down next to the rest pulling out another box.

Joe had joined her and was looking at the ones she had laid out.

"Where did this one come from?" Dottie asked holding up what looked like an unhappy brown hippo made out of cotton balls and paper with googly eyes.

He reached for it and smiled, "A Winter Festival when I was five. We hadn't moved here yet, and I was with my cousins. Our parents made us do them, even though I was making a giant protest about crafts. We sat down to make these, and I didn't want to. I was told if I made an ornament, I could play catch with the big kids. I glued the parts on so fast, and then ran off to play. It was always one of my mom's favorites," he chuckled and got lost in his memory.

"Baseball even pulled you away then," Dottie teased.

Feeling Dottie's eyes on him, Joe looked up. Clearing his throat, he set down the fluffy ornament, and said, "Well, should we go get that tree?"

"Sure," Dottie said, seeing a side of Joe that she hadn't in a very long time. She missed that softer side of Joe. She grabbed her discarded vest that she had taken off while she was unwrapping ornaments. They walked outside together. Large fluffy flakes of snow cascaded from the sky and sat on their clothing for a moment reminding that each flake was an individual miracle. The falling snow dampened the sound outside, so it was comfortingly quiet on the driveway.

"I didn't know it was snowing, "Joe said, looking up.

"Must have just started," Dottie stated, "It wasn't snowing when I... uh," Dottie blushed remembering.

"Walked in on me in a towel?" Joe suggested.

"Well... yes," she said walking to the car and clicking the unlock button.

"Dottie, it's really ok. I'm used to it," Joe shrugged as he opened the rear passenger side door and started to test the rope.

"You might be, but I'm not," Dottie said. "You might live in a big city and be in a locker room all of the time with lots of... other players," she gulped as she quickly pushed that thought out of her brain. "But I am not used to men walking around less than clothed in..." She looked over at him. Joe was ducking trying to stifle a laugh. "Never mind." Then trying to change the subject, "They're tied on to the top. There are two trees. The other I'm taking up to the museum to put in the ballroom after this."

"Great," he said pulling a pocket knife out of his

jeans and starting to cut the knots. "So," he said with guile, "Harold doesn't walk around much in a towel?" A sly grin spread across his face.

"No, he... we... No." Dottie shook her head. She said a lot without saying or revealing anything. Now wasn't the time to question her relationship with Harold, she thought to herself. Nor did she want to talk about relationships in general with Joe. Especially when she was here on a mission to save the museum. "I hope you like the tree," she diverted the conversation.

"I'm sure," he said cutting through the last knot, "I'm sure I'll like standing next to it, once it's all decorated. Standing in my towel," he said coming around the car making eye contact. He always loved teasing her. Hiding her embarrassment with a chuckle, she backhanded him on the shoulder. "Stop it! I haven't blushed like this in..." she looked at Joe. He was looking at her with a goofy grin. "What?"

Shaking his head and rubbing the back of his neck, "Nothing," he said and looked at her again. He then looked up to the sky. "Seems like the snow is coming down harder, we should get this inside, so you can get the other one up to the museum."

"Right," Dottie grabbed the top of the tree from the front of the car. Joe grabbed the back and they carried it up to the house.

"Let's stop here for a moment," Joe said as he set down the tree. "We can tie the other one onto your car and then take this one in."

"Oh," Dottie said, "I'm just going next door. We don't have to secure it too well."

"Well, I—" Joe protested.

"Joe, I don't drive like a maniac. Let's just loop the rope around the base of the tree and through the doors."

"I don't know—" he questioned.

Walking over to the car, Dottie started to do just as she suggested, "It will be *fiine*. You worry too much," she threw over her shoulder at him.

Sighing Joe walked to the car and helped Dottie tie up the tree. When they were done, they carried the tree to the front room.

They started with the lights but didn't get far as they both had a different technique. Hers circled the tree from the base, while his was more of a vertical striping technique.

"You can't do it that way," Dottie laughed.

"Who made you the lighting police?" Joe asked.

"It's just that you should go around and around to echo the tinsel," she demonstrated making circles with her finger that pointed down to the floor.

"Echo the tinsel? Who says that," Joe asked?

"It's a technical term," Dottie smartly retorted. "It's faster too. You stand on that side," she pointed where Joe should stand, and I'll hand you the lights and we can get them up easier."

Just like she suggested, Dottie and Joe passed the lights back and forth and they quickly wrapped the tree twice with lights. Then together they wrapped the tree in silver tinsel. Together they hung all of the individual ornaments. Decorating the tree took longer than Dottie expected it to, but she was having so much fun she didn't mind.

"You have to put that one in prominent spot," Joe said when Dottie was bending down to put an angel ornament around the side of the tree. She had a chip out of her wing, and her face had rubbed off. And there were a few feathers left making it look like it was molting.

"Why?" Dottie judged scrunching her nose.

"It was my mom's favorite. She got it when she did her first Christmas pageant when she was a girl. She was an angel."

"Oh, well then," Dottie stepped to her left looking at the tree. She thought Joe had moved to get another ornament, but she ended up stepping right into him. Stepping away to avoid stepping on his toes, she lost her balance. She twisted, trying to catch herself and she fell onto Joe, her hands on his chest. His arms wrapped in a bear hug around her as he caught her. Dottie froze. For the second time this week she found herself in his arms. And she couldn't lie to herself, it felt nice. She took in his fresh spicy scent, his warm arms and felt a glow rush her through entire body.

"Thank you," Dottie sputtered as she self-consciously pushed her way out of his arms.

"Sure, no... problem."

They both laughed nervously.

"I'll... just... put the ornament—" Dottie stammered as she kept his eye, but then quickly looked away.

"Here," Joe said pointing to a place in the middle of the tree, and right at eye level. "See, that's perfect. Now we can see her. Imperfections and all."

"Oh, speaking of which," Dottie bit her lip, "bringing you this tree was sort of a bribe?"

"I knew you had to have ulterior motives," he accused her with delight.

"I couldn't ever keep anything from you for long." Dottie blushed and tried to hide it by hanging another ornament. "As you know the museum is having problems."

"Yes…"

"Well, it was suggested by the board, and Hetty mentioned that you would likely that you would be willing to help out because you're a nice person." Dottie started to pace. She hated buttering people up, thinking they always saw right through her. "Even though I said that you were only here to fix your family's house and didn't want to be bothered. And really, we've, well I've bothered you enough already and—"

Joe laughed. "Dottie, spit it out. It's just me."

"Oh, it's not because you're famous. Well actually it *is* because you're famous—"

"Dottie," Joe stood in front of her and held her by the arms. "Really, I'm still your friend. The one who rode bikes with you. The one who would hide out with you in the woods when times were rough. The one who used to beat you badly at Monopoly."

Her breath catching, Dottie covered with a smile as his never-failing habit to comfort her kicked in.

"Ok. Well, it would really be great, well more than great. It would be really helpful," she looked at her feet, "That's only if you won't mind—"

His finger lifted her chin. Their eyes locked. She took another deep breath.

"Would you come to the museum and allow us to post on social media that you've been seen there? And then maybe come back every so often just to prove the rumors?" She spoke quickly.

A confused look crossed his face. Then it seemed to turn to anger. Joe dropped his arms and turned away from Dottie and rubbed his neck.

"I'm sorry, I shouldn't have asked," she rambled again. Dottie picked up the last of the ornaments and put them on the tree. "It was a silly idea, I tried to tell them that—"

"Yes," he said, his back still turned.

"Right? I mean you have so many things to do while you're in town. And you said you're trying to keep a low profile and—"

He turned and cut her off, "No, Dottie. Yes."

"I know. I didn't mean to—"

"Yes," he said raising his volume so she would hear him over her rant. "Yes, Dottie, I'll do it."

She hung the last ornament and then ran over to him and threw her arms around him. She was overjoyed and felt like in this moment all would work out. She felt a little overzealous in hugging him and pulled back only to have him hold her for an extra moment and she had to gently wiggle away. Her awkward smile met a familiar smile of his, one that had a secret. Although she was curious, she turned back to the subject of saving the museum.

"Thank you so much! I'm sure it won't fix everything, but maybe it will give the place a little boost and we can get more traffic. Maybe I can get people to rent out the space for events, that always makes us more money."

"Do you always ramble this much?" he smiled.

"No, I... no." She blushed.

"Good. Because you know what time it is?" he asked with something clearly on his mind.

"No. I have no idea," she answered hesitantly.

He walked over to the tree and looked at her. "It's time for the grand finale," he winked at her and lowered himself to kneeling below the tree. He dove under the bottom branches as she turned away.

"Oh right, the star!" she said, grabbing the remaining box that sat on the sofa. "Here, you do the honors."

"Yes! I forgot about the topper. Hold on to it for a moment," he said from under the tree.

"What are you doing down there, Joe Thomas?"

"A secret my dad taught me, and I always like to do. Making the lights flash," he said.

"How do you do that? These are just regular lights," she reminded him.

"Yes, but they all come with a flasher bulb. The red tipped one, if you replace one of the bulbs with it, they will flash," he said with a grunt of exertion.

He then stood up. "Ok, star first then the grand finale." He smiled at her, and she handed him the star and smiled back. Dottie liked him like this. She put her hand on his back to steady him while he reached up and put the star on the tree. When he was finished, excitedly he dove down under the tree.

"Drum roll please!" he shouted.

Patting her legs quickly to sound like a drum, Dottie encouraged him. And then, suddenly the tree twinkled.

She took a couple of steps back to take in the tree. Mesmerized, she didn't realize he had joined her and stood to her side.

"Wow! This looks amazing," she said.

"We did a great job." he said.

"The flashing lights make it really festive," she said.

Minutes passed as they both took in the magnificence of the tree. It was one of those moments when the only thing that mattered was just to be.

Joe turned to her and said, "Thank you. I needed this."

"Oh, it was nothing," she waved her hand to brush away the thanks. Then she turned to him. "It's really me that should be thanking you. What you're doing for the museum, no for me, is amazing."

"Don't you know I'd do anything for you Dottie?" he said quietly and vulnerably. She couldn't believe all of the honesty coming from him and wondered if he meant to be this open with her. He shook his head and rubbed his neck, "I think I care for you more than you care for me."

Dottie laughed, thinking he was making a joke. She looked up to see him intensely focused on adjusting a Santa ornament.

"Oh, Joe I—" she started to apologize. But then the question that had been burning inside of her for over a decade just slipped out. "What happened all those years ago?" Dottie asked.

"What do you mean?" Joe replied, knowing exactly what she meant but played dumb.

"We used to be great friends. All three of us," Dottie said sadly. "Then one day, junior year, you just stopped talking to me."

"Well you know how kids are, and baseball—" he deflected and started to walk away.

"No!" she chased after him and stood in the

doorway blocking him from leaving the room. "Joseph Thomas you know exactly what I mean. It might have been years since I've seen you, but I know you much better than you think." Dottie surged on. "You stopped talking to me. It was right around the time—"

"Harold asked you out." he finished for her and sighed with defeat.

"Wait, what?"

Joe turned away from her and walked back to the large picture window in the room and looked out at the falling snow. He sighed deeply before offering his confession, "The day you said yes when Harold asked you to the dance was the day I felt like I had no business talking to you anymore."

A stunned silence hung between them. The lights from the Christmas tree glinted as if they had secrets that they afraid to let go of as well. She took a couple of steps into the room, more to regain her balance as the floor didn't seem as steady as it was moments ago when she started this conversation.

"But... but, why?" Dottie finally stuttered.

Turning back to face her, his confession poured out of him. "I thought that if you wanted him, you wouldn't want me. He and I are so different. And I just couldn't take that," he paused to rub his neck. "You see, I have loved you from the moment I met you Dorothy," he said using her given name adding weight to his admission. He lightly stroked her cheek with the back of her hand as he looked deeply into her eyes. "You and your mother knocked on our door and had cookies just like the ones you brought me. Your hair was in pigtails, and freckles dotted your face." Joe blushed. "When I met you, I thought you were named for your freckles," he smiled and met her eyes. Her knees started to give, and she started to walk to the sofa. Joe leapt to her, putting his arms around her just in time. Joe caught her as she started to collapse and he lowered both of them to sit on the sofa. As if she were on fire, he jumped back up again going back to the safety of the picture window.

"Wow the snow is really coming down out there," he commented.

"Don't change the subject," she said weakly trying to use a little bit of humor. "Why did you..."

"Why did I stop talking to you?" He said looking back at her and then rubbing the back of his neck with his hand. "Because the day before he asked you out, I told Harold how I felt."

CHAPTER FOURTEEN

Silence filled the room as he tried not to give away more of the story that might rip apart her future and soil her happiness. Dottie tried to put the puzzle together, but couldn't she asked, "Why would that make any difference?"

"The day before he asked you out, I told him how I really felt about you."

"What?" she was still confused.

Joe's lungs ached. He wished she just knew the rest of the story and he didn't have to speak it. Many years of holding it in made his heart pound and his head ache. He could feel the knot in his stomach getting tighter with every moment that passed. Well, he finally thought to himself, looking out at the snow, I haven't spoken to her in over twelve years. If tonight she never talks to me again after finally hearing the truth, maybe it's for the best. Joe had been harboring a broken heart too long.

His voice came out in almost a whisper. "After practice, it was a Tuesday. You were helping with the quilting ladies and didn't need a ride home. I was sitting in the bullpen by myself. Harold had showered and came out to find me."

"You look down. What's up chum?" Harold had asked.

"Ah, nothing." Joe said as he just sat there.

"I know that look. Its either baseball or a girl," Harold guessed.

Joe's head snapped up to look at his friend and squinted as he scanned Harold's face. He wondered; did Harold know? Joe got up and started collecting his things.

"Nah, it's nothing." Joe said hoping Harold would take the hint and walk away. Slowly and deliberately he took off all of his pads and packed everything away in his oversized duffel bag to carry them to the locker room. Joe turned around to find Harold standing in the doorway of the chain link fence that led from the bullpen to the field.

"Let me out, man," Joe said with an edge of pleading. He really didn't want to confess how he felt to Harold of all people.

"Tell. Me. What's. Going. On." Harold replied brightly like a kindergarten teacher.

Throwing his bag to the ground, Joe sat back down on the bench and crossed his arms over his chest. "Nope."

Trying a different tactic, Harold sat down a foot away from him and crossed his arms as well. "Come on man. Your game is off. Has been for a few weeks now. Is it because those scouts seem to be coming back more regularly?"

Joe said nothing but took a deep breath in and out. Harold's freshly showered scent made Joe long for a shower. His muscles were so sore and tense.

"Okay," Harold continued his inquiry. "So, it's not the scouts. Then it's a girl."

Joe had one tell about his feelings. Hetty was too close to the whole situation, being friends with Dottie, too. Joe didn't dare talk to her. It was a weird feeling to not share his feelings with Hetty or Dottie, the two people he always confided in.

When thinking, Joe rubbed the back of his neck. No movement so Harold deduced he was on the right track.

"Well then," he said intrigued and turned toward Joe with his arms still crossed. "Hmm... is it Samantha?"

Joe thought of Samantha, the cute girl who was at every game. She was a year behind them, and quite obviously had a crush on him. That wasn't who he was attracted to, though.

"Not Samantha, huh?" Seeing no movement from Joe to indicate anything, Harold got up and paced a few steps.

"April?"

Joe chuckled. Harold was way off base. The girl who sat by Joe in biology was not even close to his type. She was a really nice person, but Joe was pretty sure she wasn't interested in him either.

"Hetty?"

His beauty queen best friend should be the obvious choice for Joe, but she was not the girl of his dreams. Harold was getting too close to the truth now, making Joe fidget in the smallest way. Harold, a pitcher trained to home in on the smallest of his catcher's movements saw it.

"Not Hetty then. But I'm getting close!" Harold paced away a few steps, then quickly turned around. He knew. Joe tried to make himself stay as still as possible. He would not give his biggest secret away. Joe hadn't had time to weigh the options and outcomes. How could he possibly talk about this to Harold before he knew what he would do himself.

Harold sat down leaning into Joe. Harold stared at Joe for an interminably long time. Not being able to stand it anymore, Joe slowly started to turn his head toward Harold. Taking it as his cue, Harold whispered, "Dottie."

With a double blink of both eyes, Joe gave away everything.

"You have feelings for Dottie?!?" Harold laughed. Joe couldn't be sure if Harold laughed because he was so delighted that he had figured it out or because Joe had revealed he had feelings for Dottie of all the girls in the school.

To hide his embarrassment, Joe stood up and grabbed his bag, only to find the resistance of Harold holding on to the strap as well.

"She's... Dottie's beautiful, Joe." Harold confessed. "Why haven't you told her yet?"

Joe rubbed the back of his neck and sighed. "I don't know," he said looking out at the field. "We've been friends for so long, I didn't want to complicate it. And now with these scouts every game..."

"So... are you going to ask her out," Harold prodded.

Joe looked back at his friend who seemed genuine. "I don't know. Do you think I should?"

"Why not? I don't know how she feels. She certainly doesn't look at you with goo-goo eyes, like the other girls do. But maybe that's a good thing."

"Yeah," Joe said looking off into distance. "Or maybe it means we're just friends."

"Big dance is coming up. Ask her and see what she says," Harold suggested and dropped the strap of the bag.

"I don't know," Joe said as he yanked the bag toward him and in one practiced move swung it over his shoulder and pulled the strap over his head. He walked out of the bullpen and onto the field toward the locker room.

"Just ask her," Harold yelled after him. Joe rubbed his neck all the way to the showers. "If you don't, I will," Harold shouted as he was almost in the locker room. Those words echoed through Joe's mind for almost two decades.

Joe shook off the memory as he shook his head.

"And so," Joe said after he retold Dottie the entire story, "I had made up my mind to ask you that next day. Harold was talking to you at your locker. Then Hetty came over to me and broke the news that Harold had asked you to the dance. And you accepted." Joe sighed before he continued. "You smiled and started to laugh at something he said to you at your locker. You were so happy, and I didn't want to take that from you. The dance came and went, and it seemed like every time I went to talk to you, there was Harold by your side."

Dottie didn't know what to say. She thought she

should return his confession with her own truth and feelings, but when she finally found words, all of the wrong things tumbled out. "So, when you saw that Harold made me laugh, you just decided to stop talking to me? You decided to throw away years of friendship because I said yes to *one dance*? To the first boy, in fact, who had ever taken the time to ask me out. Because no one would ask me out because you were always around." The gaping wound she had ignored for years finally opened up and gushed feelings. She was standing now, flung all of these feelings at him. Why couldn't she say something that was helpful? Why couldn't she tell him how she really felt about him? It was almost like she wasn't herself, and someone else had inhibited her body. Someone with years of rage and anger and passion who needed to let it all out. "How dare you, Joseph Thomas, to decide for the both of us all of those years ago."

Dottie whipped around and stormed out of the house grabbing her coat.

Conflicted, he stood at the window watching her leave. He wanted to run after her because he loved her. The snow was coming down really hard and she might get stuck. But he knew her well enough to know that she needed time. Also, if her reaction was to scream at him when he told her his feelings, well that made his choice many years ago just that much more right. He needed to finish what he came to do and get out of this town, once and for all.

CHAPTER FIFTEEN

And he would have succeeded in doing just that if the other Christmas Tree hadn't fallen off of Dottie's car as she peeled out of his driveway in her car. He stared out the window at the tree for a while. An innocent bystander, the poor tree didn't deserve to just be left out in the cold. It was almost completely covered in snow before he decided what to do. The brilliant idea would work. But he needed help. Grabbing his coat from the hook and his keys and cell phone off of the front table, he threw his coat on and dialed. This was the move he should have made years ago.

* * *

Dottie drove off pressing the gas deeply into the floor. She felt the car kick in the snow. Blind with anger or passion, Dottie thought it was the car and the snow that kicked as she drove at speeds, she didn't know her father's old car could go.

It wasn't until she had parked the car, marched up the stairs to her apartment, opened a bottle of wine, poured a glass and took her first sip that she realized what happened.

"Crap!" she hollered so loudly that Mrs. Johnson next door probably heard it. "Sorry, Mrs. Johnson, she said in a singsong whisper, hoping the essence of the apology would float through the wall. The tree she had bought for the museum was now probably in Joe's front lawn covered with snow or smashed with bits on the road.

Well, who cared? She certainly didn't she told herself. There were other Christmas Trees in the farm! And she slammed back her glass of wine to punctuate the thought. She poured another glass. Trying to calm herself, she went and sat on her sofa, crossed her legs and took another sip. It didn't help. She jumped up and started pacing the room like a caged tiger.

"How dare he decide for the both of us!" she said out loud, echoing the sentiment she felt earlier.

Dottie's quiet life was upended. To find out that her big dream wasn't really hers at all, but Harold's. And then to find out that Harold had known Joe liked her and asked her out.

"Hetty!" Dottie growled her friend's name in anger. "She's known all along!" She paced and drank her wine as she tried to unravel her thoughts, feeling like everyone was against her and out to get her all of her life.

"Ok, wait. Think this through," Dottie kept talking to herself, taking in a deep breath through her nose, making her nostrils flare. She set her glass down on the table. Paper. She needed paper. Doing a quick gaze around her living room, she spied her box of wrapping paper laying on the floor. She popped open the top and grabbed a roll. Then she took three steps to the junk drawer in the kitchen and grabbed a handful of permanent markers that were there. This small apartment was perfect for finding many things quickly. She picked up her glass, paper and markers, then swept everything else off the coffee table to the floor. It was a very dramatic gesture, but in reality, it was two coasters, a remote control and a magazine that proclaimed it could tell you the secrets of worriless holiday decorating.

"Yeah, don't try decorating someone from your past's house!" Dottie said to the magazine. With a practiced air she crossed her ankles and sank to the ground cross legged. Dottie was down on the floor in two seconds. The markers she tossed on the floor next to her knee, and took the paper set it on one end of the table with the white side up and let it roll away, so the table was now covered in paper. The cardboard tube skittered across the floor being free of the paper and hit the wall. Taking a red marker, Dottie started writing in no particular order or placement:

Joe has had feelings for me since??
Harold knew all along.
HETTY knew all along.
If I were Hetty would I have told me?
Joe left, so apparently his feelings weren't <u>that</u> <u>big</u>.
Harold wants me to move to New York.
Did I ever want to live in a big city?
What is <u>my</u> <u>dream</u>?

Picking up the green marker she started to write answers next to the questions or just somewhere on the paper.

NO, if I were Hetty, I would have known it would be better to figure out for myself. Besides, she is Joe's friend too. Maybe he asked her to keep it a secret.

Harold knew, and he always had a rivalry with Joe. Maybe I'm just a prize?

No. I don't want to move to New York. I don't think I want to move anywhere. Except maybe the New York Public Library.

My dream is…
My dream is…
My dream is… to travel to places, but to return home and teach others about them.

If someone loves you, they give you enough space to make your own decisions.

I love

Dottie didn't get to finish her last thought because there was a knock at the door. It's Joe! She thought. He knocked again. Her heart raced with the thought he was just outside her door. Wait, why was she suddenly excited? Shouldn't she still be angry, she thought. A knock pulled her out of her introspection.

"Just a minute," she said toward the door as she

quickly balled up the paper and tossed it over into a corner. She didn't realize until after she had tossed it, it was the size of a large snowball. As it hit the wall and rolled, it was falling open already. He knocked again, louder and faster this time. She grabbed the markers, tossed them on the kitchen counter, and ran to the door.

"I'm so glad you came over Jo—Harold!" quickly correcting herself as she actually looked at who was behind the door.

"Hey, Dot," he said as he walked in past her. "Oh good, you have wine open already." Harold set the poster boards down that he was carrying, leaning them against the back of the sofa and walking to the kitchen. He grabbed himself a wine glass, and the bottle with the same hand. He took Dottie's hand with his free one and led her to the sofa, adeptly setting her down and pouring wine into both glasses. Hers was a little shorter pour than his, she noticed. But it was the end of the bottle. She was focused on the fact that he didn't bother to even the glasses, but instead leaned over the back of the sofa and grabbed the poster boards and set them leaning against the far side of the coffee table, out of reach of Dottie. Harold then picked up both glasses, handing one to her and then clinking.

"We're celebrating, baby!" he took a quick gulp, set his glass down on the table, and clapped his hands and rubbed them together. "Now, you might be wondering why I'm over here so late." Dottie tried to look around to the microwave to see what time it was but was at the wrong side of the sofa to see it. Deciding it was best to just go along, she noncommittally said, "sure."

"Well, I hope you don't mind, but while I was at the interview for my new company, I told them about your cookies. Turns out they have a company who wants a new baked good, and—" he said with great dramatic pause, and turning to grab a poster, "They want to buy 'Grandma Dottie's Ginger Chew Cookies'!" He said flipping a poster around and showing Dottie a hand drawn picture of an elderly lady with crinkly eyes and gray hair sneaking a bite of a cookie with one hand and holding a plate out to the viewer with one missing with the other hand.

With a mixture of confusion and dissatisfaction Dottie looked from the poster to Harold's face and back to the poster. She opened and shut her mouth, and then took a large swig of wine.

"I know the photo looks nothing like you, but research shows that people would rather buy cookies from a sweet grandmother then from—" Harold went on and on. He showed her the other three posters that showed profit margins, a commercial mock-up and a plan for launching the cookies. His voice droned in the background and Hetty caught highlights.

Interwoven while he spoke, her own thoughts poured out. At first, she was self-effacing thinking the cookies weren't good enough to be a national product. Then she was angry at Harold taking the idea to his new company without asking her first. Suddenly she realized that she could use the money to save the museum and caught Harold's excitement. The cookies really were the solution to keeping the museum open! She thought quickly through the origin of the recipe and wondered if any of her maternal ancestors would mind if she passed it along. Her mother's voice came through like a bell, "If it will save something you care about, we will always support you."

"How soon?" Dottie asked stopping Harold in his persuasive speech.

"What?" he did a double take. "Well, I... Dottie, don't you see that this is a great opportunity you have here? With the money—"

"Yes." Dottie said looking at him expectantly.

"Yes, what?"

"Yes, I see that it is a great opportunity." Harold turned toward her with his hands on his hips. A baffled look crossed his face. "Well, I—" his hands fell limply at his sides. Poor thing, Dottie thought. Harold had his big plan to try to convince me, and I didn't need as much persuasion as he planned. He is adorable, she thought as she looked at him. No, she corrected her own thought, he actually looks a bit weasley and plotting. She wondered if this was the same feeling Joe had all of those years ago about Harold. Joe...she shook him out of her head and became present in the room again. Harold's excitement snapped her back completely.

"I... I... I think we can get it out and rolling soon, I just need... contracts, and..." Harold started fumbling around her small living room, gathering up the posters. As he grabbed the last one, he grabbed for his wine glass to toast Dottie again. Then tipping the glass back to drain it, he dropped all of the poster boards. In regathering them, he noticed the wad of Christmas paper and picked it up. "Interesting decorating," he said holding it up and looking at it. The thing was unfolding and about the size of a large mixing bowl now. Dottie cringed as she hoped he wouldn't notice any of the writing on it. He looked around the room, doing a small circle in place, "Babe," she winced as he called her the pet name, "Why don't you have your decorations up yet? Don't you always give the guys at the hardware store a run for their money? Usually yours are up before December."

"Well, there just hasn't been time, what with trying to help the museum and baking the cookies and—"

"Cookies, right! Well, there will be plenty of time for decorating soon." He tossed the ball of wrapping paper at her then gave her a quick peck on the top of her head. "I'm going to get out of here before you change your mind. Call you tomorrow with the details."

And with that he was gone. Dottie hadn't moved from the sofa the entire time. She should feel better since one of her problems was solved, shouldn't she? But what about Joe, her brain prodded. What about New York? What about the museum? If you move to New York, who will run it? More questions poured through the floodgates that had been opened. She reached for her glass, but finding it was empty stood up, wadded up the ball of paper more, and tossed it toward the boxes of decorations.

Looking around for her phone because she felt the urge to call Hetty. Then she stopped because at this moment she felt Hetty to be a traitor.

Dottie didn't want to talk to her mother about any of this either. Instead she plugged the phone in and set it on the kitchen counter. Turning around to face the living room, she sunk even lower thinking about how she hadn't made time to decorate. Then, it was almost if the box twinkled at her, the idea to set up the miniature town and the train set hit her. Normally she set it up under the tree as the last thing. But she really wanted to put out the miniatures, even if she didn't have a tree yet. If she set it up around the tree holder, she could just plop the tree in when she picked it up later this week and she'd get an answer for the museum! She could avoid Joe.

The evening passed as she set up all of the buildings, the trees and the miniature people all around the tree skirt. Her troubles dissipated as she drifted into the memories of collecting and setting this up every year with her father. The red train was a North Pole Express. It was a vintage looking train with an older black locomotive and pulled red and green passenger cars. It had a flatbed car that she always put at the end where Santa, in his sleigh, was being pulled by reindeer. Dasher and Dancer already flying into the air. When she finished, she grabbed a pillow from the sofa and lay on the floor. She put her head down on the cozy pillow admiring her work and in wonder watched the train go around and round the track, until it lulled her to sleep.

CHAPTER SIXTEEN

When the alarm went off the next morning, Dottie found herself fully clothed in her bed. She vaguely remembered waking up at some point during the night, turning off the train and climbing in bed. Shuffling to the shower, Dottie peeled off yesterday's clothes and the irritation of the day as she climbed in and let the warm water wash all the worries away.

Feeling revived, and hopping into her cozy robe, she shuffled to the kitchen and started a cup of coffee to brew. Coffee erased all kinds of ills. As soon as the coffee started to drip into her cup, she dashed to her room to get dressed. Always one to sleep until the last possible moment, Dottie only allowed herself about twenty minutes in the morning to get ready, and she jumped in jeans and a shirt and threw a nice sweater over. She was headed to the high school first today to do more yearbook research on the horseshoe competition. In her normal pace, she was up and out the door, coffee in hand in twenty minutes.

Arriving at Bacon High School, she went to Robert's office and waited for the first bell to ring and his morning announcements to finish.

"So good to see you Dottie, welcome back!" Robert said. He wasn't the principal when she was in school, he was too young. But he was a fixture at this institution. "I'll walk you down to the library and we can stop in on Mrs. Rhuel, she oversees the yearbook," he said as he walked down the hall, commenting over his shoulder. Dottie didn't make it out to the high school much, she had only been here twice since graduating, but the place didn't age. The bricks and the smells and the carpets all looked the same. Voices from the past rang in her ears as they walked past the cafeteria and her old homeroom. As Robert stopped to talk to a teacher, Dottie looked over to see she was standing in front of her junior year locker. Crystal clear, the memory of that day played in her head. She had worn overalls that day with a pink collared polo shirt. Her purple three ring binder clasped to her chest; the inside cover had Joe's baseball number doodled repeatedly. She remembered Hetty standing right next to her as Harold walked up and asked her to the dance. Feeling the bile of fear rise up in her throat again. Remembering Hetty's face cringe as Dottie looked to her for reassurance. Guiltily, she remembered everything slowing as her brain churned. Back then she thought that maybe if she said yes it would make Joe jealous. That was a funny thing to remember. Why would she want to make Joe jealous, she wondered?

"Dottie?" Robert said as he looked at her

questioningly. "Everything ok?"

"Oh, yeah." she smiled. Just remembering this was my old locker and how I got stuck—"

Robert interrupted her misunderstanding and chuckling, "Yes, those old lockers did stick. We put new mechanisms in them a couple of years ago. So many students were using the 'my locker was stuck' excuse to be late to class. We tested all of the lockers that summer to find out they were right." He smiled at his own effectiveness over the change. "Well, shall we move on?"

Leading her down the hall, Robert stopped and held the door for Dottie to enter into a classroom. The bell had just rung so second period had started. An introduction to Mrs. Rhuel and her beginning journalism class was brief. There was a quick announcement that Dottie was visiting, a mention of the museum, and then the class started on an assignment.

Robert escorted Dottie aside and Mrs. Rhuel joined them. She told Dottie, "If you come back around fifth period, I have only my editors then. As we aren't on a deadline at the moment, we all can help you sort through the digital versions of the yearbooks."

"Digital?" Dottie asked.

"Yes. A few years ago, one of my more industrial classes suggested we scan every yearbook we had so we could have a digital back up. It's become a great research tool and we would love to make it more accessible to everyone. We tried to do a fundraiser to get a website but couldn't raise enough. It costs a lot to have a server hold that much data that is accessible from anywhere. So, we have them on the hard drives here only." Mrs. Rhuel said a little disheartened. "It also isn't completely catalogued. I have students come in from time to time, those who are interested or those who need to get their grades up," she winked at Dottie, "to do extra credit. It's a big job, but it will be a great resource when its finished."

"Sounds like it. I wish we had something like that at the museum!" Dottie said. "I'm sure I could get you more volunteers to help catalogue it."

"I thought you didn't get a lot of traffic," Robert said.

"That is true. We don't get a lot of paying customers, or people wanting to rent the place for events. I do get a lot of people, especially retirees, that want to volunteer. There is now a "cleaning day" once a week, and a book organizing day. People come in, help for a couple of hours and leave. It's to the point I have so much help, I make things up to do around the museum because I don't want to turn them away," Dottie shrugged.

"Well, then," Robert replied to move things along, "we should get over to the library so you can make headway."

"Right. I'll see you in a bit Mrs. Rhuel," Dottie waved as they walked out of the classroom.

The library was only a few more feet down the hall. Robert started to push the door open, and then he stopped and turned toward Dottie. "Do you have your cell phone with you?"

Dottie nodded.

"Would you mind turning it to airplane mode or off? We have a no cell phone policy on campus, except in the cafeteria or outside of the building."

"Sure, sure," Dottie replied, fumbling for the phone in her jeans pocket. She was practiced at hitting the two buttons to turn it off so by the time she raised it to her face it was the "are you sure you want to turn off your phone" screen. She swiped right and powered down.

"Thanks," Robert said as he held the door open for her.

Shortly after he walked her into the library and introduced her to the librarian, he left Dottie in the library asking her to stop by and say goodbye when she was leaving campus.

A very cute woman in her early thirties who went by Miss Harmon, was not your typical librarian. With a blue streak in her hair and a dress with lightning bolts all over it that said in script across the chest something about being sorted into a house Dottie knew that she was a "fun librarian."

"You can call me Jen, if there aren't too many students around," Miss Harmon whispered as she led Dottie back to a far corner that had now windows. "Here," she pointed, "is the reference section that is barely used in our computer age. I moved it over here when I first started as not many people come in for the old yearbooks. Mostly its only alumni who use it, and its less distraction for everyone over here." She winked at Dottie. "Help yourself to any of them, and feel free to use the table," she pointed behind her. "Just don't worry about shelving anything. I'll have my aides do it. They need the practice."

"Thanks," Dottie said grabbing a few of the tomes in front of her. "I'll let you know if I need anything."

As Jen walked away, Dottie thought about asking if she could take pictures. But then she remembered the no phone rule. If there was anything she needed, she could always make notes and ask Richard to take care of it later. Or she could come back, after school was out so that way, she wasn't a bad example for the students.

Cracking the first yearbook, Dottie was sucked into the pictures and the recent history. All of it was so fascinating. Dottie wondered to herself why she never looked at the old yearbooks before. There was so much wonderful information about the school and the town here. Her mind started to build an exhibit for the museum in her mind that showcased the yearbooks. The oldest she could find was one from 1819, but the oldest with pictures was 1912. The table was piled with books when the bell ending fourth period rang. Jen walked over and said, "Just so you know, that was the end of fourth period, and I usually get a rush of students during fifth, using their lunch break in here to study or just escape the cafeteria."

"Oh, thanks for the heads up," Dottie said, just as she was pulling from the shelf a few yearbooks from the 1920's, "I'm supposed to go back to yearbook class and check in there."

"Did you find what you were looking for," Jen looked hopefully at Dottie.

"Not yet." Dottie closed a book in front of her. "Are you sure I can't help clean up?"

"Don't worry about it," Jen said, "Really. I have so many aides in sixth period and they want things to do. They'll have a blast going through all of this. In fact, I might mess them up a little more and make it a

145

challenge," Jen said with a twinkle in her eye.

Laughing, Dottie said her goodbyes and walked back to Mrs. Rhuel's classroom. She spent the next two periods gazing through the 1920s on the computer. A couple of the student editors helped on other monitors. Apparently three of the computers were linked to the hard drive with the scans on them of past yearbooks and school published newspapers. Dottie described to them the photo they were looking for. As they scrolled and scrolled, time ticked by. This mystery was becoming more and more intriguing the more she hunted. Dottie's eyes became tired and she started to worry that they wouldn't actually find the picture of the two holding the horseshoes.

"Hey, is this it," asked a girl who looked barely old enough to be in high school, with her brown hair pulled back by a fabric headband revealing her freckles and big eyes.

Dottie walked over, blinked when she saw the image on the screen and then started jumping up and down. She hugged the girl around the shoulders briefly then leaned over her shoulder to look, "Yes! Yes, that's it Kara! You found it. What does it say?"

Rigidly the girl read, "Winning the annual winter horseshoe competition with a ringer, Virginia Yolls and Samuel Edwards, seniors, show off their winning shoes. Although the game is usually played in summer, this tradition of winter horseshoes dates back to the opening of the school. With the centennial celebration this year, the game was brought back with the hope to remain a tradition in the future."

"That is so wonderful. Can you print this out for me?" Dottie asked.

"Already done," Kara said smiling. "Would you like it emailed as well?"

"Sure," Dottie grabbed the print out from the printer baffled by the young lady and her expedience. "Did you notice anything else about horseshoes in that edition?"

"I didn't, but I can keep looking," Kara said.

The bell rang.

"But it will have to be tomorrow. I have to go to Calculus," Kara said as she grabbed her backpack off the floor next to her. "This was fun! Thanks," she said as she dashed out the door.

Dottie leaned on the table she was standing next to and sighed as she looked at the picture of the smiling couple on the screen. "It's too bad I can't keep looking on my computer."

"You can come back anytime. And if we can figure out how to remote our server over to the museum, I'll give you a call," Mrs. Rhuel said.

"Thanks," Dottie said with a sigh. "What time is it?" she asked realizing that she had been at the school all day. It was a good thing she had put a sign on the museum door yesterday saying it would be closed for the day.

"We're just about to start last period, so it's two-fifteen pm."

"Well, that would explain why I'm so hungry," Dottie said. "I think I'll be going. Thank you, and your students, for all of the help. I'm sure I'll be back," Dottie said as she walked out of the door.

Meandering through all of the students was slow as if walking through drifts of snow through. Eventually Dottie found her way back to the office.

"He's in with a parent," said the secretary. "You're welcome to wait, but I have no idea how long they'll be in there."

"That's alright. Just let him know I found what I was looking for, but I think there is more research to do, and I'll call him later."

"Will do," said the perky, curvy older lady with a short and spiky blond pixie cut. She seemed genuinely happy.

"Thanks. Have a great day!" Dottie smiled, feeling the secretary's effervescence spread to her as she drove away from the school.

CHAPTER SEVENTEEN

When she arrived at the museum, she ran up the steps and around to the kitchen entrance, reaching up for the key she hid over the door frame. It wasn't on the corner where she usually left it. She felt across the doorframe, feeling the rising panic. That was odd, it wasn't there. She tried the knob. It was open. The door creaked as e she opened it then quickly closed it behind her. She opened and closed a couple of drawers looking for the key. She shrugged it off. It was probably in a pair of her pants in the laundry. She would check when she got home. Excitement of the picture in the yearbook pushed the thought of the missing key out of the way and Dottie quickly unlocked the door then quickly put the key back on the frame and walked in. She rushed up the stairs. At the top she turned left and walked into the Logan room, it shared a wall with the much larger Baker room. The photographs were all on the floor leaning up against the walls. Dottie walked directly over to the photo, pulling the printout from her back pocket and unfolding it. Already knowing it was the exact same photo, she wanted to make sure.

"Hello Virginia and Samuel!" she greeted the picture and waved. She crossed her legs at the ankles and lowered herself to the floor and leaned back on her hands. Dottie felt so proud and carefree in this moment. Pushing herself up, she took the paper and set it on the floor in front of the picture and sat back again. An idea started to form. Looking around the room at the blank walls, Dottie felt inspiration flowing from them. Voices from earlier today echoed through her mind.

"Anything you need," said Robert.

"These are never looked at except when an alumnus comes..." said Miss Harmon.

"Centennial celebration," read Kara.

"We could share the server..." said Mrs. Rhuel.

Everything seemed to snap together at once, if only...

Dottie hopped up and dashed out of the room. She ran down the stairs, and a flashing light made her glance through the doorway to the ballroom. Preoccupied with the need to find paper, Dottie ignored the feeling something was different. She ran into the kitchen, rifled around for a pen and the spiral notebook she had left on the counter with some of her brainstorming for the exhibit and a to do list for Hetty's exhibit.

Hetty. Traitor! The thought flashed across her mind, and she said out loud, "No, she is my oldest friend, and there must be an explanation. I just don't have time for that right now."

Grabbing the notebook, her eye caught the tub of cookies that were left, and she grabbed for it. Taking one cookie and putting it in her mouth, then grabbing a second thoughts, of Harold and cookie contract flashed across her mind.

"I don't have time for that either," she said waving the thought away like a fly.

Roughly she snapped the lid back on, sealing away that idea until she had time to process it. Leaning on the counter she roughly drew a sketch of the room and started drawing the flow of the exhibit. Would the room be big enough for what she wanted to do? She chewed on both the cookie and the idea. Maybe.

Full of vigor, Dottie grabbed the book and went to the maintenance closet and threw the door open, leapt in and pulled the cord on the light. She reached for the toolbox, but it wasn't in its normal space. In fact, nothing was. She looked around the room to find that shelves were now labeled, and everything seemed to be organized. What volunteer would have done this, she wondered. Squatting down, she found the toolbox was on the bottom shelf. Opening it, she found it too was organized. Pondering how this happened for a moment, but then filing it away to deal with later, Dottie grabbed the tape measure and ran up the stairs, seeing a flashing light again, as she passed the ballroom. Later. She had to get this idea down before it escaped.

Measuring walls and pictures, then sketching and taking notes, the idea blossomed. Dottie scrambled to the floor and lay on her stomach on the floor kicking her feet up. She was in the position just like she used to do when she studied many afternoons in this very museum. She wrote it all out and reviewed the plan. It would work. She even jotted down some alternative ideas just in case she couldn't get all of the pieces to fall into place. Taking a deep breath, she sat up and reached for her cell phone. But it wasn't in her back pocket. Feeling a bit like she was missing a part of herself, she looked all around the floor. It wasn't there. She ran down to the kitchen. Checking the drawers and the counters she found nothing. Dottie ran to the maintenance room. She hadn't left it on the shelves and didn't see it on the floor. She traced her steps, up and down the stairs. Nothing. Wait! It must be in the car. She ran to the front door and fumbled with the lock, seeing a flashing light again coming from the ballroom, but still ignoring it. Dashing to the car, she threw open the driver's side door, but it wasn't on the seat. She leaned over and felt in the crevices and the seam of the seat. Nothing. Pulling up on the bar and yanking the seat forward, she saw it! It had dropped under the seat and slid back. Hitting the lock button on the door, she unlocked the back and grabbed the phone. It was still off. Waiting for it to power on, she closed up the car and walked back into the museum.

Suddenly, her phone was a deluge of noise and notifications. Apparently, Dottie had seventy-two notifications in the time her phone was shut off. Seventeen were from Harold, four from Hetty, one missed call from Frank, a few texts from Robert. The list went on.

Not wanting to deal with any of it at the moment except to talk to Robert about yearbooks. She selected his number and hit the green call button. Dottie held her breath until she heard his voice at the other end.

"Dottie—"

"Robert," Dottie was so excited she cut him off. "I have a crazy idea, and I need your help to make it happen."

CHAPTER EIGHTEEN

Hanging up the phone Dottie felt hopeful. A "we'll see what we can do" from Robert was a good sign. She walked around The Logan Room again in a circle to see if she could gather any more inspiration. This would work. If she could just borrow some of the yearbooks from the school. Frank and Murray always said they would make display cases for her. More elaborate plans like enlarging pages of yearbooks and hanging them flew into her mind. Or, she could even get those poster turnstiles, putting blown up copies of yearbooks, so visitors could turn the pages of the year books. With the newer yearbooks, there might be extra copies that visitors could turn through, but the older ones she would display in glass enclosed bookcases lining the walls as they were more fragile. She would move the glass covered cases in from the library and put them out in the middle of the floor in this room.

"That might be a little congested," she said to herself. Suddenly she was hit by a great idea. "What if I used both rooms for the exhibit?" Dottie exclaimed out loud. Throwing her arms up over her head as if she was rejoicing a goal scored. Racing with excitement, her heart beat like it was trying to get her lungs to dance. Dottie felt hopeful for the first time in weeks. Despair had set in earlier this month with the board deciding to close the doors, then the roof needing patching and replacing almost crushed her spirit entirely. Dottie didn't want to assume that this idea for this exhibit could fix everything, but if she could just show the board that there was hope for the museum. The museum could attract guests. She wanted to prove that this museum meant something to the community, whether or not they remembered the museum still existed.

Feeling parched and overloaded with ideas, Dottie went to the kitchen for a glass of water. Every idea spurred a different one and she was so filled with ideas and excitement. This exhibit could have several phases. Her mind churning with ideas, Dottie unconsciously grabbed a glass from the cabinet, then walked to the sink and let the cool water run. Not turning off the faucet, Dottie chugged the glass of water letting both the water and her ideas absorb. Filling up the glass again Dottie took another swig.

Feeling as if the thrum of ideas was settling into her mind and coming together as a big picture, Dottie wandered back to the staircase. She took another sip at the bottom of the stairs and through the clear bottom of the glass she saw the flickering light again. Lowering the glass, she looked into the ballroom and almost spat out her mouthful of water.

There in the middle of the ballroom was a fully lit

and decorated Christmas tree. Dottie's jaw dropped. The sparkling magnificence was breathtaking. As she looked at the flickering flashing lights her eyes teared up a little. She had been wanting to decorate for about a week. In fact, she itched to put up Christmas decorations the day after Halloween, but her father's birthday was November twenty-second, and there was a family rule that no Christmas decorations could go up before his birthday. Even though he lived in a different state, Dottie still upheld that tradition. And then with the notice the museum would be closing she had been focused on trying to keep it open. And she had yet to put up a tree.

This tree was perfect. She was so mad at herself for driving off and leaving the tree in Joe's yard. It was probably still there, covered with snow. It upset her to think about that night. To think about him in general was frustrating, in many definitions of the words. The tree lights flashed again as if to demand her attention. It was an amazing gesture. But who could have done it? How? When? Tons of questions flashed through her head.

Circling the tree, Dottie took it all in. These were her ornaments from her apartment. The angel she made in second grade. A droopy looking reindeer. Santa with a large sack of toys thrown over his back. Several train ornaments that had been collected over the years given to her by her father. Her great literature ornament collection that Joe had given her one of five every year from when they were nine years old to fifteen, and this was her father's train running around the bottom. Unable to help herself, Dottie lay down on her stomach and watched the train go around and around. Mesmerized watching the train underneath the flashing lights on the tree, she felt like a child again. Her mind relaxed and her concerns flitted away as her brain recalled stories her father used to tell her of all of the people who lived in the miniature village under the tree.

After about fifteen minutes, the phone beside her buzzed. It was a text from Robert. She could have the yearbooks! On loan, of course. But if the events went well and the museum stayed open, they would discuss making the museum the high school's official archives.

Pushing herself up and off the floor with her arms, Dottie sprang into action. Ignoring the content of Hettie's texts, Dottie sent a quick: Can you help me with the exhibit tonight?

She sent off a quick email to Mrs. Rhuel and Miss Harmon over at the high school asking when she could come by and pick up the items the museum was borrowing. As a final thought she put her cell phone number at the bottom. All of her emails had the land line for the museum at the bottom, but she didn't know how close she would be able to be to the phone in the office or the kitchen. After hitting send she turned the phone's ringer on.

Dashing upstairs, she wrangled the "exhibit closed for renovation" curtains out and put one in front of the room where the yearbook exhibit would be. Then she carried one up to the Baker Room. As she was setting it down, she looked up at the ceiling. It looked as good as new. Happily, she sighed. Something seemed to be going right. Taking her phone out of her back pocket, she searched for a number and hit send. As she put the phone to her ear, she knew exactly who

was responsible for the tree.
"Frankincense and Myrrh Hardware."

CHAPTER NINETEEN

"**W**hy, hello Murray. You meddler!" Dottie's voice answered sugary, then icy cold through the phone.

"Dottie, howareya?" Murray replied as if she only weren't throwing disdain at him.

"Murray!! I just can't believe you!"

He started to chuckle to himself. "That is what my wife says all of the time. What did I do this time? Or what didn't I do?"

"Murray, you know why I'm calling," Dottie tried to finagle a confession.

"I have no idea what you're talking about," he said shutting up.

Dottie had a feeling he knew exactly what she was talking about, but she also needed a favor.
"Mmmhmm. Alright," she gave up and changed her directive. "Murray, so I need to call in that favor from you and Frank.

"I hope it's not putting lights up on that museum roof. You don't think you can beat me or Frank in decorating, now do you?" he joked with her.

Dottie laughed, "No. It's not lights for the roof. I need a bookcase or five." As she explained her plan and her vision, Dottie heard Murray scribble some notes. Pencil on paper makes a very distinct sound, it was one of her favorites. "So, do you think it's possible?" She asked at the end of her explanation.

"I think so," she could now hear the thoughts churning in his head, even though the phone. "As a matter of fact, I think we just got some premade book shelving in that we could snap together. It was for J— another customer, but I'm sure they won't mind if it's for a good cause. We will just say these came in damaged or something, and assemble them in the museum, and order him another set."

"Amazing. You know where the spare key for the museum is, don't you?" She said trying to see if she could catch him off guard and get a confession.

"Yup. I'll see if I can get these over to you today or first thing tomorrow," Murray said into the phone. Then to someone in the store he replied, "It's Dottie. She, uh... is looking for bookshelves. I was thinking we could use the ones for ..." she could tell he put his hand over the speaker, because the voice got muffled. "...has a clue but doesn't know yet." Murray said as he removed his hand.

"Who doesn't know yet?" Dottie asked, pretty sure he was talking about her.

"Uh... Mrs. Barnes. She doesn't know yet if she's having a boy or a girl," Murray said.

"I didn't even know she was pregnant again,"

Dottie said distracted.

"Shoot, I wasn't supposed to say anything—"
Murray said with a drop of worry.

"Don't worry, Murray," Dottie said soothingly.
"Everyone knows that the hardware store is better
than the beauty parlor for getting gossip. Plus,
everyone knows that you can't keep a secret. I'm sure
she told you on purpose to let everyone know. It's just
like her!" A text message came in and took Dottie's
attention. It was Hetty replying about coming over
and helping set up the beauty queen exhibit. "Hey,
Murray, I've gotta get going. Keep me posted about
those shelves!" Dottie shouted into the phone
distractedly as she texted Hetty back.

"No problem, gal." Murray said. "Oh, and you
really should start locking your apartment door.
Anyone could walk in and take things. Like, I don't
know, Christmas ornaments. Goodbye," and he hung
up before Dottie could ask anything else.

* * *

A few hours later Hetty and her husband Don
caravanned to the museum with Frank. Don and
Frank carried the bookshelf parts upstairs and started
to assemble. Dottie and Hetty carried the dress forms
and the garment bags of dresses upstairs in several
trips. They laid the garment bags out on the floor in a
sort of "V" formation in front of the rounded
window.

"I'm so glad the roof damage was just in the
corner and we can mask it with curtains and use the
room still," Hetty smiled.

"Me too. It's really perfect for this," she smiled back at her friend. "What should we start with first," Dottie asked, ready to get to work.

"I've got a couple of hat boxes in the back seat on the floor. Those are the crowns," Hetty said. "You go get them and I'll start getting these dresses out and putting them on the forms," Hetty instructed.

"Will do," she said walking out of the Baker Room. Passing The Logan Room where Don and Frank were working, she heard a bit of a squabble, she popped her head in.

"Hey, guys! How's it going over here?" Dottie asked.

Frank cleared his throat. His hands were on his hips and he had his back to the door.

Don looked over at her. "Fine, fine, Dottie. We were just—" Don said.

Quickly, Frank turned at the waist to face her. "We were just talking about where we thought the bookcases would go," Frank spoke with intention toward Don and seeming to cover up what he was really going to say. Don also conveyed this by suddenly finding the carpet in the room extremely interesting.

"Oh?" Dottie said, "I thought that would be pretty clear from the drawings I left, and how I've lined the walls with the photos over there," she said to Frank knowing he was up to something, but she just couldn't put her finger on what. "They go over here," Dottie said, pointing to the blank wall to her left.

"Great," Don said as he leapt to one of the boxes and started pulling out the pieces. "We'll get started. You... you don't have to worry about a thing." he said overly chipper.

Frank just shrugged, and then started to instruct Don on how to build the shelves. "Frank, you don't want to read the directions?" Don asked.

"Listen, boy, I've built more shelves in my lifetime—" whatever Frank said next, Dottie didn't hear because she was halfway down the stairs to go get the crowns. The tree in the ballroom winked at her on her way out and back in from Hetty's car. She paused to look at it briefly both times. It made her so happy.

By the time she got back upstairs, Hetty had dressed three of the five dressmaker dummies with her stunning gowns. She was struggling to put the fourth on because it had such a full skirt, and she was drowning in it. Dottie set the cases on the ground and dashed over to Hetty, "How can I help?" Dottie asked.

"Oh good, you're back," Hetty said. "Here," she said grunting and handing over a lot of tulle and beading, Take this. The bottom of the zipper is there," she said pointing as she drew Dottie under the dress she held up like a tent. "If you can make sure that gets over the head and is centered on the back. This one is a bit tight. Had to lose a lot of weight for that one—there!" she exclaimed as they got the dress over the model. Hetty stood back and Dottie came around to look at it.

Sighing, Hetty continued. "I call this one 'Love letter to all the pizza I missed' because of the heart shaped neck. To fit in it, I didn't eat carbs for months," Hetty looked at Dottie, "And you know there are two things I can't keep my hands off of: pizza and my husband," she shouted the last part.

"Love you too, honey," drifted from the Logan

Room.

Both ladies smiled.

"Hetty, they're all gorgeous," Dottie said.

"Yeah, and they've just been sitting in bags in my closet. The crowns I can display all over the diner, but the dresses are a fire hazard," Hetty replied. "Here," she said unzipping the last garment bag, "Let's get this last one on the form, and then we call for pizza."

"Which one is your favorite," Dottie asked.

"Dress or pizza?" Hetty joked. "No, but really. I couldn't say, they're all so beautiful," Hetty replied distantly.

"Fair, but which one do you like the most?" Dottie tried a different direction.

"The most?" Hetty repeated.

"Yeah," Dottie chuckled. "You've got to have a favorite."

"Well, I mean..."

"Hetty," Dottie said looking at her friend's face, and seeing that it now resonated with angst. "Are you alright?"

"Kinda—I..." Hetty drifted off. "Well, asking me to pick a favorite dress, it's like asking me to choose a favorite memory."

"Favorite memory?" Dottie queried. "I don't think I understand." Her friend was always quick to disclose the work she had to do to fit into each outfit for every pageant. She would talk about moments from the pageants from time to time. But Dottie had not heard Hetty get this emotional over the dresses before. Usually she told the stories of the pageant and talked about the funny moments or the flubs.

"I can see how all of your pageants weren't always

great memories, especially the ones you didn't win," Dottie tried to ease her friend's anguish. "But with all of these dresses, I can only imagine how great of a success you were. And the whole town knows that you did such great things using prize money. Like gaining scholarships for yourself and using some of your earnings to upgrade the children's center with new playground equipment and computers."

"Yeah, well 'Molding the Future for Our Children' was my most successful platform," Hetty said as she took the last gown out of its bag. It was a beautiful sapphire gown. Form fitting and beads only up around the bodice, with flowing silk chiffon as a frothy overlay for the skirt. Effortlessly Hetty took it out of the bag and as if she were a magician showing a trick with sleight of hand, tossed it onto the model and had the dress in place in seconds. She smiled but then sighed again. "Each of these dresses represents a sacrifice that lead to a memory. In fact, two of these were dresses I didn't win in."

Dottie said nothing. Hetty walked through the garments readjusting a strap or shifting a bead that seemed to be in the wrong place.

"You say there is history in everything," Hetty said quoting Dottie, "Well the truth is that not all history is pretty. Even if it glitters and sparkles," Hetty smirked, standing by a form. "Pageants are gritty and hard work. There are invisible and unspoken rules that we all adhere to. Some are good, and some… aren't."

"You've mentioned some of this before, but I've always wondered…" Dottie drifted off caught in Hetty's musing.

"I was never unhealthy; I just want you to know

that. I didn't do… that," she said directly. "But sometimes you lose a toenail and have to get one glued on. Or a strap breaks and you have to give an interview to someone who just looks down their nose at pageants. Or someone you think is your best friend just turns their back on you so she can win."

"Hetty, I would never—wait, what?" Dottie said walking over to her friend who was now looking out the windows. "You had a best friend on the circuit? Why didn't you ever tell me?"

"I… I just didn't want you to think… I mean you and Joe… and then Harold—"

"Hetty, you can have other friends. And I didn't ever mean to discard you or make you feel second to anyone. Especially not for Harold or Joe," she put her arm around her friend's shoulder.

Laying her head on Dottie's shorter shoulder, Hetty explained, "It's hard to explain the pageant world to anyone not in pageants. Sure, I can tell you stories, and everyone wants to hear the highs and the lows. But there are only so many times I can tell a story that starts with, 'because I needed to tape my boobs together' or 'my shoes were too small, so I had to…' ya know?" Sighing she continued as she drifted away down a river of memories. "And Jayden was always so seemingly helpful. She's the one that suggested the pizza dress," Hetty pointed at the red dress Dottie helped her put on the form. "I always said the night I won a national title. I would eat an entire large pizza by myself to celebrate. That dress was to win me the crown." She sighed and petted the sleeve. "But Jayden kept me just close enough to get me trusting enough. That pageant," she said pointing at the red dress again, "I was determined I would win so I lost as much weight as I could. And to add insult to injury, I tried waxing for the first time." Hetty made a painful face.

"Oh Hetty, no! How old were you? Does your mom know?" Dottie asked.

"She does now, but I didn't tell her at the time," Hetty smacked her free hand to her face. "I was allergic to something in the wax and had welts all over my legs from it. I tried to cover them up with two pair of tights, but it was just bad. I stammered in my interview because the tights were chafing, and my legs burned. Obviously, I didn't win that one."

Dottie started to laugh. "I'm sorry, I shouldn't laugh. It's just so——"

"Funny?"

"Yeah, but in a sad way. And I get that it's better to have someone with similar experiences or a similar past to share things like that with. I'm just sorry you had another woman you trusted treat you so terribly." Dottie felt remorseful.

"So that dress, needless to say, is not a favorite, but it's full of reminders of what I went through, and although it seems like it should be my least favorite, I think I love it most. It reminds me of the competitor I could be."

Smiling, Dottie felt prouder of her friend in this moment then when she knew she had won her first crown. "After that, losing a friend, my heard just wasn't so in love with the crown anymore. I still competed, but it wasn't as fun," she looked poignant for a moment more, then a Cheshire smile broke out on her face. "And I wanted pizza back in my life."

They both laughed.

Hetty sat up and wiped the dripping tears and mascara from under her eyes with her pointer fingers, then wiped them on her jeans. She blew a big breath out of her mouth as to blow away the frustration she was feeling. "Now, enough of the tears, let's get out the sparkles." She walked over and picked up a case, handing one to Dottie, who followed behind her.

"Speaking of sparkles," Hetty said with an agenda, as she opened the case and started taking the crowns out of their velvet traveling bags, "Tell me about the tree downstairs."

"I've been meaning to talk to you about that!" Dottie exclaimed louder than she meant to. "The thing just appeared."

"What do you mean, 'just appeared.' And why didn't you text me about it sooner?!?" Hetty raised an eyebrow.

"Well," Dottie shrugged, "I meant to, I just went to the high school and then had the ideas about the exhibit and just started running with it. I got so absorbed—oh Hetty! The Logan Room is going to look amazing!" Then she veered from the subject, her brow drawn up in confusion, "I don't even know when the tree got here, because I was out most of the day."

"So, the tree just appeared?" questioned Hetty.

"Yup, and its someone who knows me, and I'm pretty sure who it is," she squinted as if she had deduced everything.

"Who?" Hetty excitedly asked.

"Well, I'm pretty sure," Dottie conspiratorially leaned in and lowered her voice to a whisper, "that our two favorite curmudgeons did it."

"And why would it be them?"

"I called the store earlier today. Murray answered and I was trying to pull it out of him. He wouldn't admit to it, but just before I hung up, he told me I needed to start locking my apartment door," Hetty looked blankly at Dottie so she continued, "The tree has all of my ornaments from home. So, I think that Frank and Murray, feeling sorry for me and the way the museum is going, got a tree, snuck into my apartment and decorated for me."

"You don't think it's a romantic gesture by Harold," Hetty teased dripping with sarcasm.

"Ha. Nope. He thinks a romantic gesture is selling my cookies to a conglomerate. Oh! That's another thing I have to tell you about!" Dottie remembered.

"Ok, wait. So you think that those two took time away from bickering at the hardware store, to sneak into your apartment, to take down the train set you put up in the last couple of days and grab your Christmas decorations, and know how to set it up exactly as you like it, with the angel ornament in the front and the store shops lined up in alphabetical order?" Hetty questioned knowingly and paused. "And what is this about selling your cookies???"

Distracted and guilty for not sharing sooner, Dottie shrugged, "Well, Harold said he had a plan to solve the museum's problems. He said that if I sold my cookie recipe to one of his new company's clients then it would be enough money to help fix the roof and keep the museum running. But then he said we would move to New York to work on the cookie deal, so I just don't know who would take over for me, maybe—" Dottie floundered.

"And you're moving?" Hetty turned to face Dottie head on, "Girl, you really need to loop me in faster. Hello? Best friend," Hetty waved her hand as she tilted her face in frustration.

Dottie sighed. "Yeah, well. Like I said, I was more focused on getting the museum exhibits going and I really haven't had time. Plus, you've been pushing Joe at me—"

"It's ok, Dottie," Hetty waved her away.

"Don't be upset at me. Please Hetty," Dottie pleaded, changing her tune as she realized she wasn't really mad at Hetty. "I am so overwhelmed. You know I am and I—" Dottie stopped when something clicked in her head. Something that Hetty said about the train set. "Wait, how did you know I had the train set up? Did you—?"

Just then Don walked in, "Looks nice in here, ladies! Shelves are all built next door. We took the trash out, too." He looked at Hetty, "Oh and you and Joe did a really nice job with that tree in the ballroom, Hetty."

Dottie turned to her friend and stared in disbelief. "You? And... Joe?"

CHAPTER TWENTY

Heat rose up through her veins. Later, Dottie would realize in this moment she was totally irrational, but right now she was mad. She was more than mad she was vehemently angry. A raging bull was "happy" compared to the angst and irritation inside of Dottie. She started to walk toward the door.

"Dottie, where are you going?" Hetty called after her. This was the second time in a week that she felt betrayed by her best friend. It was a very odd feeling and she didn't like it. But she would deal with Hetty later.

Walking to the front door, she grabbed for her coat from the hall tree. She heard steps coming down the stairs and she didn't care. Suddenly, the front door opened, and Harold came through it. Wild with excitement, he threw his arms around Dottie in a giant hug. "We did it!" Harold exclaimed.

Not wanting to be trapped by anyone at this

moment, Dottie wiggled out of his arms a little more roughly than she meant to. "We did what, Harold?" she accused.

"Dottie, what's wrong?" Harold noticed she was upset. He pulled the door closed just as Hetty reached the ground floor.

"Dottie, I—Oh, hey Harold." Hetty spoke with draining enthusiasm.

"Hetty!" he shouted. He truly was ignorant to how much Hetty disliked him. Harold and put his arm around Dottie's shoulders. Once they were past the threshold, he removed his arm from around Dottie why she exchanged a look with Hetty. Taking off his coat, he tossed it over the banister.

"Hey, Harold, I thought I heard your voice," Don acknowledged coming down the stairs. "How are you, man? I haven't seen you in ages?"

Both men tempered politeness as Harold put out his hand for Don to shake, "Good to see you, Don. Things are well. How is the diner?"

Sharing another look, Hetty asked Dottie with her eyes what was going on. Dottie raised her eyebrows and shrugged.

"Fine, fine. To be expected," Don answered politely.

"Well, look what the cat dragged in," Frank said has he descended the stairs. "Never see you around here," Frank lightly admonished Harold. Dottie was unaware until now just how much all of the people currently in this room didn't care much for Harold. It was very obvious in their voices.

"Frank! You're here too, great!" Harold was getting more excited. "Well, since you're all here, I have an announcement!"

"Harold, what—" Dottie was cut off.

"We are moving to New York!" Harold's excitement was met with a stunned silence.

Frank finally broke the tension. "Well, congratulations, he said reaching out to shake Harold's hand. Then turning his attention to her, he said, "Dottie, I didn't know you were wanting to leave."

"Frank, you know that Dottie has always talked about traveling around the world," Hetty said both trying to clue Frank in, and pointedly spoke to Dottie.

"Well," Don cleared his throat, "That's... great. We will certainly miss you... Dottie." Hetty glared at her husband. "What? What did I say?" he asked innocently.

"Thanks, Don!" Harold beamed. They all stood in silence waiting for Dottie to say something, but she just blinked a few times. "Dottie, they're still working on the contract for your cookies, but I'm sure it will come through. Now, I have to start next week, but I know you are attached to this," he looked around the front hallway odiously, "place. So, I told them you would have to call in remotely in on any meetings. I should go and start getting packed up. I have to move in the next four days!" He reached for his coat and started to shrug into it. "When did you put up the Christmas tree in the ballroom?" Harold asked when he caught the sight of it.

Still standing in the middle of them all, Dottie said nothing.

"Uh, this morning," Hetty answered Harold.

Confirming to Dottie she really did help put up the tree.

"Harold that is great news," Dottie snapped out of her stupor and walked to him and kissed his cheek. "You should get going, and we can talk later about all of the details," she oozed with sweetness as she led him by the arm out through the door.

"I knew you would be happy!" he exclaimed. "Ok, honey, I'll call you later."

Dottie held the doorknob as Harold walked out of the museum. He put his phone up to his ear as he got into his car. She turned to Hetty and with irritation spat, "We will talk later." Then she walked through the door and slammed it behind her.

As she walked up her driveway and down Joe's, the words formed and reformed in her head. She was moving, and he was leaving, and it was time once and for all to tell him how she felt. Years of feelings rose up and congested her head with frustration and hurt. Memories of the last few days flooded her brain as well. Why did he bother doing nice things for her, and looking at her the way he did, if he was only leaving again? Most likely leaving town for good this time. Dottie stopped walking as her heart had a shot of pain as she realized she had always held the hope he would be back. As long as he still owned his parents' house, she knew he would come back someday. But now he would be leaving and for good.

"Well good riddance!" she shouted at no one in particular. Snapping back out of the pain and into her frustration she took a few more steps and reasoned, she was leaving, too. New York was calling and—she stopped walking again. Just a few moments ago when Harold announced it, it felt wrong. Looking to her left she could still see the roof of the museum. Her heart warmed. That felt right.

Shaking her head, she told herself that moving on was good. Heading toward a future with Harold in New York was what was planned, and the museum would be fine. She would get these new exhibits up and volunteers could run it. It didn't matter that she stayed. Someone else could run it. Then she could travel the world and study other history as she always had planned to do. Besides, the world went on without Joe here, she thought. And he was a bigger deal to the town then she would ever be.

The audacity he had to come and put a Christmas tree up in her museum! The thought heated her blood again, and she marched down toward the front door. Knocking hard with her fist, Dottie hollered, "Joe! We need to talk!"

CHAPTER TWENTY-ONE

He had been on edge all day. The excitement was palpable. From the moment he got the idea he was just waiting to hear what Dottie thought. His phone was quiet. Nothing from Dottie. He hadn't heard anything from Hetty, Frank or Murray. They were all in on it, so he thought he would hear something by now. He had texted them all but had gotten vague responses. Hetty said she was headed over to the museum around six-thirty but hadn't texted after that. Dottie must have seen it by now. It was getting late. The sun had set at least four hours ago. Looking out the windows in the kitchen, he tried to see the museum, but between the rise of the hill and the row of hedges, he couldn't even see the roof of the building.

Yesterday the plan seemed simple when he called Hetty.

"We should meet at the hardware store tomorrow early," Hetty had in reply when he spouted the idea to her.

"Great," he exclaimed, "We can get supplies and decorations."

"Nope, we're gonna get hers," Hettie schemed. "Frank and Murray are gonna know exactly what to do. They know everything."

When they met thirty minutes later at the hardware store, Hetty had the blueprint of a plan in her mind. Joe remembered her being a planner, but not this much of a force of nature.

"According to Robert, Dottie is supposed to be at the school in the morning looking through yearbooks," Murray commented from his seat behind the counter. "He's gonna let me know when she is leaving which will give you two a couple of minutes heads up if you're not done yet."

"And if you need, I can always call her and make a distraction," Frank proposed as he stood up from leaning on his hand that was resting on the outside of the counter. I was over there and finished fixing the roof, so I can always call her and make something up."

"Remind me never to get on your bad side," Joe said smirking to the team.

"We only use our powers for good, not evil, Joe," Hetty clarified while smiling. She continued "Great, now, I want to get her decorations out of her apartment."

"I've got the key to the building. I helped Art, the owner, do some repairs a few months back. He said to keep the key in case anything else came up," Frank added.

"Dottie doesn't lock her front door unless she's sleeping," Murray divulged.

"How do you know that, old man?" Hetty

challenged.

"None of your business," Murray turned away. They all stared at him. "Fine. She told me about a year ago that she needed a new doorknob that didn't automatically lock. She wanted something she could leave open. Growing up out here in the country she got used to not locking her house, so she would forget to take keys, and lock herself out. I told her the way to flip the settings so it wouldn't lock. Then," his informative tone changed to reassuring, "I gave her a lecture that she should lock her door. She reminded me that no one can get into the building without a key. But after giving her my sternest look," Murray demonstrated the face, and they all stifled a laugh as he continued, "that if nothing else, she should lock her door at night when she's sleeping. She promised," he finished looking smug.

"And... you know she's doing it because..." Hetty led him to answer.

"That girl does what people tell her to. She's a good gal," Murray said.

All but Murray bust out laughing. Tears started falling out of Hetty's eyes from her gasping guffaws. "You know that's not true," she choked through their chuckling.

"Yeah," Joe agreed. "Dottie is worse than either of us when it comes to doing what she's told. She just makes you think she'll do it."

Hetty turned to Joe, "Great, so wear all black, and we will sneak in during the night and nab the ornaments." They laughed harder.

"I've totally got your back," Joe took on a serious tone but played along and even squatted down on one knee with his back to her, making a gun with his finger and thumb.

Hetty took his lead and with her back to his lunged out and made a gun with her hand; both took on spy poses.

"Are you two done clowning around?" Frank asked.

"Sure, sure," Joe said as he got up groaning. Then rubbed his knees out of habit.

"Those knees of yours, they gonna last another season?" Murray questioned.

"Doc says they'll last me a while longer, but the knees say otherwise. We'll just pretend it's from all the work on the house," Joe said.

"You trying to get the inside scoop on the season," Frank pointed at Murray.

"No, no. Just making conversation," Murray retreated. "Can't a guy just care about his friend's well-being?"

"I don't trust you, ya old coot. Everyone knows you're a gossip," Frank accused.

Murray picked up the silent store telephone. "Hello?" he spoke into the phone, dial tone loud enough they all could hear it. He handed the phone over to Frank a moment later, "Hey Pot, its Kettle to tell you, you're black."

"What does that mean?" Frank asked.

Murray rolled his eyes and hung up the phone without breaking eye contact, "It's like the pot calling the kettle black," Murray explained slowly.

"I... don't get it," Frank played stupid. "Explain it again, would ya? A little slower this time."

"You two are incorrigible!" Hetty exclaimed.

"So," Joe changed the subject, "do you think she has a tree stand?"

"I think that we should take one from here just in case, and maybe a couple of new sets of lights," Hetty suggested. "It's always a pain when you start to decorate, and you only have one set of lights that works."

"I'll go grab them," Frank hustled off.

"Hey, Joe," Hetty changed to a cautious tone, "This is a great thing you're doing, but I hope you're doing it with the right intentions."

"What do you mean?" Joe raised an eyebrow, questioning her.

Murray jumped in, "Son, everyone can see how you feel about that gal, well everyone who is paying attention. She won't admit it, but she broke like an over turned bureau of delicate china when you left town."

"There's no way that Dottie—" Joe started to protest

"It's true, Joe." Hetty confirmed by stepping closer to her friend and putting her hand on his shoulder. "She might not know it, but she has harbored feelings for you for years. You didn't come back until now, so she pushed them way down deep inside and ignored them. All the while telling herself for years that Harold was the one. This is a very delicate situation."

Starting to protest, Joe's breath hitched as things seemed to snap together. Dottie's appealing eyes appeared in his mind. He thought about all of their interactions lately. She was always waiting for him to say... something.

As if answering his thought, Murray said, "She's

waiting for you. Even though she doesn't know it."

"So, think long and hard, because after this, there is no going back, Joe," Hetty agreed. "You know you should have done something back in high school, but—"

"I'm in it for the right reason, Hetty. We're going through with it," he determinedly clenched his jaw.

"What did I miss," Frank walked back feeling the tension.

"Just making sure Joe knows he is reigniting fires by putting up this tree," Murray said.

"Oh, good," Frank said to Murray. Then turning to Joe and putting a hand on his shoulder, he said, "Yup, that gal loves you. I'm glad you're doing this."

"Great, so we have a plan," Joe tried to end the awkward conversation. "What do I owe you for the lights?"

"I'll put it on your tab," Murray waved off the cash Joe started to hand over. "Now get out of here and get going. You're losing time."

"Thanks," Joe smiled and put away the money. He grabbed the lights and tree stand. "Should I pick you up?" he asked Hetty.

"Nah, I'll take my car. We can both go to the apartment, then I'll follow you home. You park at your house. I'll follow you and drive us and the tree up. This way if she does come to the museum, it won't be suspect. I'm there all the time," Hetty explained.

"Great." Joe nodded.

They both started to walk out of the store when Frank called out, "If you need to get into the museum, there is a key above the kitchen door directly above the door knob. Just make sure you put it in the exact same place, or she'll think something is up."

"Thanks," Joe and Hetty hollered in unison.

CHAPTER TWENTY-TWO

It was surprisingly easy to sneak into Dottie's apartment and into the museum. Joe and Hetty had no real problems. At her apartment, her next-door neighbor, an agreeable old man who came over when he saw the door open. He was standing in the doorway when Hetty turned around to take the first box of ornaments downstairs. She jumped.

"Oh hey, Mr. Norman," she tried to regain her breath and heart rate.

"Hey Hetty. Did Dottie leave me those cookies?"

"Oh, uh," Hetty struggled with the box, and tried to look over her shoulder into the kitchen. "Um, I don't see anything, but you're welcome to go take a look."

The man that was a foot shorter than she. He was dressed in a brown sweater vest with his long seventies collar popping out of the top. His brown corduroy pants and brown suede slippers completed the outfit as he blinked through his rectangular wire rimmed glasses that doubled the size of his eyeballs. It seemed they had a standoff in the doorway.

"Mr. Norman, this container is kinda heavy could you—" Just then Joe rescued her as she tried to get out and he waited to get in.

"Let me take that, excuse me sir," he said taking the box from Hetty and turning started to walk down the stairs with it.

"Hey, I know you," the old man shouted as he shuffled to look over the railing. "You're that baseball kid."

Joe stopped and looked up, "Yes sir, that's me," and stood frozen as if he were caught and was thinking up an excuse to get out of trouble.

"We're helping Dottie decorate the museum," Hetty told a little white lie to Mr. Norman. She crossed her fingers behind her back and hoped he wouldn't see through it.

Squinting an eye at her, Mr. Norman finally said, "Well that's nice of you. Tell her I'm waiting for those cookies," and he shuffled back inside his apartment.

Hetty quickly took a picture of the train set with her cell phone, and then started to gently put all of the pieces in the box, carefully wrapping each up in tissue. Joe came back up and helped her. They were done in no time and headed to Joe's house to drop off his car, then drove up to the museum. Hetty pulled up close to the kitchen door. They saw the "Closed" sign on the front door and decided just to go in through the kitchen. The key was just where Frank said it would be.

After loading all of the decorations into the

ballroom, they began. The thing that took the longest was getting the tree straight. Hetty spotted it by holding it at the top, while Joe was underneath. After about fifteen minutes and both of them taking turns to stand back they decided it was straight enough.

"There is power over here," Hetty said walking over to the left of the fireplace. She opened a box and pulled out an extension cord.

"How did you know that would be there?"

"When they do events with music, they have the band set up here in front of the window. So, Dottie just leaves the extension cord here to make it easier to plug the keyboard and speakers in," Hetty explained.

"Maybe we should divide and conquer. If I work on the tree, you can set up the village underneath," Joe suggested.

"Sure, that sounds good. Why don't I help you do the lights so you're not tripping over me, and then I'll dive into the trains," Hetty replied.

"Great!" he said.

"Fantastic!" she agreed.

They set to work. It wasn't as much fun as it was setting up his tree with Dottie the day before, but it was great to be this close for this long with Hetty again. They caught up on all kinds of things, his career, her diner, his apartment, her attempts at having children.

"So, tell me about this girlfriend of yours," Hetty prodded.

"Not much to tell. We met at a celebrity fundraiser gala. She was there and a mutual friend introduced us. A few pictures were snapped of us together laughing. Her publicist called me the next day and suggested we go on a date," Joe disclosed.

"So... not a fairy tale. No horse, no castle, no swooning," Hetty teased.

Joe chuckled, "Nah, nothing like that. She was just so driven to get the career she wanted. I knew all along I was a stepping stone. A good public relations move. At the time, I didn't care. I had lost my parents and was tired of being the party boy. I was also tired of women trying to throw themselves at my feet. So, in a way she was my protection while it lasted," Joe mused.

"So... it's over?" Hetty clarified.

"Yeah. It's been over. I'm waiting for her before we announce it. It is a business decision for both of us. You see rumors and the press will eat it up and we both have contracts in the balance. But the relationship," he sighed, "has been over almost as long as we were together," he said hanging a snowman ornament and watching it spin on its string in front of him. "I lost it right after I moved in with her, I thought if we lived together, I would feel closer. But the moment I moved in I just felt... stuck." He drifted a little. "Teammates all said that having a girlfriend or wife helped them settle into their game, because they had family. So, I tried it. And it just wasn't working. In fact, I was getting in more fights than before on the field. I knew I was being used. Her relationship with social media takes precedence over anyone or anything. I decided I don't want a girlfriend who has a more important relationship with social media. I just didn't want to compete with her fans." He sat on the floor and started to help Hetty since the ornaments were finished. He smiled and his shoulders shook in a quiet laugh. "Did you know I tried to give Heather my grandmother's ring? She laughed and said it was dated. She wanted something bigger and newer, and not the antique that has been in my family for three generations."

"Dottie always loved that ring. She would talk about coming over here and your mom letting her try it on sometimes," Hetty knew exactly what she was doing, and she just kept planting the seeds. "Dottie was always yours, you know that, right?"

"I was about to ask her to the dance. I had it all planned," he answered. "But then I told Harold one day after practice and he beat me to it. I figured if she really wanted me instead, she would have said no."

Hetty stopped decorating and turned to Joe. "She always said that if you wanted her, you would have asked and she would have told Harold where to stick his invitation," Hetty bluntly laid out the facts she had known for years.

Joe felt like there was a fist around his heart squeezing tighter and tighter.

Hetty sat up on her knees. "Don't you worry," she said patting him on the leg. "There is always a long quest to find the right lady in all of the stories. You just have to fight the battle. And with Dottie, it's going to be tricky." Turning so she could look him dead on, Hetty urged, "But you can do it, I know you can. You will help each other."

Hetty's phone rang. "Hey Murray, what's—"

Joe could hear Murray's voice, he spoke loudly. "Dottie left without saying goodbye. She is on her way back and will probably be there any minute."

"Thanks, Mur. We're done, just need to tidy up,"

she said and hung up the phone. "What are you doing?" She asked Joe who was fishing up in the tree for something.

"Just putting in the flasher bulb. And, voila!" Just then all of the lights on the tree started to blink at them.

"Never knew you could do that!" Hetty said as she tossed things back in the containers.

The creak of the kitchen door made them both look up. They hear some rustling and drawers in the kitchen open and close. Both unintentionally held their breath. Joe started to take one step toward Hetty and opened his mouth to say something. She quickly stopped him.

"Shhh!!!" Hetty waved Joe over to a corner as she pulled the empty boxes toward the other corner. They motioned to each other hand signals to try to figure out what to do. Hetty knew that her best friend was somewhat oblivious, and they might have a chance to get out without Dottie seeing them. On the other hand, was it so bad if Dottie caught them red handed after Joe had done such an adorable thing for her? Hetty thought about hollering out to Dottie, as it would be just the thing to get them together. But she hesitated. Joe had a plan. Suddenly she heard footsteps headed in their direction.

Dottie dashed in to the museum and went right up the stairs. They both stood stock still just in case she came right back down. Hetty put up her hand and mouthed, "Stay here." She tiptoed to the bottom of the stairs and looked up. Coast was clear. She motioned Joe to follow her and they quietly snuck out the kitchen and into her car. Hetty drove Joe back to his house,

"See you later partner!" she hollered at him as she drove off.

Shoving his hands in his pockets, Joe realized he still had the key to the kitchen door. Dashing up the hill and wiggling through the bushes that had overgrown, Joe snuck up to the kitchen and was about to put the key back, when the lights snapped on. Dottie got a glass, poured herself water. She chugged the first glass, then refilled. He smiled. She was thinking about something, planning something. He wanted to walk right in, like in the old days and ask about whatever crazy plan she had going this time. But he didn't. Both their argument from yesterday and the surprise he just created for her held him frozen in place. He just watched her for a moment. She was so beautiful. Dottie moved out of his view, and the light went off in the kitchen. Not wanting to get caught, he slapped the key up where the found it. Joe put the key back took one more glance hoping she'd come back into the kitchen. When she didn't, he smiled at the warmth he felt just being close by. He walked off the porch heading home and started to whistle "The Way You Look Tonight." This ceased immediately when he walked into his house to find the woman waiting for him.

* * *

Joe was now restless and stalked the living room like a snow leopard searching for something. Maybe he could go out in the driveway again. From the top, the lights from the museum could be seen. Banging at the front door startled him out of his thought.

"Joe, we need to talk," Dottie's voice was angry.

Although those words are usually terrifying, his heart sang hearing her voice. Then his mood quickly flipped. Why couldn't he have caught her in the driveway? Why couldn't she have come earlier? And now he had an unexpected guest. Joe heard the pipes in the house groan as the knobs turned in the bathroom and the shower started. Good. Joe would have a few minutes. He would get Dottie out of the house and explain about his unexpected houseguest. Unless she already knew and was upset about it. But why would she be upset? It didn't matter anyway, and he was sure if he could just explain—

She banged again. "I know you're in there, I see all of the lights."

He jogged to the front door. "Hey, Dottie," Joe was sheepish and rubbed his neck as he opened the door. She just stood in the doorway. This was unlike her. "Um, do you want to come in?"

"I'm trying to decide," Dottie spoke through gritted teeth.

"Ok, well, I'm gonna go get a coat if you're just gonna stand—" Dottie cut Joe off and barged in.

In a huff she turned, crossed her arms and stood in the middle of the living room. He worried for a moment that they might be heard if they stood right here. Then again, he didn't care.
"Would you like a drink? We could go into the kitchen—" he tried to lead her into the other room, away from the stairs. Dottie didn't budge.

He waited. She stood boring her eyes into him.

"I'm moving," she declared boldly.

"Okay...."

"So, there was no need to do that," she held hear arm straight out in front of her and pointed in the direction of the museum.

"Put up the painting?" he asked looking at the wall that she was actually pointing at.

"No," she slapped her arm down. "The *tree*. And don't deny it. Those flashing lights have *your* name all over them," her temper rose. "And I don't know how you roped Hetty into it, and I'm sure Frank and Murray have their fingers in this pie too, but you *shouldn't* have done that. I'm engaged to another man, and whether we like it or not, that is just how it's going to be," she huffed and crossed her arms back over her chest.

"I... don't quite know what to say to that... but you're welcome?" Joe was confused. This wasn't how she was supposed to act. Why was she mad at him? Wait, she said engaged? "Wait, you're *engaged*?" Joe repeated his thought out loud.

"Well," she looked at her feet dropping her guard. "Well... not technically," she went on the defensive again, "but it's bound to happen."

"So, Harold hasn't asked you."

"Yet. But since we're moving to New York, I'm sure it will happen eventually," she stated with a twinge of disbelief and distraction. Joe knew that she was starting not to believe in that idea as much as she used to. The corner of his mouth lifted and gave away the smallest of smiles.

Taking a step toward her, he asked, "So when are you moving?"

"Harold has to start on Monday, so he's going

up—"

"I didn't ask about Harold," he said taking another step closer, "I asked when *you* were moving.

Dottie took a step back. Joe was closing the four-foot gap between them, but it felt like it was just inches. "Well, sometime... in the new year... I suppose." She was grasping at straws now; he could feel it. "And what does it matter," she fought back. "You're leaving town as soon as this house sells, probably sooner."

Joe knew from years of playing competitive sports that in any competition or fight, when a person knows they are losing they pull out all the stops, including fighting dirty. His mind was suddenly on that last game again. His team was losing and there was nothing he could do for the team he loved. He would have done anything then to win that game. He kept it clean. Well almost clean. He said a few things to batters that he probably shouldn't have. It was all part of the game though. Outside of the playing field, he wouldn't have said any of it. Because when it came down to it, his team was more than a team to him. It was his family. He felt the same way about his teammates that he did about his parents. The way he felt about Dottie. They were all his family.

How to play this game he wondered. How could he win her? What was his strategy? He could see she was scared, too. She was a fighter, and she truly believed she wanted to go to New York. Joe wanted to help her, but maybe if he pushed her toward that New York dream, she would see it wasn't really what she wanted. Harold wasn't what she wanted. It was a big gamble, but he could always to the run-after-her-

and-confess-everything moment if this didn't work.

"Ok, so I put up a tree with Hetty, so what? Hetty and I thought it would be a fun antic for old times. I mean, you did drive off and leave the tree in my driveway. So, I figured I could do what I wanted with it. Plus, you love Christmas, so what is the big deal?" Joe crossed his arms and challenged her with his eyes.

"Well..." she let her shield of anger drop and she smiled. "It was a pretty good trick," Dottie admitted. She continued in disbelief," I can't believe you two got the ornaments out of my apartment. But then you and Hetty together were always a good team."

"We were a good team," he said dropping his arms and taking a few steps closer. He was only two feet from her now. A close enough distance that they could touch.

"That's what I just said," Dottie put her hands on her hips.

"No," he smiled and rubbed his neck. He dropped his head toward the floor as he could feel the blush rising in his cheeks, "I meant you and me," he peeked up at her again.

"Oh..." A slow blush started to rise in Dottie's cheeks, and she glanced down at the floor. He wasn't sure if she was still angry or if she was blushing. Either way, it filled his chest with pride and hope.

Joe liked when he threw Dottie off balance a little, especially when she was angry. Even more when she was angry to hide other feelings. When she was this angry, it meant she was vehemently passionate about something. He hoped it was him. He wasn't sure before, but to have Murray, Frank and Hetty all confirm that Dottie did have feelings but was keeping them so hidden that she herself didn't know they were still there. Joe was ready to dig those feeling up and fight for her. His heart which had been crumbling for years suddenly felt like it was resealing and healing. He had the feeling he was stepping into the batter's box of the biggest game of his life, and he just had to keep his head; to wait for the right pitch and then lean in and swing. This moment in the last few games had him rattled and unsteady. Right now, he was a rock. Nerves diminished, and he saw her clearly. He just had to stare her down and wait. Coach always said that the relationship between a batter and a hitter was like a dance. Joe really understood that now. He just had to wait for the right moment. She was ruffled now, so she was about to throw him something. Come on Dottie, throw me the heat, he thought.

"Well," she crossed her arms again. "It doesn't matter what kind of team we *were*. You are leaving again, don't pitchers and catchers report in February

He smiled because she paid enough attention to know this fact. She was interested. "Yeah, the eleventh, but—"

"See, you're leaving. And the tree is beauti I'm sure you can throw your money around a that kind of thing for any girl, I mean anyone wanted," she grasped at straws.

Joe just wanted to reach out and hold started to step toward her, but she put o "Stop! Don't come closer," she said. I her. He knew it.

"Dottie, I—"

"Don't say anything you'll regre

"Regret?" He opened his arms

chuckled nervously. "The only thing I regret is that I walked away and left you all behind."

"Speaking of which, why did you do that?" she painfully asked. "Why did you just walk away? You discarded us like we were nothing to you. Must be nice to have so many friends that we're all disposable," she spat at him.

"Disposable? DISPOSABLE?" He echoed his temper starting to rise.

"Sure, you keep us all for a time and then toss us away," she said standing and facing him now. Her pain radiating and filling the whole room.

"I think you should leave, if you think that," he said. Protecting himself. Again. He instantly regretted it. Instantly he contained his anger, shoving it away and tried to find the right words in his head. Dottie was precious. China. Delicate situation. All of the words he wanted to say to her came to him in a deluge. The ones he really should say now. The ones he meant to say to her over the years when he dialed her number or started emails. The words that he should have said to her before Harold had.

Nausea threatened. Focusing his fear and nervousness down to his toes like his coach had taught him to do many years ago, he took a deep breath in through his nose. Opening his eyes, he didn't realize were closed, courage soared through his veins. He cleared his throat and began to speak, "I have loved you for as long as I can remember—" the front door slammed. He realized she had done exactly as he suggested. She walked out. Joe's newly repaired heart cracked into a thousand pieces.

CHAPTER TWENTY-THREE

Dottie stepped outside and fought with the zipper on her coat. She was so upset her hands were shaking and she couldn't connect the ends together to zip the jacket. The wild gusts of wind didn't help her either. It blew a handful of hair into her face, blurring her vision. She huffed and took a few steps up the driveway to go back to the museum. Suddenly a gust of understanding hit her, and she couldn't breathe. She bent over and put her hands on her knees as she tried to tell her lungs to move. This feeling was exactly how Joe felt when he heard about Dottie and Harold. This was a terrible feeling. Why she had walked out? Dottie didn't know. It was not at all how she really felt. She didn't want to run away from Joe. She wanted to run to him. Joe wasn't throwing her away, he was waiting for her to make a choice. She hoped.

It was worth a shot, though. Courage surged through her chest and then burned down into her legs.

Joe was worth fighting for. She should have fought for him sooner. But pride and pain led to blindness and ignorance.

Before she knew what was happening, she stood up and turned on her heel. This time she didn't knock when she got to the front door. Taking a deep breath, she flung open the front door and marched back into Joe's house. Joe was standing in the same exact spot when she left him. Slowly he looked up and revealed his handsome face filled with anguish. His still hopeful eyes met hers. Her breath left her as she opened her mouth to speak. When words finally found their way out of Dottie's mouth, she spoke at the same time he did.

"I didn't mean anything I—" he said.

"We shouldn't have let so many years—" she said.

They both laughed with nervousness and excitement.

"You first," they both said at the same time.

"You know what, it doesn't matter," he said and in three steps he was across the room. He cupped her face in his hands and looked in her mossy green eyes searching quickly for permission. She looked right back. He took that signal as the go ahead. Lifting her chin up a little to meet his, Joe gently placed his lips on top of hers. She leaned in falling deeper into the kiss while he wrapped his arms around her.

Everything seemed to be aglow and grow fuzzy around the edges. Nothing else existed. It was just the two of them with their arms wrapped around each other. Finally. Together as they should have been for years. Terror and fear no longer existed between them. In this moment they stared into each other's eyes and saw the whole world, and their future all at the same time. Touching their foreheads together communicated every apology that needed to be said. Everything was perfect. Until they heard footsteps on the second floor.

"Joe," called the foot stepper, who was female by the sound of her voice. She was obviously in ill-fitting heels clomping across the second floor and started down the stairs.

Dottie pushed Joe away, "Who—?" she looked at him, then up at the ceiling.

"Dottie, I can explain. Give me a moment to—"

Joe was interrupted by a thin waisted, bleach blonde woman who had so much makeup on, it would probably take hours to wash off.

"Joe, where can I—Oh!" she cut herself off as she noticed Dottie in the room. "Joe, why didn't you tell me we had company?" She looked to Joe then crossed the room to Dottie offering a limp hand, "Hi, I'm Heather. Heather Smolen? You might recognize me from my season of 'Real Lives'," she said as if everyone knew her reality show as if it was momentous, groundbreaking television.

Completely shaken, Dottie trembled.

Heather gave Dottie a warm smile, more than just the one she used for good public relations with fans. Heather took Dottie's fear as excitement at seeing a celebrity. Although Dottie was terrified to be caught.

Dottie spoke first then awkwardly extended her hand, "I'm Dottie, I just came over to… I…I'm Joe's—"

"DOTTIE! The *Dottie!*" Heather squealed and then hopped up and down while clapping. Then she almost tackled Dottie with a hug. "It's so great to finally meet you! Joe often talks about his friends he grew up with here in West Hattum."

"East Haddam," Joe corrected, then looked between the ladies as if he were waiting for one or both to fly off the handle at any moment.

"Riiiight," Heather giggled as she let go of Dottie. The woman was all bones, and Dottie felt all of them dig into her in the tight embrace from the tiny woman.

"I was just about to go," Dottie said. "But Joe, it's so nice to finally meet your fiancée," Dottie said as she started to retreat to the door.

"Dottie don't go—" Joe started to say. He looked like he had something he needed to tell her, his eyes pleaded.

"Yes! You can't go yet! We've just met," echoed Heather, seeming to get Joe's intention incorrect. "We were just about to go out to dinner, to The Queen's... something. You should come with us!"

"NO! I'm..." she shouted, but then tried to cover her unnecessary loudness with extreme politeness. "I need to get back to the museum. I have... things to do. For the museum." Dottie squirmed. "Exhibits. I need to build the new exhibits. You see we're trying to get them open soon to get more visitors. You see the museum is closing," Dottie continued to ramble. "We don't get as many visitors as we used to, and we need a new roof..." She looked at Joe who just beamed at her. Dottie blushed both from his look and from her incessant chatter. Then she kindly declined and shook both of their hands as she said, "But you two have a nice time. Joe, it was great to see you again, I..." Dottie had so much that she wanted to say as well, but now wasn't the time. "I'll see you later," she said and without waiting for a goodbye from either of them, she walked out the door.

As her feet crunched in the snow Dottie's mind spun about what just happened. That kiss! And Joe liked her too. Of course, they were interrupted. Did nothing between them go smoothly? Oddly she didn't feel upset, just confused. She was halfway up the driveway when she heard someone running after her, footsteps crunching in the snow.

"Dottie wait! Dottie, I—" Joe shouted.

She turned around with a blank face and looked at him. He searched her face with his eyes. Joe looked like he was ready to be slapped.

"What's the matter Joe?" she broke the silence. "Did I forget something?" she said as she checked her pockets.

"I can totally explain," Joe was panicked and started to reach out for her hands, but then looked back at the house behind him.

"Ok…" Dottie waited.

"She just showed up. Without warning. I couldn't send her away. We… we've been broken up for a few weeks. It's really over between us. We decided it right after I arrived here." He rubbed his hand on the back of his neck. "I don't know if I ever really felt much for her, and I'm pretty sure for her I was just her stepping stone to the next great thing. We haven't mentioned anything to any one because she has a big contract looming. I care about her enough that I don't want her to lose that opportunity. And my contract is due for re-signing this year. Becoming fodder for the gossip papers might be bad for both of our careers at this moment. We both agreed that staying out of the spotlight was the best thing. We would wait until we both had our affairs in order to have our agents make a statement." He looked at her, pleading for her understanding.

"Ok." Dottie said. Still with a blank face.

"I just want you to know, I kissed you as a— wait...Ok?" Joe was trying to register her answer. "But you... Aren't you...? Can we...?" Joe was completely thrown that she believed him, and he sputtered, "Can we talk about this later? I'm sure you have questions and I want..."

"Sure." she smiled and shrugged her shoulders as he was apologizing for just stepping on her shoe.

"Sure? That's it? You're not going to go crazy or yell or slap me or anything?" Joe was confused.

"Nope. We can talk tomorrow or whenever," Dottie complied chipperly and smiled genuinely.

"Wait. What? Why do I feel like I'm missing something," Joe stated.

Taking a moment to look in his eyes to confirm to herself, Dottie shook her head and smiled. Reassuringly she reached out and put her hands in his. Although she was in slight disbelief, a warmth filled her. "Honestly, all you say makes sense. And you have no reason to lie. You've never lied to me. Kept things from me, yes. Lied, no," he was taken aback, but she continued. "You knew she was upstairs, told me how you really felt and kissed me anyway, knowing she could be down any moment and catch us. You're not the type of guy to do that to any woman. So..."

He waited for her to finish, but after a few moments he prompted, "So... what?"

"So, I choose to trust you," Dottie was in such shock over the whole evening that she saw everything clearly. What she would do from this point forward, who was to say. But at this moment, everything was clear to her as a morning after a fresh snow. She smiled at him, and then leaned in and kissed him. Just a light kiss, but one that assured him she meant every word she just said. "Besides," she continued, "we both know Hetty is the dramatic one."

They laughed and then Joe's face turned serious and searched her eyes.

"Oh, Dottie," he murmured her name as a thank you. He had so much he wanted to say to her.

"I know," she replied to all he wasn't saying. "We will have so much time to talk about it all and figure it all out."

"I should... get back inside." he said, not letting go of her waist which he took hold of when she kissed him.

"True," she laughed and wrapped her arms around him, "you don't have a coat on."

"Well, and a house guest," he joked. "Sure, you don't want to join us for dinner?"

"Nah, I really do have things to do at the museum. You should come over tomorrow and see all of the progress. Hetty's exhibit is mostly done, and we're working on the yearbook exhibit. Tomorrow they're bringing over the computer and a lot of the yearbooks." She paused for a nervous moment before asking what she really wanted to. "And, maybe, if you're willing, you could possibly, let us maybe photograph you and, you know... put it on social media?"

She scrunched up her nose and looked at him questioning. He looked back and said nothing. Then a smile cracked across his face.

"Then I will see you tomorrow," he murmured as he touched his forehead to hers. "Good night."

"Good night," Regrettably she pulled away from him, giving his hand one last squeeze before she turned and walked up the driveway.

On her short walk back to the museum, she replayed the last thirty minutes in her head. Although many things were answered, Dottie was now even more confused.

She loved Joe! He loved her! But Harold. New York. The museum. And Joe had a contract and move back to Los Angeles in a few weeks. Confusion echoed in her mind until she got back to the museum and locked the door after herself. "What WAS that?!" Dottie hollered her question to the empty hallway and leaned against the door, listening to the silence and waiting for an answer to come to her.

CHAPTER TWENTY-FOUR

"**W**hat was what?" Hetty hollered as she came running down the stairs.

"You're still here?" Dottie jumped from her leaning stance as she was startled out of her daze.

"Of course, we're still here," Frank echoed. "Robert called me just after you left saying he was bringing a load of the yearbooks over. We've started placing them, maybe you want to come look?"

"Sure," Dottie said taking off her coat and snapping back into business.

"Wait a minute!" Hetty barred the way up the stairs, "What just happened over there?" She was concerned.

"Well—"

"Wait a minute, I want to hear," hollered Don from inside the room.

"Me too," hollered another voice.

"Who is up there? Oh! Hey, Robert," Dottie's

face went red with embarrassment. There were so many people here tonight, and she probably shouldn't tell them all. She wasn't sure if she was ready to have everyone know the feelings, she just realized herself. Well, she resigned, this was a small community. It would be all over town, soon enough. "Why don't you all come into the kitchen. I need a drink, and I'm sure if you've all been working, you could use a break." Without waiting for anyone, she walked into the kitchen, flipped on the lights and grabbed the cocoa powder, milk and cinnamon.

"Hot cocoa, huh? This must be serious," Hetty spoke somberly, looking over the island as Dottie grabbed a pot and measuring cups. Hetty started to get cups out as Dottie prepared the drink. Turning from the stove, she saw that everyone had assembled.

Putting her hands on the island and taking a stance and making a serious face Dottie began. "You all have to promise you won't say anything about this. Including Harold stopping by and the cookies. The mystery of the Christmas tree in the ballroom, and anything I'm about to tell you. Just until I've got it all figured out."

"But—" Frank said.

"I don't care if Murray doesn't know. I'm well aware that you can't keep a secret to save your soul, but careers are at stake. And maybe the fate of this museum. Got it?" After meeting everyone's eye as they individually nodded. Satisfied, Dottie took a deep breath and continued. "Joe is in love with me." And she smiled the biggest smile.

Echoes of "I knew it," and "Yes!" and "Told you," were a cacophony in the room.

"Do you want to hear what happened or not?" Dottie hollered over them.

"We do!" exclaimed Don, who Dottie thought was the least interested in her life, until now. But it made sense, being Hetty's husband that he would be invested.

"Well…" Dottie continued to regale her friends with the story as she passed out hot chocolate. "At first I walked in and was really angry at him. But then he looked at me and…" She told them how she was so touched by his gesture of decorating the tree that she couldn't stay mad. She blushed when she revealed that Joe kissed her. And was even more embarrassed when they were interrupted by Heather his fiancée, who is actually no longer engaged to him.

"I guess she is visiting him to work out the details of their breakup. Apparently, Joe's contract is in negotiations and Heather is up for something big in New York. She was out this way and came up to see the town," Dottie said. "You know I've read in books and seen movies where this moment happens, and the gal gets all upset. But it was funny, when the moment was happening, I just knew that it all didn't matter." She turned to Hetty and said, "It was like when we made those forts when we were kids with the sofa cushions and blankets. It felt cozy and safe inside, no matter how precarious it looked from the outside," Dottie remarked. She mentioned how they invited her to dinner, but she declined, because she wanted to finish at the museum. Then she smiled slowly and blushed. "And he followed me out and kissed me again in the driveway." She looked around at her silent friends. They were all looking at her with hopeful faces that were swept away in her romantic tale. Even Don had become a little misty eyed and wiped his eyes with the back of his hand.

"I can't believe you were so rational," Hetty remarked. "Especially since you were about to tear someone's head off when you left here."

"True, I was irrational. But you were acting sketchy," Dottie motioned to Hetty, "and Harold here only moments before, it was just…too much. Throw in all of these feelings I've had forever for Joe that I've ignored. I don't know anyone who would have been rational."

"Speaking of which, what are you going to do about Harold?" Don asked, as he leaned in on the island. He was definitely the one most engaged in the whole saga.

"Harold. Oh no! What am I going to do?" she looked up at her friends with pleading eyes and put her hands on her cheeks.

"Well, you can't stay with him," Don argued. "You have to be with Joe."

"Yeah, but he's going to go back to Los Angeles, so either way Dottie is leaving town if she does go with Joe," Frank theorized.

"Then you still have the problem of the museum," Robert reminded. "Who will take care of it? With these new exhibits, I bet you'll get more foot traffic, at least for a little while."

"Yeah, but with the cookie money, Dottie will be able to save the museum, and probably can pay someone to run it, at least a few days a week," Hetty suggested. "She can come back and check in on it, won't ya, honey?"

"Ugh, the cookie money. If I break up with Harold before the deal goes through, then we won't get the money to save the museum," Dottie felt trapped. "But not breaking up with him later only to get the money makes me feel dishonest." She continued, "Plus this was a big deal for him. It helped him solidify the job, he said." Dottie put her head in her hands.

"I still vote for Joe," Don chimed in.

"My love, no one here is voting for Harold," Hetty frankly replied to her husband. Turning to the group she threw her hands in the air and clarified, "Not that I'm saying anyone is against him. He's a nice person... at times. But he tries. He's just not right for Dottie."

There was a hubbub of agreement in the kitchen. It was weird for Dottie to have all of these people chatting about her relationship, but at the same time it was nice to have a community to talk all of this out with. Or what are they calling it these days she thought to herself, a hive mind?

"You don't need Harold's cookie venture. I agree that it's the wrong reason to stay with anyone. Plus, if you're that worried about it, Joe has money," Robert stated. "Why not ask him for help for the museum?"

"I'm sure Joe would help. He is very generous. I know he bought a lot of your cookies and gave them away," Frank added as they all looked at Dottie.

Her head was still buried in her hands and so she spoke muffled, "I already told him I didn't want his money for the museum."

"Yeah, but that was before you knew he had feelings for you. It's different now. I'm sure you can take it back," Don said.

"That is exactly why she can't ask," Hetty reiterated Dottie's sentiment. "If she goes back now asking for the money again, as in 'Sorry Joe, I was wrong. Now that you've professed that you love me, can I have your money for my failing museum?' It just wouldn't be right. And it puts a damper on the mystique out of their newly budding romance," Hetty said.

A cell phone rang. They all checked their pockets except Dottie. Somehow, she knew that her bliss wouldn't last long. She also somehow knew exactly who was calling. After the second ring she announced to the room, "It's Harold." She didn't have a special ring for him, she just... knew. On the third ring she took it out of her pocket and answered downtrodden, "Hello Harold. Yes.... Wait. Before you..., Harold!" she was almost shouting now.

"We should go," Frank whispered as he shooed everyone out of the kitchen.
Hetty held her hand up making a phone gesture and mouthing, "Call me later."

Dottie nodded and then hung her head hearing his voice through the phone. She squared her shoulders and said into the phone while sighing, "Harold, I need to tell you something..."

* * *

The call lasted only four minutes. Four minutes to undo everything Dottie had thought mattered for years. Things she thought mattered until a few weeks ago. The only romantic relationship she'd ever had. Their plan of moving to New York. But now she knew those weren't her goals anymore. Hope for the museum died midway through the call. Harold said he would discuss the deal with the partners, but he wasn't sure that they would see Dottie as a good risk, if she wasn't moving to the city to be readily available for consultations. She wasn't sure if it was a retaliation or if he just realized it wasn't a good idea. Dottie hoped Harold wasn't vindictive enough to just pull the rug out from under her. At the same time, she understood and was a little glad.

No cookie deal meant that it would be a clean break between them and they both could go on with their lives. She would just have to wait and see. When Dottie finally hung up the phone, she felt drained. She wanted quiet comfort.

Joe's face flashed into her mind. He was the only thing keeping her sane at the moment. Dottie wanted to call him, to go cuddle in his arms, but he was out with Heather. Hetty had texted saying mentioning that they were at the diner, and invited Dottie to stop by when she got done on her call, but Dottie wasn't in the mood for people at the moment. She definitely wasn't in the mood for explaining anything that happened to anyone, not even to Hetty or Joe.

Instead she went upstairs, taking solace in her beloved museum. As she walked through the hallway, she found herself petting the walls as she went. "Old girl, you've been good to me. I'll be sad when we end as well."

When she got to the yearbook exhibit room, she was stunned. "Wow,' she gasped out loud.

They had lined the bookshelves with the yearbooks. Every other book was open to a different page. The alternating books had the cover showing. At the ends, five to ten were shelved so they could be taken off the shelves and looked through. On the alternating wall, somehow Frank had mounted frames with hinges on the walls, so they turned like oversized pages. Robert had also texted her when he left mentioning that the school was printing large poster sized reproductions of several momentous pages from the yearbooks for those hanging frames. It would truly be like a giant yearbook that visitors could flip through.

Against the back wall, the computer had been set up, so people could sit and search through the database scans. There was also a sign that said "Please let us know if you would like to volunteer to scan. Yearbooks from 1803-1879 still need to be scanned."

Dottie smiled. It was amazing what could be accomplished by asking for help. Rubbing her hand over the top of the computer screen she quietly praised everything surrounding this exhibit. The help. The technology. The art of the idea. Even Joe falling through the roof and finding the photos to begin with.

Turning around to take it all in, she saw that they had flanked the doors off the Logan Room with the glass table cases from the library. A pair of white felt gloves sat on top of one of them. It was open and a stack of yearbooks were on the floor. In the case a few were laying open. Dottie walked over. Putting on the gloves she gently took each yearbook from the pile and gently turned the pages of each one until she found a page that made her smile. Selecting an open page where there were interesting pictures or some sort of community event, she placed every one of the remaining ones in the case before closing it. Stepping back, she looked around the whole room. With a sigh of contentment, she walked toward the door, but turned around for one last look before turning the lights out in the room.

This was a simple joy she felt. Making an exhibit that showcased her community. Something that taught a different viewpoint to visitors. Her mother always said that if one person learned one new thing before they exited the doors for the day, they were doing their job. A history teacher Dottie had in college said, "History teaches us where we've been and points us to where we should be going." Dottie hoped that was what she was doing. Running this museum might not have been what she dreamt of doing with her life, but she knew it made a difference in the community.

She walked over to the library and set the gloves on her desk. She took out her phone and saw it was past eleven.

It was time to go home, Dottie thought. She would handle everything else tomorrow. Laughing to herself, she realized she just quoted one of her favorite heroines, Scarlett O'Hara. If there was anyone who could get out of something like this, Scarlett could. Dottie tried to channel her all the way back to her apartment, and even picked up that book when she got home. Only a few pages in, Dottie fell asleep reading.

CHAPTER TWENTY-FIVE

Joe confessed his feelings, and everything seemed to be falling into place. The museum started to get busy, and with the plans for her upcoming event and exhibits Dottie didn't have much time to process her feelings completely. Or maybe she was trying to ignore the fact that he had a career in Los Angeles. However, every time someone mentioned Joe, or she thought of him, his smiling face invaded her thoughts and a blush burned her cheeks. How had she gone this long without realizing her feelings she continually thought to herself. Well, at least now she knew, and they were doing something about it. But the museum's resurrection was taking her primary brain space.

Robert had arranged for school groups to visit claiming they all needed to see the yearbook exhibit. Dottie got busy scheduling all of those to happen in December. But he called multiple times a day saying he had another group to add. The museum could only hold about 80 people at a time, so she could only take two classes every few hours. Robert had also put in calls to neighboring school districts, recommending they get in to view the new exhibits as well.

"Dottie, I have another group for you to schedule," he stated, for the fourth time this day.

"That is great, Robert, but I don't have any more room this year," she said triumphantly. "But if you'd like I can start to schedule them for January?" She said the last with a question, not knowing the fate of the museum, but hoping this interest was enough to keep it open, at least for one month more.

"Do what you have to do, Dottie. I'll have meetings with the school board and with the museum board. We will make sure all of these kids get their groups in. We will also mention something to the parents. I'm trying to get all groups to have some sort of assignment they need to complete, so they will have to come back at least once more without the group."

"Robert, you're despicable!" she chided with a laugh. "Please let them know when they return, I'll give an extra dollar discount for students. Two if they bring someone else with them that isn't a student!" "Now you're thinking like a business woman, Dottie," Robert said proudly.

"We're going to make it, aren't we Robert?" she said quietly.

"Dottie," he said strongly, "you have done a phenomenal job and if it were up to me, I would make sure the East Haddam Historical Society stayed open for as long as you were around to run it."

Dottie smiled over the phone. "Thanks, Robert.

It's nice to know I have you on my side."

"You're welcome, Dottie. I'm sure I'm not the only one you have on your side. This museum has reminded a lot of people about a sense of community they had forgotten. I think the ball will also help solidify that," and just before he hung up, he added, "You have more friends then you thought you did."

Dottie smiled acknowledging that he was probably talking about himself, although once again Joe's face smiling at her slid into her mind.

It was nice that her love life actually felt like a love life. Dottie now realized that her relationship with Harold seemed more and more like two people just not wanting to be alone. She sighed feeling guilty every time she thought of Harold. She should have ended it so much sooner.

Harold texted Dottie many, many times over the next few days. Each text getting more desperate or desolate. And then they just stopped. She told herself it was better this way. Just to let him go. Harold was a good guy in a big city. He would find someone more suited for him.

Joe came over as promised and Dottie showed him the exhibits.

"These are great, Dottie. They should bring people in," Joe said.

"We can hope," she sighed.

"Oh, here, take a picture of me," Joe said, handing her his cell phone, then grabbing a yearbook and pretended he was looking at a page. He made sure to pick one that had East Haddam, bolded on the cover and that it was easy to read by the viewer. Dottie snapped the picture and smiled. Joe smiled back. As he took his phone back from her, he almost held her hand with as long as his fingers lingered.

Dottie pulled back and shrugged away.

"What is it, Dottie?" Joe asked with concern.

"Joe, I—"

"It's Harold, isn't it?" Joe cut her off.

"No. Yes. Well, not in the way you think." Dottie collected her thoughts. "He, well I, called it off."

"You're no longer together?"

"Nope," she said and sighed.

"Well that's great," Joe said walking over to her and setting his hands reassuringly on her shoulders and started to lean in to kiss her.

She leaned back a little and looked up at him with pleading eyes. "Joe, I... I don't think we should pursue this," she motioned her hand back and forth between them and walked out of his embrace, "until you get everything settled on your end, and we figure everything else out."

Confusion was written all over Joe's face. "What do you mean 'this,'" he echoed her hand gesture.

"I mean, I think we shouldn't kiss and whatnot," she blushed, "until you announce you're not with Heather." She turned away from him. "We've waited this long, I really think that the air should be clear, and things should be figured out. So, no kissing for now. Besides, you're a big star and I'm not ready for media to be jumping down my throat, yet."

Chuckling, he said, "Well, I'm not *that* big of a star. Media tends to follow Heather much more than they follow me, but... I understand." He sighed. "I agree, we need to let it all rest a little before we jump in to this. Plus, you need to get this place, and what you're doing with it, figured out."

"Right." She turned back to him, "And not to put the cart before the horse, you are still moving back to Los Angeles and selling your house, right?"

"Well, if I can... there doesn't seem to be too much market for it at the moment. I can't seem to get anyone out to look at it."

"Wait.... Maybe. Well, it could work," she mumbled to herself.

"What?" he asked.

Dottie turned to Joe. "You said your dad had those horseshoe pits in the barn, right?"

"Yeah..."

"Well, what would be a good way to raise money for the museum, and show off your property at the same time?" Dottie's excitement rose. Not waiting for him to answer, she replied, "Having a celebrity horseshoe tournament to celebrate the opening of the new exhibit! We could have an open house, and we could have the tournament, with a big cash prize. Maybe we could even charge people something small, like, I don't' know, five bucks to tour your house? Proceeds going to the museum, of course."

"But what about the ball?" he remarked.

"That could still happen. They could even both be on the same day. Hey, maybe you could get Heather to come to that? Oooh, you could come together and maybe it would get in the papers for a bit. We could, with her permission, of course, start a rumor that you two were thinking about getting married here!"

Joe shook his head, "No."

"No?" Dottie stopped in her tracks. "But why, I—"

"Not about the wedding and Heather. I'll ask her,

and I'm sure she will do me the favor." He walked over to her and cupped her cheek with his hand. "I mean, no, I have waited too long to kiss you, and I'm going to wait longer," he said and kissed her. It was a light gentle kiss.

Dottie sighed. "Joe. I really want to kiss you too, but to the world you're an engaged man. You said yourself you didn't want to distract anyone who might have control over your contract to make a decision based on media images," she reasoned. "Plus, I don't want to come off as a homewrecker. I can't do that to my parents."

"True," he sighed and removed his hand from her face. "Ok. I guess I can wait a few more days. Let's get these plans in motion." He pulled out his phone and scrolled through numbers. Finding the one he was looking for he tapped it to connect. "Hey, Heather, what would you say about getting married at Dottie's museum?"

* * *

Four days later, it was viral that Joe and Heather were hiding away in Connecticut making plans to get married at the East Haddam Historical Society.

The day after, when Dottie arrived at the museum, there was a line to get in. It was early on a Saturday, and she was so excited to have all of the visitors. Many whom she recognized from the town. Most were hoping to catch a glimpse of Joe Thomas, or even discuss the exhibits with him while they walked around the museum. Joe didn't show up that day.

However, Joe visited the museum the next day,

true to his word. Even though it was a Sunday morning, there was again a line when Dottie showed up. She had texted Joe on her way to the museum to tell him about the line the day before. He agreed to visit. Joe showed up around noon. Swarmed by excited visitors, he got stopped right inside the entryway at the front door and no one could get in or out. There was such a clamoring for his attention, no one actually saw the museum. In fact, twenty minutes after Joe arrived, the parking lot was packed. It was as if everyone within a fifteen-mile radius showed up to see him. Joe had gotten to understand the power of social media from Heather and was asking everyone he took a picture with to post it and tag the museum in the photo using hashtag Save The Museum. After about ninety minutes of photos, Joe excused himself and made an announcement he would be back.

"Check the website for the East Haddam Historical Society in the next twenty-four hours to get updates on Joe's next appearance," Dottie told the fanatic group.

That evening Joe and Dottie planned two other visits for him that Dottie just announced on the museum's website and Facebook page. Joe was set up in the library to sign autographs. This would allow congestion to be on the second floor and would allow people to still enter and exit the museum easily without congestion. Dottie had to schedule more volunteers for those days to make sure she could manage all of the visitors. Joe was to be at the museum Tuesday and Wednesday. There was a sign-up link on the website for assigned autograph times. People were given a time window and were encouraged to arrive early.

They somehow managed to get over three hundred people through the museum on these days. This was good for business.

While he signed memorabilia provided by the guests Joe suggested that they view the other exhibits. He would encourage everyone to find old photos of him as he started his career on the local team. And he also promoted the beauty pageant exhibit.

"Hetty was one of my best friend's growing up. She was famous before I was," he would tell people. Dottie would chuckle to herself every time she heard it. Once he caught her and smiled. It was nice to have a private joke with Joe again, she thought to herself as a warm tingly feeling filled her inside and a smile crossed her face.

The museum stayed open two extra hours both days to allow all the visitors in. Amazingly, people would stop in to snap a picture with Joe or get an autograph and then they stayed to meander the museum. People would get their autographs, and then would be caught up in the exhibits. It warmed Dottie's heart to see both the Baker Room with the Hetty's exhibit and the Logan Room with the Yearbook exhibit were both packed at closing time. She kept the museum open an extra couple of hours after Joe left just to let people browse. Dottie was also thrilled that she had finished both exhibits finished just in time for the rush. This was the reason she stayed. People coming to learn or be inspired by the local community.

She was so glad that she had built the exhibits even though the museum was set to close. However, with such interest, closing was hopefully being postponed indefinitely.

Although originally Dottie and the board were wary about the ball attracting attention and raising enough money, they had a waiting list. She was saying yes to everyone at first, but then tallied the incoming reservations. Currently this list was way past one hundred people who wanted to attend. Dottie was also figuring out logistics of the whole thing. Would they need room for tables for food? How large would the bandstand need to be? These questions and more were filling her time and was keeping her from letting the whole town attend.

As of this morning Dottie had over sixty paid bookings for the Christmas ball the following week. This meant she had enough money for the roof. She sashayed into Frankincense and Myrrh hardware with a check. Dottie had never been more delighted to pay for a repair for the museum. When she walked up to the counter, Murray was in his normal spot sitting on a stool behind the counter working on today's crossword puzzle in the newspaper.

She said hello and handed him a check stating she was paying for the roof.

"It's already paid for," Murray stated.

"What do you mean, it's paid for," Dottie questioned. A shocked look crossed her face.

"I mean its paid for."

"But I… I don't understand. How is it already paid for?" Dottie puzzled.

Murray looked at her. "I don't know how else to say it," he pondered. Murray always seemed to think deeply about the strangest things. "Someone else already gave us the money for your roof."

"Who?" Dottie blurted.

"Can't say," Murray said grabbing his crossword and looking at nine down.

"Come on Murray. Everyone knows you can't keep a secret," Dottie poked.

"Apparently so does your donor," Murray was being cryptic. Dottie wasn't sure if it was on purpose or not.

"What? I don't understand. Why do you say that?"

Murray looked over the rims of his glasses at her, "They left the money, cash, in an envelope. It was behind the counter sitting on this shelf," he pointed down in front of him.

Leaning over the counter as if she didn't believe him that there was a shelf there, or maybe looking to see if the money was still there. Dottie just couldn't wrap her head around it.

"I…" she was still stunned with disbelief. "And no one saw them," she looked around the store up around the ceiling.

"No use in looking, we don't have cameras. So, there would be no way to know who left the money. I'm rarely away from this stool, unless Frank isn't here," Murray offered.

"How… Why… But…"

"Yup, Frank and I said that exact thing," he confessed. "There was no note or anything, I'm sure you're going to ask that next. Just "Dottie's Roof" was printed by a computer on the outside of the envelope that was sealed and had more than enough for the roof. In fact, there is some left over, in case you have other repairs," he reported. "The museum has a credit of about three hundred dollars here, so let us know when you need something, and we'll deduct."

Shaking her head and standing wide eyed, Dottie was still overcome with disbelief. Who could have done this? Someone who knew Murray and Frank well enough to know that they gossiped to everyone about everything. And it had to be someone who knew that the museum needed a new roof. There were so many people it could have been, but few who had that amount of cash.

"No sense in trying to figure it out," Murray said as if he had been reading her mind. "Frank and I tried to poke around and see if we could suss out the answer the last few days." He leaned toward her conspiratorially, "Frank likes to think himself an amateur detective. But even with his wily ways, we determined that it's not Joe, any member of the school board, Hetty or Don, and I'm assuming by your befuddlement that it's not you either," Murray was eying her as if to double check that she didn't leave the money.

"Well, then… I guess I need to get decorations for the Christmas ball while I'm here, instead." Dottie was mystified. Who could the mysterious donor be? Puzzled about the money, she turned and walked into Joe's chest.

"Just don't go for any more wreaths. Or if you do, please let me know and I'll stay out of that aisle," he grinned at her.

She was so glad to see him. That smile made her fall head over heels all over again. Dottie hated that she was the one who suggested that they hold off on their relationship until things got straightened out in his life. It was all she could do to keep her hands at her sides and not throw them up around his neck and kiss Joe.

"Hey," she said, and punched him lightly in the arm instead.

"Hey," he laughed at her and shook his head.

"You two don't have to pretend around me," Murray said with his head down in his crossword.

"Joe, did you hear about my roof?" Dottie asked watching him to see his reaction.

"Oh no, did it leak again?" he asked in earnest.

"No, the opposite. Someone paid to have a new roof put on," Dottie stared at him trying to see if he would give anything away.

"Wow. Who?" he asked and then seeing her inquisitive look, put up both hands and took a step back, "It wasn't me. I wish it was. Wait, how do you know that the roof was paid for, but you don't know who did it?"

Dottie retold the story Murray just told her. Joe seemed genuinely surprised.

"You really don't know, do you?" she asked, double checking.

"Dottie," he said comforting her by softly stroking her upper arms with his hands, he didn't care who saw. "I've tried to help you with the museum, and you've told me you don't want my money. I know you better than to be sneaky and trying to do things for you behind your back. Do you not remember your fifteenth birthday? We tried to give you a surprise birthday. You thought Hetty and I were dating when we were just trying to keep your party a secret. You wouldn't talk to us and wouldn't come over for the party. After multiple calls from both Hetty's and my mom, your mom finally dragged you kicking and screaming. You were more upset than surprised. I swore that day, never again to surprise you. It only turns out badly," Joe confided.

"Okaaay, I believe you," Dottie groused. "I still feel bad about that, by the way. The party. And accusing you both of dating. I should have known better," she said taking his hand in hers for just a moment and looking up into his eyes.

"Hey Murray," Alvin Marks, a teller at the bank walked in. He had two daughters in school that visited the museum last week. "Oh, hey Dottie," he acknowledged, waving as she was facing the front door. "Murray, I need new plates for my outlets. Sarah wanted to paint, and…" Dottie didn't hear the rest of the conversation as she focused on Joe.

"I should go pick out decorations," she cleared her throat and took her hand back.

"Yes, you should," he agreed.

Looking over her shoulder at him as she passed, she caught him looking back at her. And he winked. She wasn't in the clear yet, but everything was going to work out. Somehow.

CHAPTER TWENTY-SIX

At Joe's house, plans were underway for the open house and the horseshoe tournament. Joe thought it would be a good idea to hire some security for the open house, and also someone to manage it, just in case there were an issue, or someone wanted to put in an offer. Frank, with some assistance from high school kids who needed to do a service project, provided by Robert, helped clean out the barn, which was more of a large storage space. They found two horseshoe pits and made four more. Murray had done some research about indoor horseshoe games and found that clay in the pits made it similar to outdoor play. So, they poured a thick gray clay in all of the pits. This stopped the bounce of the horseshoe and made it much safer to play indoors.

Heather even helped. She and Joe were to be a team. This was to make them appear to still be a couple to the public. Heather also got two of her celebrity friends to come into town and play as well. Ashley Mills was a star on a popular TV show about lawyers, and she played the high-profile secretary. Kevin Gray was an up and coming pop star. Both were living in New York, so they were only a few hours' drive out of the sleepy river town in Connecticut. Ashley needed to polish up her image. Kevin was a friend of Heather's from the reality show. His band played at a club they frequently visited on the show. The three shared the same agent and Heather was glad to have a little more star power around her as well. She tweeted her fans to come and watch.

They borrowed temporary bleachers from the high school and put them up in the barn to accommodate up to two hundred seated spectators. Additional security was hired for inside the barn as well.

Dottie's research into the school tournaments said that the best two out of three games and the team advanced. With the last two teams competing against each other for the trophy. Donated by the local horse farm, the trophies were a pair of real horseshoes spray painted gold, one for each member of the winning team. They sat displayed in the front room at the museum with a sign that said, "sign up for your chance to play in the first annual celebrity horseshoe tournament." The clipboard got over seventy entrants. To make it fair, the names were drawn out of a hat both to see who would play and who was paired.

Hetty's husband Don was picked and was paired with fireman Aaron, who rescued Joe from the roof. Kaitlyn from the museum board was selected and paired with Kevin Gray, the celebrity musician. Ashley Mills was paired with Bart who owned the oldest bar in East Haddam. There was a wide selection of contestants including the owner of the pet food store, and the band director from the high school. The owner of a kitting store was paired with an architect. Some of the match ups made Hetty and Dottie laugh when they called them out. Some of the pairings were so mismatched but would be very entertaining to watch. Both Hetty and Dottie excused themselves from the competition, as they were running the ball that evening and Hetty was to be the Master of Ceremonies. Six pits in total were available in the barn, so a total of twelve teams were selected.

Plans for the ball were going well too. An additional security team was in place. No one was allowed into the museum that night without tickets or were on the list. The mayor insisted on all of the security as a precaution for the celebrities in attendance. Hetty was closing the diner for the night and offered Dottie her cooks and wait staff, all four of them, to work as the catering crew for the event. They were only having light hors d'oeuvres and canapes. Some of the high school journalism students volunteered to run the coat check as long as they were allowed to photograph the event for the school paper. Bart offered to bartend, as he said it would give his bar good advertising. It was less professionally staffed than what Dottie had originally wanted, but Hetty talked her into it.

"If you use volunteers, that is more money that goes into saving the museum. True it isn't the high caliber of the events you would like to do, but you keep saying that this place is the backbone of the community. It needs the community to thrive. Well, how better to have the community help it thrive then to take their offers to volunteer and help with your party?" Hetty urged. "The great thing is that you've already had most of the guests pay in advance. So, they aren't expecting glitz and glamour. They just want a fun party with famous people in attendance. More importantly, they want to support the museum and you," she reminded her friend.

"You're right. And we're serving hot cocoa, and eggnog at the bar. Passed simple comfort food, like cookies and savory puff pastries, so it's nothing crazy." Dottie took a deep breath. "Ok, let's do it," and the plan was set in motion.

Frank and Murray volunteered to decorate the ballroom, under the condition Dottie wasn't to see it and wasn't to peek. A big reveal of the room was to happen just before the guests arrived. Dottie wasn't one to allow someone else to take over for something this important. Hesitantly she agreed.

"Well, it seems like everything is handled," Dottie said to Hetty over the phone, as she collapsed on her sofa the night before.

"What are you wearing?" Hetty changed the subject matter-of-factly.

"Tomorrow? Probably just jeans and a museum shirt," Dottie replied thinking Hetty was talking about the tournament.

"No. Tomorrow night?"

"I don't know," Dottie sighed. "I haven't really thought about it. I have my black dress and gold heels. I'll probably wear those," there was a knock at Dottie's door. "Hold on Hetty," she said into the phone and then hollered to the door, "Who is it?"

Hetty's voice boomed in stereo, "It's your stylist, open the door."

Dottie got up to open the door and half said into the phone and half and the door, "You know it's open, why—" Dottie's mouth dropped when she opened the door to see Hetty holding two garment bags.

"You're wearing one of these," Hetty pushed past Dottie and laid them over the back of the sofa, then walked into Dottie's room. "What do you have in the way of foundation undergarments?"

Closing the door, Dottie hollered, "I should have some compression shorts in there somewhere," She started to unzip the first bag when Hetty came back in the room holding gold heels, nude Spanx and a strapless bra. "Put those on," Hetty instructed.

"Here?" Dottie questioned standing in her living room.

"Why not? Drapes are closed and it's your apartment, isn't it? No one else is here, and I've seen everything there is to see backstage at beauty pageants." Hetty remarked.

Dottie turned her back and changed, feeling a little self-conscious, as Hetty unzipped the first dress. She set it on the floor so Dottie could climb in.

"I'm not sure one of your pageant dresses would fit me, you're so much taller," Dottie worried.

"These aren't my pageant dresses."

"They're not?" Dottie questioned with surprise.

"No. They have this magical thing now called the internet and you push some buttons and things arrive at your door. It's amazing," Hetty quipped sarcastically.

"You bought me dresses?" Dottie asked.

"Nope, there is this great company that I wish was around when I did pageants. You can rent designers and keep them for a week so you can wear things to events, and then return them," Hetty said zipping Dottie up, "It's really a miracle. Wow." Hetty did a circle around Dottie. The dress was a floor length halter, platinum beaded gown that was fitted all the way down with a slit from the right ankle to knee. "Go take a look!" Hetty urged.

Walking into her bedroom, Dottie went right to her floor length mirror next to her closet door. Hetty was right behind her. "Wow," the said in unison.

Grabbing Dottie's bright auburn hair, and gently twisting it said, "we can easily toss your hair up and make you look very dressy.

"I didn't know I could be..." Dottie stopped and looked up to the ceiling trying to stop the oncoming threat of tears.

"Hold that thought," Hetty ran into the other room. She brought back the other dress out of the garment bag. It was an emerald green gauzy Grecian dress. "Shall we try on the other one before you lose it? I mean decide!" Hetty winked at Dottie, who quickly wiped the tears from her eyes.

As she climbed into the green, guilt overtook her. "Hetty, you're so good to me."

"Of course, honey. The street goes both ways," Hetty replied finishing up the zipper. Dottie turned and grabbed her hand.

"No, I mean, you're so good to me always. And I'm sorry I ever doubted you or suspected you," Dottie remorsefully admitted.

"I don't... when did you...? Honey, I'm confused. When did all of this happen?" Hetty had stepped back and placed her hand on her hip.

Dottie brought her hands to her face and flopped down on her bed. "There were a couple of moments lately that I thought you were against my decisions. To be honest, there were moments lately that I didn't trust you. When the reality was, I didn't trust myself." Dottie took a deep breath and turned away from her friend. "I have just been so confused. And you've been nothing but supportive and wonderful," Dottie let out a small sob.

"Now stop that," Hetty grabbed her friend by the elbows and pulled her off the bed. "No, I'm serious," her tone was now matter of fact, "If you cry your face will be puffy, and if you sit the dress will wrinkle and I didn't bring my steamer." Hetty said wanting to hug her friend. "Aww, screw it," she said and hugged Dottie anyway.

Letting out a contented sigh, Dottie said, "Thank you. I think this is the one, by the way."

"I think so too; I was hoping so. You look amazing in green. Honestly, I'm jealous. With my dark hair, that color makes me look like I'm sickly," Hetty grumbled.

"Thank you," Dottie repeated and started to cry.

Putting her finger in Dottie's face, Hetty snapped, "I'm serious. Your face will be all puffy tomorrow if you cry! Stop. That." Her face softened to a smile. "Now, get out of that so we can hang it up and have a drink. Heaven knows we deserve it." Hetty retreated to the kitchen and was clinking around in the refrigerator.

Dottie undressed and then got into comfy reindeer pajamas. Ones that Hetty got her last year for Christmas. It was really nice to have a best friend who took care of her so well. Even if she did meddle a little at times.

CHAPTER TWENTY-SEVEN

Dottie awoke the morning of the ball and horseshoe tournament to a text that said: CALL ME from Joe. Rubbing her eyes, and not really able to think clearly, she hit send and called Joe. The clock on her bedside table said it was only 8:30. Six hours until the horseshoe tournament and just under twelve until the ball. Plenty of time to figure out any emergency or difficult situation.

Three rings and Joe picked up.

"Hey," he said out of breath.

"Hey," she repeated.

"Did. You. Just. Wake. Up?" he panted.

"Yesh," she yawned as she shuffled out of bed into the kitchen.

"Oh. Sleep well?"

"Joe, are you running?" Dottie asked.

"Oh, yeah. I do ten miles every morning, there is a great—"

"I don't mean to be rude, because I really do want to learn everything there is to know about you, especially your super fun, early morning runs," a little sarcasm dripped into the last sentiment, "but, I doubt you texted me in all caps to ask how I slept or tell me that you run every morning," she took a sip of coffee.

"Right," she could tell he stopped running.

"Uh, oh. What's wrong?" she asked quickly waking up.

"Well, Heather got called into New York to do a photo shoot. She had a car pick her up really early this morning. It's for a clothing designer's new line. This was the big contract she was waiting for."

"Wow." Dottie marveled. "That's... amazing!"

"Yeah, well... it means I don't have a partner for horseshoes. And you're down one celebrity. She promised to tweet all day and she wanted me to text her pictures that she will post on Instagram for us but—"

"That's great Joe, but who can play in her place?" she cut him off.

"Well, I was thinking... you."

Silence fell on the line.

"Dottie, are you there? Did the phone disconnect? Hello?"

"I'm still here," she sighed. "Don't you think—"

"No," Joe stopped her thought.

"But—"

"Dottie, I want it to be you," Joe said resolutely.

"Joe... "Dottie whispered.

"I know," he comforted. "I am scared too, but it's

going to happen eventually. People will see us together. And now that Heather has her contract, and Harold is off in New York with his big job, you and I are free to be together."

Silence again.

"Okay," Dottie both gave in to his request and felt her smile radiate to her toes.

"Okay," he agreed. "Oh, Dottie, it's my agent. I... need to take this. I'll call you back in a little bit, ok?"

"Sure! Bye." she longingly said.

"Bye," he replied warmly then took the other call.

She turned on the TV and waited for Joe to call back. Around noon she still hadn't heard back from him. Instead of worrying about it, Dottie decided to get dressed and headed over to his house. Before she left, she packed up the dress, makeup and hair products. She would stop at the museum, drop off the dress and her other things upstairs so she could get ready there and then would walk over to Joe's.

When she arrived, she was greeted by Murray, who had found a stool and was doing his crossword in front of the pipe and drape that was sealing off the ballroom.

"Don't trust me, Murray?" She sighed.

"Nope, we don't Dottie," he said not looking up from his crossword. "Hetty said you might be by to drop things off, so here I am. Just in case."

"Fine," she laughed. "Is Hetty in the kitchen?"

"Yes, I am!" Hetty yelled.

"Great," she hollered back as she started up the stairs. "I'm just dropping off my dress, and I'll be heading next door. Did you hear? I'm playing in the horseshoe tournament today!"

There was a small bedroom upstairs that had a bathroom attached. They had left it this way in case they had anyone needing the room as a bridal suite or something like that to get ready. There was a daybed and a few chairs. Mostly it stayed locked. Dottie opened the closet door and hung the dress from the top of the door. Unzipping the garment bag, she let the dress out, so it wouldn't wrinkle. She set her canvas bag carrying her accessories down on the daybed and then hurried back down the stairs.

At the bottom, Hetty stood like a prison matron with hands in fists on both of her hips. Her entire head moved with Dottie as she descended. "What did you say?" Hetty turned back asking the question as she neared the bottom of the stairs.

"I'm playing horseshoes." Dottie was matter-of-fact about playing a sport, when Hetty knew she was not the athletic type.

"But we agreed that you needed to get ready and supervise things going on here," Hetty reminded her.

Gently brushing past Hetty, Dottie walked into the room where the bar was set up. A pair of khakis greeted her as she walked in the room, "Hey Bart," she said, and the man stood up, revealing a gray head of hair, and a broom mustache on his face to match.

"Dottie, good to see you," he said waving. "Eggnog is almost done, and we've prepped the hot cocoa. I've got a crock pot back here to keep the cocoa warm, and as you can see the glassware is all set up on the bar. I'm already to go." Hetty groused at Bart's admission. He leaned in and whispered, "I also have Irish Cream and Whiskey back here for the adults," he winked. "After all, happy people are more likely to open their pockets and give donations!" He lightly patted her on the shoulder.

"Great, thank you," Dottie smiled. Then turning to her left she saw the two silver garment racks had been assembled and hangers were hanging from their single bars. Numbers hung from the hooks.

"And I see our friends from the yearbook committee have already been here," she mused.

"Yup, I think you just missed them. They were upstairs looking at the exhibit for a bit, and then I think they went to go get pictures of the house next door," Bart relayed. "But they said they would be back by seven-thirty at the latest."

"Fantastic," Dottie exclaimed as she turned on her heel and walked to the kitchen. Hetty's face was getting a little grumpier. "And how are things in here, Don? Oh, hey Mel. I didn't know you were going to be here so early," she asked the skinny waitress with the mousy blond hair and big eyes that usually worked breakfast on the weekends.

"Everything is great. I just came to give Don a hand, since he is headed over to the tournament, but we prepped a lot at the diner yesterday. So, I think I'll get to go over and watch some of the games!"

"See," Dottie turned to Hetty, "Everything is going to be fine if I'm not here."

"Oh, fine!" Hetty conceded.

"Besides, Joe will be good at horseshoes because he's got the baseball arm, but me... I couldn't hit the broad side of a barn! I doubt we will make it past the second round! I'll still be available to make everything ready over here. Everything will totally be ready on time. Promise me you'll stop stressing! I'll see you in a bit?" Dottie said the last over her shoulder as she headed out the kitchen door.

"We'll be over soon!" Don said.

* * *

Dottie climbed through the bushes, for old times' sake which was harder done than said, with the all of the bushes grown back together. That plus the snow that had fallen overnight had built up around the bases of the bushes creating a drift. Joe's property could sell today, and this might be her last chance to walk through them. She made her way down to the house. A security guard stationed outside on the porch opened the front door for her.

"I'm glad they've got you under cover," she stated. He looked at her confused. "I mean because it's supposed to snow more today."

"Yes, ma'am," was all the stoic man in an all-black suit and tie said.

"Hmm. Just like they are in the movies," she muttered to herself about the stoic security guard as she was walking through the living room. "Joe?" she called up the stairs.

"In here," he said from the kitchen. Dottie walked in to find him on the phone, trying to pace, but he was tethered by the cord. "It's my agent," he mouthed.

"Oh, I'll..." she looked at her watch. It was just after two in the afternoon already. Where had the time gone? She pointed at her watch and whispered, "We need to get out there."

"Be there in a minute," he mouthed.

Dottie led herself back through the house and ran into a smart looking woman who was dressed in a burgundy suit and matching lipstick, with her brown hair up tied up in a neat chignon. "Hey Dottie," the woman exclaimed giving her a hug.

"Hey Kate, I didn't expect to see you here," Dottie was surprised to see one of the best realtors in the county in the house. "Well, Joe didn't want to mess around. There are five security and me to let people into the house look it over. And then a couple of the high school kids volunteered to take shifts for the donations to tour the house."

"Oh. That's... great." She realized in this moment that she had equally mixed feelings about Joe selling his house as she did about giving up the museum. "We think so. I'm gonna do my darndest to sell this house today. He's done so much work and it looks amazing. I'm sure it won't be on the market long," Kate was just a little too perky about the whole thing, Dottie thought.

"Well great. If you see Joe, tell him I went out to the barn," Dottie said walking out of the house.

"Great. See you later!" Kate shouted after her.

The chatter in the barn could be heard from thirty yards away. The great building still amazed Dottie. From the outside, it was all graying wood that although aged, still was strong and durable. Walking inside through the doors that had been thrown wide open to welcome anyone and everyone, Dottie looked around. She was amazed to see all of the bleachers were packed.

"It's a ten-dollar donation to get in, ma'am," a teenager squeaked from the opposite side of the table at the front of the barn.

"Oh, I'm—" Dottie started,

"She's a contestant. In fact, she's my teammate."

The stunned teenager stood and tried to salute and put his hand out to shake all while contemplating jumping over the table when he saw Joe standing in front of him. "Mr. Thomas, it's a great honor to meet you. My name is Kenny. I want to be a catcher just like you," squeaked the gangly teen who grinned through his mop of a hairdo.

"Hey, Kenny," Joe held out his hand. "I'm Joe Thomas."

Kenny looked nervously between Joe's hand and Dottie's face. Dottie nodded letting the young man know that it was ok, and it was all really happening. Kenny took Joe's hand with both of his and vigorously shook it. "Wow. This is… I just can't…Mr. Joe Thomas, sir. This is one of the best days of my life. Wow. Do you have any pointers for a guy like me? You know, a catcher."

Joe smiled. This was a regular way for him to be greeted. He had appreciated being in the small town around people who had known him before the fame. Although, he had to admit, it was a proud moment to be able to reach kids who had a similar dream to his own.

"Keep doing all the things coach tells you, especially the taking care of your body," Joe suggested taking the kid's hand and shaking it, as well as putting his other hand on the kid's shoulder. Kenny started to shake out of pure amazement that his hero was talking to him. "Also, be kind. And always, always respect women," he smiled at Dottie. Then letting go of

Kenny's hand he offered his elbow to Dottie. She looked at him in amazement and looped her hand through his elbow and they walked into the middle of the ring.

CHAPTER TWENTY-EIGHT

To her amazement, Dottie was much better at horseshoes than she originally thought. When the tournament began all of the pits were full. Two people on each team. The barn was a buzz with excitement. Many friends she knew and had grown up with had shown up to support, both the tournament and the museum. A true feeling of community was in the air, and Dottie cherished it. After feeling like her beloved museum had been forgotten, this turnout meant that it, or at least she meant something. This community wouldn't let her down. They would put on a great show for them today, she silently promised as she looked around the barn.

It was already established that Hetty should be the master of ceremonies for both the tournament and for the ball this evening. Dottie disliked public speaking and Hetty was more of the public figure with all of her pageant experience. Both owning the diner and all of her experience in pageants made her right at home with making public speeches in front of many people.

"Ladies and Gentlemen," a hush fell over the crowd as Robert called to the crowd. To make it a festive occasion, Robert was to introduce Hetty. She insisted on being announced. Robert took the honor proudly, as his community spirt was high as both the high school principal and a board member for the museum. "Welcome to the first annual celebrity horseshoe tournament." The crowd cheered excitedly. "Some of you may be wondering why we're playing a summertime game in the winter. Well, recently during an accident involving the roof of the museum, photos were found of a tournament over a century ago. As many of you know we just had our two-hundredth year anniversary at the school, which is the oldest high school in the country. This tournament was part of our history. Winter horseshoes were an East Haddam tradition that started when a horse got stuck in the pond on campus when it froze. The horseshoe team was nearby and used the horseshoes to free the horse from the ice. The next year to commemorate, they started the winter horseshoe tournament. And those photos can be seen at a new exhibit at the museum. I invite you all to go visit early and often!" The crowd cheered again. "And now I would like to introduce you to the lady of the hour, Hetty Lynnd."

To raucous applause, Hetty walked to the center and took the microphone from Robert. "Thank you, Principal Sampson!" Loud cheering greeted her again. "Thank you all for coming out today to help raise money for the museum. Now, your entrance fee has done a lot already, but we still have goals to meet to keep this treasured museum open. History costs a lot! So please show your community spirit by purchasing snacks and beverages donated by local restaurants and there are plenty of Dottie's famous gingerbread cookies, too! And of course, you can just give us your money! There are red donation buckets at the entrance. Feel free to drop in any and all of your cash! And now, without further ado, let me introduce our competitors."

Announcing the competitors by teams, she introduced those with celebrity pairs first, then the town teams, which got more applause. Saving Dottie and Joe for last, Hetty announced Joe first to a standing ovation. As the applause died down, which took a few minutes, Hetty announced Dottie, "And now the woman of the hour, Dottie Henry." Loud applause erupted again and Hetty handed the microphone off to Dottie.

"I'm completely overwhelmed," said Dottie. "Thank you all so much. As you know the East Haddam Historical Society has been around for over a century. The house it is in was donated many years ago, and recently was supposed to close due to a lack of funds and visitors. Although I'm told that we're very close to meeting our goal to keeping the museum open," loud cheering greeted her again. "As Principal Sampson said, please come visit the museum. We have an amazing new yearbook exhibit where you can look through and browse the actual yearbooks of more recent years. We also have a database that is on loan from the high school that has scanned yearbooks in it from the turn of the century and farther back so you can explore and research our town history." Applause broke out. Dottie waited for it to die down before continuing. "We also debuted this week an exhibit starring our own crowned beauty, Hetty Lynnd. You can see her rise to queendom and some of her crowns and gowns!" More cheering. "And, Joe Thomas," loud cheering required her to pause again. Dottie laughed at it, and Joe waved to the crowd, which made them cheer louder, "Joe has opened his house, and you can walk through for a five-dollar donation. So, if between matches, you want to go tour a house that a major league baseball player grew up in, just head out to the house. It's also for sale, so if anyone wants to buy it—" more wild applause, "unfortunately, that money doesn't go to the museum though," Dottie looked over at Joe and smiled. He winked at her. Dottie handed the microphone back to Hetty.

"Now contestants, head to your pits," Hetty addressed those standing with her. She then talked to the audience as everyone moved to their playing positions. "Some of you may know that Heather Smolen was supposed to be with us today, but she had a last-minute engagement that she was needed for. Now, to the rules," Hetty described how the game was played and a quick review of how scoring happened. She also introduced the referees. Then, the play began.

At first Dottie's throws were very short. Joe coached her telling her to raise her arm just a little more before she let go of the shoe to get it to go farther. By the end of her first game she had hit the post once and gotten very close the other times. Joe, of course had three ringers.

With twelve teams, six advanced. Dottie and Joe barely won their match. If it wasn't for a ringer on Joe's last throw, they wouldn't have made it. Both of the other celebrities made it into the top six. A planned twenty-minute break was announced between each round. Right as their match ended, Joe's phone rang. He looked at the screen and then at Dottie.

"I... I have to get this. I promise, if it takes more than twenty minutes, I'll hang up and will be back to play the next round," he winked at her, then answered the phone and dashed off.

Dottie decided that she needed to occupy her time with something, so she walked up to Joe's house. It was packed.

"I've started to have the security guard hold them at the front. If one person leaves, they can let another in. Too many people in a room and you can't actually see the house," Kelly mentioned to Dottie when they found each other. Kelly had stationed herself in the kitchen. Her stack of fliers was getting low.

"Have you had any real interest in buying the house?" Dottie asked.

"Actually, there was a family who have two young children that were interested. They like all the land," Kelly reported.

"Wow, that's great. A family would be great here," Dottie replied.

"And one of your celebrity guests said he was interested in the place. He likes how close, yet far away from the city it is," Kelly continued, "both took information on the house, and said they would get back to me."

"Pardon me," interrupted a shorter lady in her early

thirties, with brown shoulder length hair, "but are you the realtor? I hear this house is for sale."

"Yes," Kelly said to the lady. Then to Dottie she whispered, "I'll keep you posted."

As Dottie meandered back to the barn walked behind two ladies that she recognized from but didn't remember their names. One was a blonde and the other a brunette Dottie was pretty sure they were two or three years behind her in high school. Their conversation drifted back over their shoulders and Dottie heard every word.

"It's so great to see Joe Thomas back in East Haddam again," said the blonde.
"Yeah, I know my husband loves that one of his favorite baseball players is from here," replied the brunette.

"My husband can't believe I went to school with him. Mark couldn't believe that I just walked right up to him and said hello," laughed the blonde.

"Oh, right! Your husband has always fit so well in the community, I always forget that you met him when you were away for college. He fits in so well in the small-town life here," commented the brunette.

"Well, it's too bad Joe has to go back to Los Angeles," replied the blonde.

Yeah. It's a shame he's selling his house. We probably won't ever see him again once he sells the house and goes back to baseball," sighed the brunette.

Dottie stopped walking. Joe had a job. In Los Angeles. And he was just about to sign his contract for who knows how long. She couldn't ask him to move back here to this tiny town and give up his dream. Could she do a long-distance relationship?

Everyone always said they were hard.

"You ok, Dottie?" Bart's voice snapped her out of her thoughts.

"No. Um, yes. Sorry, what?"

Bart put a hand on her shoulder as if he wanted to make sure she was steady. "The next round is about to start. Should we?" Bart offered her his arm. A chivalrous gesture. One that Dottie was pretty sure he was offering it also to steady her.

"I was pretty nervous my first football game," Bart stated as they started to walk toward the barn. "What?" Dottie turned her head and looked at him.

"You know, when I started my first game in high school. I was terrified," Bart thought she was nervous about playing the next round of horseshoes.

"Ah, right," she decided to play along. "So, what did you find helped you?" She asked.

Bart didn't have much time to describe all of the tricks he had but he got through quite a few in the two minutes it took to walk the rest of the way to the barn.

"Thanks, Bart. And good luck," she said has he dropped her off at her pit. Joe was nowhere in sight, and Hetty was walking out to the center to announce the next round.

"Where's Joe?" Hetty mouthed to Dottie.

Dottie shrugged and looked around. Then as if on cue Joe came jogging through the bleachers and Dottie pointed.

Spotting him, Hetty raised the microphone and announced the next round.

"Sorry," Joe said breathlessly as he reached Dottie.

"Everything ok?" Dottie asked.

"Yeah, just... contract negotiations," Joe admitted

hesitantly.

"Oh?" Dottie wasn't sure if she wanted to know. Instead, she picked up a horseshoe and vehemently flung it. Ding-a-ling-a-ling sounded as her horseshoe hooking around the post for ringer. Her frustration momentarily subsided. She screamed and hopped up and down and hugged Joe. Then she quickly pushed him away and threw the other one. It looked to be half an inch away from the post.

"Great job," he said and held up a hand for a high five.

"Thanks,' she lightly and quickly slapped his hand and then looked away. She couldn't stand it. He was so close. Of course, this would happen. Years after she buried her feelings and then uncovered them, he reveals he feels the same and then they have to try to manage a relationship over a distance? It wouldn't work. These things just didn't work. Dottie had to turn off her feelings now. Before they sunk in too deep and she would spend years trying to cover up this broken heart.

"Dottie? You ok?" Joe had lightly touched her elbow. She was standing with her arms crossed tightly looking out at the playing field. Her face was scrunched in anger.

"Huh?" she said only just realizing how tensed she had made her body.

"Are you ok? Are your nerves getting to you?" Joe asked coming around to face her, but still had his hand gently cupping her elbow.

"Yes. I mean, no. What are you asking?" she stumbled with her words.

"Are you nervous about this game?" Joe said softly

and kindly.

"Why would I be nervous about the game?" she said a little loudly and waved her arms around in a circle.

"You zoned out and I can't think of any other reason you would be like this," Joe was concerned. "I was trying to tell you it was time to change sides."

"Oh. No. I'm... fine," Dottie spat.

"Uh oh, you're using the eff word..."

"I don't know what you're talking about," she was getting a little irritated. "I don't swear, Joe Thomas."

He laughed. "No, I... you said 'fine.' My father always said that when a woman uses that word, which begins with an "F" that nothing is even close to resembling fine," he stepped a little closer. "So, what is wrong."

"It's nothing," she protested, "I'm—"

"Fine," they said in unison.

"Stop that." She gave him a gentle smack on his shoulder and cracked a smile. "Let's play and we can talk about it later." Because he was giving her a look of disbelief, she repeated, "I promise we will talk later. I'm just in my head, and now isn't the time to talk about it."

Joe followed Dottie to the other side. They were picking up their horseshoes and Joe's phone rang again. He pulled it out of his pocket, tapped a quick text then put it back in his pocket. They tossed their shoes again and Joe checked his phone which seemed to vibrate a lot in the last pitch. He scowled and tapped something back.

"Everything ok?"

"Fine," he said and sighed.

"Uh oh… now you're using the eff word." she said with a serious face, then smiled to show she was teasing. "So, when we're done here, we're gonna talk about my thing and your thing." Her smile made him relax a little.

"Fine," he said, smiling at her in agreement.

They finished the round and miraculously won. Dottie was so surprised her face was in shock through Hetty's announcement.

"Ladies and Gentlemen, that wraps up round two," applause rung through the barn. "Before you all leave for the twenty-minute break, I want to remind you all that we will have two more rounds. Because we had only three teams to advance to the semi-final round, a wild card position is going to the losing team that had the most points." Hetty paused for a bit of drama. "If you've been paying attention you know the point leader from the last round. And the team to advance to the semi-finals is," she paused again. "Team Kevin and Kaitlyn! Other teams to advancing are Dottie and Joe, Bart and Ashley, and Don and Aaron." Applause. "Congratulations to all of our semi-final teams. We will see you back here in twenty minutes."

Dottie turned to talk to Joe, but he was nowhere to be seen. Dottie sighed to herself. He disappeared again during Hetty's announcement.

CHAPTER TWENTY-NINE

There was banging on the door. "Hurry up, we're going to miss it," bellowed the loud voice at the door.

"I'm coming!"

Dottie leaned over the sink to put on her lipstick. There. Perfection.

More banging.

"You know the door is open, right?" Dottie hollered over her shoulder. Hetty could be so irritating sometimes.

She heard the click of the door knob turning as she walked out of the small bathroom. Hetty slipped in through the door and closed it behind her. Turning around Hetty gasped.

"Wow!" Hetty said as she walked into the room. "You look—"

"Amazing?" Dottie finished for her.

"Yes! I knew that was the right dress!" she said as she crossed the room and took Dottie by the hand.

"If you ask me, there aren't enough red heads that dress up in green these days."

"Well," Dottie said taking on a haughty voice and pretending to fan herself, "Red and green are just so Christmassy, so everyone would be jealous," they both laughed. It felt so good to be silly what with all of the seriousness lately surrounding the museum.

After the tournament, Joe dashed away again, to who knows where. He wasn't at his house. Dottie had looked. They hadn't gotten a chance to talk. Dottie was getting nervous. His avoidance wasn't a good sign.

"What? What's wrong," Hetty asked as Dottie had stopped laughing and made a scrunched-up face of worry.

"Nothing," Dottie relaxed her face and fanned it again, this time trying to keep the tears away.

"Nope. I know you too well Dottie Henry. We are not leaving this room until you tell me why you're making that face."

"Well…"

"Take a deep breath. That helps hold the tears down," Hetty suggested. Dottie did. "And another." Dottie did. "One more," Dottie's shoulders relaxed.

"Well. Joe lives in Los Angeles."

"Yes," Hetty confirmed.

"And I live here in Connecticut," Dottie stated the obvious.

"Yes," Hetty confirmed again.

"And it's thousands of miles," Dottie threw her arms up in the air.

"Uh huh…" Hetty scrunched her forehead in confusion.

Feeling her friend wasn't getting any of the problematic issues Dottie was trying to convey, she took Hetty by the arms and shook her. "This is never going to work."

Hetty wriggled out of Dottie's death grip, "Honey, you're gonna wrinkle me if you keep doing that. Now. Let's talk this through. True, Joe has a job in Los Angeles, that we're not sure he's getting again—"

"I'm sure he is!" Dottie interrupted. "His agent kept calling him all day long."

"Right, but that could be about anything," Hetty reasoned.

"Uh, I'm pretty sure that the job of an agent is to negotiate contracts and get jobs for players. So, I'm pretty sure he will be in *Los Angeles*," Dottie reasoned.

"Okaaay… well, the good thing is that you're both adults and can figure things out. Although, we've had to lead you both by the nose to each other, so the jury is still out. But don't you worry, between Frank, Murray and me, we're going to make sure this relationship gets every chance it can. It's been a long time in the making."

Dottie looked aghast at her friend. "What are you saying?"

"I'm telling you that we're not going to let you and Joe run away from each other any longer. No matter how far apart you are," Hetty said with all seriousness. "Baseball season isn't that long. And Los Angeles isn't that far. Plus, there is this crazy invention called an airplane that magically transports people—"

"Hetty! Be serious!"

"Dottie, I am," Hetty started to chuckle. "Besides, it's so great to see you as happy as you are around Joe.

This crazy relationship that should have happened decades ago!" Hetty's laugh bubbled out. She was overjoyed for her best friend. It was infectious and Dottie started to laugh too.

As quickly as the laugh started, Dottie stopped laughing and looked terrified.

"What if I made the wrong decision. What if it doesn't work out?" Dottie pained.

"Alright," Hetty stopped laughing and had a solemn look on her face. She sighed. "Well, like I said, it's not like Los Angeles is that far away. Just a plane ride. And you want to visit new places, right? So, this will give you to do that. The museum is closed a few days a week anyway," Hetty walked over to her friend and took her by the hand. "And you've lived this long without him. When something is meant to be it works itself out. Just believe. Tis the season for miracles." Hetty reassured her. Dottie still didn't look convinced, so Hetty continued. "It's obvious to anyone who was in that barn today that you're in love with each other. I had to squash rumors all day that he broke up with that model for you—"

"Really?" Dottie looked hopeful and as if she was holding in a secret. "Well, I don't think you have to do that anymore." Dottie rolled her eyes upward coyishly showing she had a secret.

"What? Why? Did Joe say something?" Hetty got excited.

"No, Heather did actually. Apparently, she texted Joe during the tournament. The thing she was in New York for today? The photo shoot was only part of it. She booked a new television show. Joe said she texted saying that in the same press release about her new show, Heather mentioned that she and Joe amicably split because she is moving to New York to film." Dottie smiled.

"That's great news," Hetty squealed like a teenager.

"I know, right?" Dottie bounced on her toes. Then calmly stated," Joe said that it won't hit the news circuit completely for a few more days. But that it's up to me if I want to start telling people."

Hetty pulled Dottie in close and started to embrace her but then halted.

"Hetty, what's wrong?" Dottie asked.

"I'm so happy for you, but... I don't want to wrinkle you," Hetty was solemn.

"Oh Hetty!" Dottie said and pulled her friend in the rest of the way. "A little hug won't hurt this dress. Friends are worth wrinkling for. Plus, I'm feeling so wonderful, I could care less about how I look!"

Pushing back out of her friend's arms, Hetty looked aghast. "Take that back Dorothy Henry!"

"Fine! Fine," Dottie threw her arms up in the air. "I do love how I look tonight," a smile lit up her face and she did a twirl in her beautiful dress.

"Good!" Hetty said looking placated.

"And..."

"There's more?" Hetty questioned in surprise.

"Yeah. It gets better. The museum looks like it will be open for a while. I received seven deposits today for weddings to be held here," Dottie said calmly.

"*Seven!*" Hetty echoed shrilly.

"Yes, *SEVEN!*" Dottie shouted and started jumping up and down. "And there are inquiries for twelve more, including some for the following year!"

They both jumped up and down and made loud giggling noises.

"Are you girls having a slumber party up there or what?" Don hollered up the stairs.

"No, honey! Dottie just got good news. Be right down," Hetty hollered back to her husband. "He hates to be left out," she winked at Dottie. "We should get down there, though. The natives are getting restless and we should probably open the doors and start this shindig."

"Right!" Dottie said. Hetty turned to walk out.

"Hetty, wait!

"What is it?" Hetty turned back suddenly with a little fear in her eyes.

"Hetty, you're my best friend."

"Yeah, honey," Hetty said as if it was a simple fact.

"I love you so much. You're always supportive and strong and just always there for me. I don't know what I did to deserve—"

"Oh stop! You're gonna make me cry!" Hetty waved a hand in front of her face to shoo away the tears and took Dottie's hand in hers. "I love you, too, crazy lady." She squeezed Dottie's hand before letting go then turned toward the door and took steps toward it. "Now, let's get downstairs!"

"Right behind, ya!" Dottie hollered as she dashed into the bathroom to take one last look in the mirror. Turning off the lights behind her, she closed the door to the bedroom and started down the stairs. A face looked up at her and she met his sparkling eyes.

"Hi," she said breathlessly to him on the fourth step.

"You look...stunning," Joe said as she stepped

down next to him.

Blushing, Dottie said, "You do too. I think I'll write to the commissioner of baseball and see if I can persuade him into making tuxedo's the league uniform." She reached forward and gently smoothed his lapels then looked up.

They gazed into each other's eyes just floating there in the foyer of the museum. But their moment was interrupted when Hetty came from around the drape that was still up in front of the ballroom. Murray was still guarding it when Dottie came back from the competition. She barely noticed as she dashed upstairs to get dressed. The tournament went longer than expected, and Dottie had very little time to get dressed, let alone peek at the ballroom. Still Murray guarded it. He was nowhere to be seen now.

"She's out here, you guys," Hetty yelled through the curtain.

Don slipped out followed by Frank. They both took one side of the drape and looked at Dottie with anticipation of her reaction.

"Dottie," called Murray from the other side of the curtain, "are you ready?" Murray asked.

"As I'll ever be, Murray," she called back, then looked at Joe and shared a smile.

"Alright, boys. Take it away," Murray instructed. Don and Frank pulled at the pipe and drape, and it came apart at the top and the fabric slipped away like magic. Joe reached for her hand as she took two steps forward and gasped.

CHAPTER THIRTY

The room looked like a sparkling winter wonderland. The rugs had been rolled up and the light hardwood floor was lit with a bright wash of light to make it look like it was whitewashed. The dark wooden walls had been covered with pipe and drape and the wooden walls were hidden by soft sheets of iridescent white and blue making the magical effect of a winter wonderland.

There were clusters of three Christmas trees of varying heights in each the corner of all wrapped around their bases in piles of what looked like snow. The tree that Hetty and Joe decorated just off to the left of the band stand. A short riser was in front of the rounded windows, and the six-piece band sat there dressed in whites and light blues. Clusters of lights and crystals hung from the ceiling making it look like icicles were hanging down. And in the center, the chandelier was wrapped with the iridescent fabric.

Over in one corner there was a photo area with a five-foot snowman and a backdrop that looked like a snowy mountain. To top it off, it had started snowing outside, so it looked like the entire room was inside a snow globe.

Dottie found she was in the middle of the room just slowly turning in awe.

"Do you like it?" Murray inquired.

"Like it?" She almost tackled Murray with a hug. "I love it," she said muffled into his shoulder.

"He wasn't the only one who did anything!" Frank protested.

"Oh, Frank! Thank you too." And Dottie gave him a big hug.

"He's taken, Dottie. Get your own," an older female voice pulled them apart.

"Marilyn, you know no one could take the same place in my heart as you," Frank said as he looked at his wife. Then took her by the hand, twirled her and kissed her deeply.

"Thank you, Don," Dottie said as she quietly hugged him while Frank and Marilyn kissed. Dottie then turned to the group and remarked, "I can't believe all of you did so much for..." she looked upward as to not let the tear that was forming in her eye drop and ruin her makeup.

"I hope you're wearing that waterproof mascara I gave you," Hetty joked.

Dottie laughed. "I love you all. I don't know why I thought I'd want to ever leave. I'd miss you all too much. I'm so glad I've decided to stay in East Haddam."

Murray whooped, Hetty clapped and the rest

joined in shouting and cheering.

"Well, we should get ready, I think people are starting to arrive," Hetty said as she pointed to the door where six or seven people had just walked into the front room. "I'll go," Hetty said, looking at Dottie then saying something to Joe with her eyes. She started to walk out of the room, and snapped her wrist at the band, and said, "Hit it boys!"

They started to play a slow Christmas tune. Don went off to the kitchen to check on the food. Murray saw a friend of his and walked over to say hello. And Frank and Marilyn started to slowly dance.

Dottie was just about to start walking out to the front, when Joe said, "That's a good idea," and he reached out for Dottie's hand and pulled her into his arms. He put her hand on his shoulder then put his on her waist and led her as they casually danced in each other's arms.

"So... you're staying in town," he asked.

"Yes. The museum needs me. And," she said looking around the room, but seeing the whole museum in her mind's eye, "I think I need it, too."

"Ah. So, definitely not moving to New York then," Joe reaffirmed.

She looked him in the eye and laughed. "No. Not moving to New York. Oh, and probably not going to be a multimillionaire anytime soon," she frowned. "Harold left a message during the tournament saying that the company went in a different direction and they no longer want my recipe."

"I'm sorry. That's too bad," Joe commiserated.

"I don't know," Dottie was thoughtful. "I've always believed that everything happens like it is supposed to."

"How do you mean?" Joe cocked his head a little and gave her a questioning look.

"Well..." she sighed thinking of an example, "Like me throwing the wreaths on your head. If I hadn't, we wouldn't be here now."

"How do you figure that?" questioned Joe skeptically.

"Well, if no wreaths, then you wouldn't have forgotten the new doorknob and gone back to get it the day that this roof leaked. So, you wouldn't have been dragged into helping and fallen through the roof. And if you hadn't found the pictures when you fell through, the ideas for the horseshoe fundraiser and the yearbook exhibit wouldn't have happened."

Joe smiled a big knowing smile. "So, what you're saying is that if I wouldn't have come home to fix my parents' house to get out of the weird funk I was in with baseball, I wouldn't have gotten hit on the head, then fallen in love with you, and then when I got the offer to move to Boston as their starting catcher for the next two seasons, I wouldn't have taken it?"

"Nope," pragmatically she replied. It took another moment for it all to register. Her eyes got big and she stopped dancing. She looked up and their eyes met. "Wait—"

"Dottie!" Interrupted Robert. "So good to see you, the place looks amazing. I would like you to meet Amber Randall, she is a local news reporter who—"

Robert started to pull Dottie into the sea of people. She looked back at Joe who just grinned happily, and he mouthed, "Go."

Reflecting his grin, Dottie was enveloped by the

party.

There were eighty people who paid in advance.
More than expected showed up at the door. They
maxed the museum's capacity and one hundred and
ten people were in attendance. Dottie just couldn't
turn anyone away. And the fire chief, who was in
attendance, said he would keep a watchful eye and
granted the overcapacity acceptable on such an
occasion as this. It was very tightly packed, about
thirty minutes into the evening. Music dropped out
leaving only voices talking loudly to be heard in their
small groups over the rest of the room. Through the
chatter, a booming voice came over the microphone.

"Ladies and Gentlemen," Hetty said looking
resplendent up on the bandstand. "Thank you all so
very much for coming this evening. I would like to say
a few things and then I will let you get back to
enjoying the evening.

"First, a huge thank you to Frankincense and
Myrrh Hardware. Frank and Murray decided this year
to combine their decorating expertise and tackled this
place instead of their own homes with the help of my
husband Don." Applause broke out over the room.
"Catering tonight is from my own personal favorite,
The Queen's Kitchen," a whistle was heard over the
clapping. "And the beverages are sponsored by Bert
from The Brick Bar in East Haddam. Thanks, Bert!"
Louder clapping and another whistle from another
direction.

"I would also like to invite all of you to tour the
museum, there are two brand new exhibits upstairs.
One featuring our fantastic high school that has two
hundred years of yearbooks," applause followed

Hetty's announcement. "As well as an exhibit featuring yours truly. You can see my embarrassing rise to stardom." Applause and whistling made Hetty blush just the tiniest bit before she continued. "And now, I'd like to bring up the woman of the hour, the one who keeps this place alive, Dottie Henry!" Loud applause erupted while Dottie made her way to the stage. The sea of people parted to allow her through. She stepped up on stage with the help of the trumpet player.

"Now Dottie," Hetty looked at her, but talked to the entire room. "I hear that people can rent out this space for events?"

Taking her cue, Dottie haltingly replied as if she was reading a script. "Why yes, Hetty. For a donation to the museum, you too could have an event just like this! And if you're thinking about having your corporate meeting, dinner, birthday party, or wedding here, you should talk to me soon, because we are booking up for this year fast!"

"Wow! I'll make sure to talk to you later Dottie," Hetty said still talking to the room but seeming to talk to just Dottie.

Nodding to Hetty, Dottie acknowledged the end of the conversation and started to walk off the stage. "Wait! Dottie, not so fast. There is a special visitor here tonight who came a little early just to see you!"

Looking around the crowd to see if there was someone she might recognize as the "special visitor," Dottie said, "Who—"

Just then a loud, "Ho! Ho! Ho!" was heard coming from the front hall. The entire room turned to see Santa with his sack over his shoulder. "Hello everyone, Merry Christmas!" he shouted as he walked into the room. Don had dressed up as Santa and looked very picturesque. He made his way up to the stage and set his sack down. It was full, and he opened it up. Hetty held the microphone up for him as he dug into the bag.

"Dottie, I hear you've been a very good girl this year. And I wanted to let the whole town know," he pulled out a big piece of foam board that was blank, "that between this event and the horseshoe tournament you've made over eighteen thousand dollars in donations." He flipped over the cardboard to reveal it was a giant check for $18, 275 that was made out to The East Haddam Historical Society.

Raucous applause rang through the crowd. Dottie couldn't believe it. She was handed the check.

"And that's not all," Santa continued. "Where is Joe Thomas?" A murmur went through the crowd as they all turned and looked to see if he was anywhere in the room. "Joe Thomas," Santa yelled loudly.

"Here!" Joe shouted as he walked back in from the front hall as he was hanging up his cell phone. "Ah good." Santa dug into his bag one more time and pulled out two golden horseshoes. "To the winning team of the first annual horseshoe tournament, I award Dottie Henry and Joe Thomas the coveted Golden horseshoes!" Santa handed the horseshoes over as flashes erupted both from the high schoolers who were photographing and from members of the crowd taking photos with their cell phones. Joe wrapped his arm around Dottie's waist, and she held her horseshoe at her side as she looked out. He held his up. They were the same image as the photo he had found only weeks earlier.

"Now," Hetty continued, "Eat, drink, dance, explore the museum, and feel free to empty your pockets into the blue donation buckets around the historical society tonight. Santa will also be giving out presents for donations in the front room where the bar and coat check are located for the next half hour, while they last!"

Applause erupted. Hetty grabbed Dottie by the arm and pulled her into a hug while she handed the microphone back to the band and cued them to start playing again. "Congratulations honey!"

"Thanks, Hetty. I truly couldn't have done it without you!"

"That's for sure. You couldn't survive without me," she said pulling back and winking at her friend. "I'm going to go set up Don, I mean, Santa to get more donations! And," Hetty said looking over Dottie's shoulder, "By the look in that man's eyes, it seems like you have something to do, too," she said. Dottie looked back to see Joe there, grinning and rubbing his neck. Something was up, and she needed to continue the conversation she was having with him earlier in the evening as the ball started.

Hetty moved by Dottie, and she couldn't be sure, but Dottie thought she saw Hetty mouth "good luck" to Joe as she walked away.

Turning to Joe, Dottie squinted at him, "That's right! We need to finish our conversation from before."

"We do," he nodded in agreement, "And I have other things I should probably say as well," Joe smiled knowingly.

"What do you—"

"We should probably get off of the stage and go somewhere a little quieter," he looked around pointedly directing her attention to at least fifty pairs of eyes looking at them eager with wonder.

Smiling uncontrollably, Dottie took Joe's hand and held her golden horseshoe in the other. Moonfaced was the perfect way to describe Dottie at the moment. In fact, if she squinted, she could imagine this very scene taking place almost twenty years earlier. When it should have. In this moment she knew that everything was right. Her mood was blissful.

But what could he have to tell her?

CHAPTER THIRTY-ONE

Joe led Dottie around the museum twice without finding a quiet place to talk. The place was packed wall-to-wall with people. Finally, he settled for the maintenance closet on the first floor under the stairs. Joe looked around them to make sure no one was watching and wouldn't think they were up to no good. With no one paying them any attention, Joe slipped through the door, pulling Dottie with him.

"Get the door!" he shouted in a whisper.

"Turn on the light first!" Dottie shout whispered back.

"Not until the door is closed. I don't want to be interrupted."

"Fine," she said pulling the door closed.

He then turned on the light. They reached for each other's hands but clanked their prize horseshoes instead. They laughed and he gently took her horseshoe and set both of theirs on a shelf. Joe reached out and clasped Dottie's now free hands in his. He sighed happily but heavily.

"So…" he started.

"So…" she repeated.

"I'm… moving," he shrugged the reveal.

"So, it seems," she smiled, then quickly dropped it. "Are you happy about this trade, or this move, or new contract, or whatever?" she asked then quickly qualified, "I just don't know a ton about baseball," she scrunched her nose in admission.

"There will be plenty of time to teach you," he smiled at her honesty. "And… I hope you'll come to see games," he timidly asked.

"Of course!" she said loudly, and he put a finger over his mouth and shushed her.

"They'll hear you if you're that loud," he admonished.

"Everyone is having such a great time, no one will hear us," she dispelled.

As if on cue, three pairs of shoes thunk thunk thunked overhead, and a loud laugh rang through the museum. Joe and Dottie put their heads closer and shared a laugh. They both felt like kids again hiding in this closet and sharing secrets.

"I guess you're right," he said looking up. Then looking back at her he said, "Yes, I am very happy with the choice to move closer to… "

"Home?" she finished for him.

"Yeah, I guess so," he laughed and rubbed his neck.

"Joe, did you…did you do this… for me? Did you change teams for… us?" She tried not to make her gulp too obvious when she said the last word. It was delightful to think that they might finally have a chance, but it was also overwhelming. Almost twenty years of repressed feelings and more years than that of hopes and dreams. Both of them had imagined finding not the perfect love but instead the right fit in love. And to find it finally. And it was literally next door. It seemed too easy. For both of them.

She hoped he would be honest.

He gulped, "Would it scare you away if I said it was for you?" he asked then quickly added, "Mostly."

"Mostly?"

"Well, Boston has a good team. It's no secret that my pitchers in Los Angeles aren't fond of me. That club has changed. Plus, one of the pitchers I trained recently that has won a lot of games is now in Boston. So, it looks like it might be a better fit. I'm actually inspired to play again for the first time in months, maybe years. I feel like a kid waiting for the season to start, instead of a guy with knees that only have a few years left hoping they'll stay good until I can get retirement plans figured out," he confessed. "I even talked to my coach; he's been like a father to me. I've been talking to him the entire time I've been here, because, well, he's the one who said I needed to come back here. To deal with my past. I thought it was because of my parents' house here. But it was more than that."

"Ah..." understanding only parts of what he said. "Well, that's...good." Her face screwed up.

"Yes, well, we both agree that it's good for me. But... is it good for... you?" he tried not to throw all of his hope next to the heart he was now wearing bravely on his sleeve. But he couldn't help it. He had loved this woman for so long. And the chance of spending every possible moment with her for the next few decades was worth sacrificing his pride at this moment. He hadn't taken the chance years ago, but he would now.

"I mean... I guess so..." Dottie was hesitant. "I mean, it will be nice to see you play in person. And if you're in Boston and I stay here, you'll be closer, and we can hang out—"

"Dottie, I don't mean to be this forward, but at this point I'm going to just put it all there. Risk it all. Dottie, I am in love with you and I will do whatever it takes to be with you. Even if that means I'll coach East Haddam High School baseball, I hear they're looking for a coach. I'd give up my pro ball career, if you want me to."

She cocked her head. He took it as her needing more convincing, so he continued.

"We can take it as slow or as fast as you need. I'm willing to commute from here, or even buy you a place in Boston even if you only stay there once a month," he let go of her hands and paced the two feet of the storage space like a caged tiger. "I don't know how to say this Dottie," he turned and stood two inches from her and looked her in the eye, "I want you. I don't want your friendship or your distant caring. I want you in my life. Tell me you don't want me, and I'll walk away and will someday forgive myself for the mistakes I made in not telling you sooner. In not fighting for you earlier in our lives. I've waited twenty years, Dottie. I'd gladly wait double that if there was even a glimmer of hope of being with you." His eyes pleaded for her to rescue him.

Slowly and gently, she placed her hands on the sides of his face. She studied his eyes and saw all the pain and fear and suffering. There was a tiny part of her in this moment that loved that she had the power to erase all of it. To make his world more peaceful, while doing the same for herself.

"I don't know what to say, Joe." He tried to look away, but she wouldn't let him. "Let me finish, please." He looked back, a little more afraid, but trying to cover it and keep himself calm inside. "I don't know what to say that could equal such a beautiful sentiment. Yes, Joe. I love you too. I'm over the moon that you signed a contract with Boston. As for real estate, yes to any and all of it. We can figure—"

As if on cue, Joe's phone rang.

"It's Kelly," he puzzled and held up the phone for Dottie to see, "I thought she was here at the party," he looked around as if he could see through the walls of the closet.

"Well answer it," Dottie said.

He nodded, and hit the button then said into the phone, "Hey Kelly!" while tapping the button for speaker and lowering the volume so they both could hear the conversation, but it wouldn't be audible outside their hiding spot.

"Hi," she replied. "I've got great news!"

"Great," he feigned. "Um, I'm here with Dottie and you're on speaker."

"Oh, hey Dottie," she plowed full speed ahead, "So, Joe. I know that its fast, but we actually got three offers on your house today. One a little low for a family of five. One for your asking price but they want to do a full inspection. And one all-cash offer to take the place as is."

Joe's eyes darted to Dottie who was mouthing "Wow!"

"How low was the family," Joe asked.

"About ten thousand under your asking."

"Hmmm…" Joe said, still trying to get a clue from Dottie who shrugged. "Do you have a good feeling on any of them in particular?" Joe asked Kelly.

"Well, I'm not supposed to have an opinion. But all cash is always a great way to go for everyone involved. It's also a friend of yours."

"A friend?" Joe replied.

"Yeah, it's the guy from the horseshoe tournament. He was saying he loves the air up here and wants to make the barn into a concert venue and make one of the bedrooms outfitted to be a recording studio."

"Hmmm… Kelly, how long do I have to think about it?"

"A few days. Have fun and let me know. I just wanted you to know the good news."

"Great! Thanks," Joe then hung up the phone.

"That's amazing!" Dottie threw her arms around Joe's neck. He remained stiff. "What?" she backed up. "What's wrong? Do you not want to sell?"

"Well," Joe asked, if I sell how does that effect you?"

"I mean, you're going to want a place in Boston, and the museum could thrive if there was a concert venue next door. Oooh! We could team up and do big events together," Dottie got excited. Then her excitement dropped, "Or is it that you want to stay in your parent's house? You know Joe, we could get our own place and make our own family and memories."

"You wouldn't... mind?"

"Which part?"

"Any. All?"

"Oh, Joe," Dottie laughed. "The sale could only help the museum. And we have plenty of time to figure out where we are going to live for the rest of our lives. There is the spare bedroom here in the museum, if you need it for the time being!"

"Well then... If you're sure...."

"Joe, my love. If we figured out how to keep the museum open for at least another year, we can figure out anything," she reassured him.

"Well, then I'll call her back." Joe started to redial her number but was preempted by a video chat request from Heather. "Why would Heather be calling?" Joe puzzled to himself.

"Maybe to see how the tournament went?" Dottie suggested.

Joe answered, "Hey, Heather," flatly. "Why are you... calling?"

"Hey Joe! Oh, is that Dottie there with you too? Hey Dee! How are you?"

"Fine, fine," Dottie moved in close to Joe so they both could see and be seen via his small phone screen.

"Aren't you two a cute picture!" Heather exclaimed, and Dottie reacted and moved away quickly, but Joe wrapped his hand around her waist and pulled her back. "Oh honey, don't worry! I already know about that!"

"Heather, did someone post it on social media?"

Joe asked.

"Well if they did, I didn't see it," Heather reported directly. "No, you idiot. Anyone looking at you two can see you are head over heels in love and if they talked to either of you for more than five minutes, you can see how perfect you are for each other," she said plainly with no ill will. "Do both of you forget I lived in a house with people for weeks and had to figure them out on a regular basis! Oooh, the stuff I could tell you—!"

"Well, thank you Heather. Maybe some other time," Joe strongly suggested. "So, what were you calling for?"

"Oh! I hear that Kevin Gray wants to buy your house. He has tons of money and needs a tax shelter, so don't be afraid to play hardball with him," she winked at them both. "Especially now that the property value in that neighborhood has gone up."

"Gone up? What do you mean," Dottie asked?

"Didn't anyone tell you?" Heather asked. "I thought for sure those two gossips would have told everyone by now."

"What are you talking about?" Joe interjected.

"Well, I guess I've spilled my own beans!" Heather laughed at her own joke. Seeing that neither Joe nor Dottie joined in she stopped. "Well, Dottie, I know you didn't want Joe's money to help the museum, but I thought that a mysterious benefactor to donate a new roof would be helpful. Joe told me all about how he fell through it. Then when you said you would help keep our cover by letting me mention that the wedding would be at your museum, I thought it would be a nice gesture on my behalf to make sure you had a good roof. Plus, I couldn't have the old shabby one in my social media posts," she winked as she meant the last part sarcastically.

"Heather, I can't believe you did this for me. For the museum. That's... there is no way I can repay... I just don't..." Dottie couldn't form a sentence. She was so overwhelmed what with the money from the tournament and ball, and Joe confessing his feelings and now this!

"Oh, honey don't mention it... but if you want to post on social media hashtag divas help divas and tag me in it, I know it would help us both," Heather gave another knowing wink.

"Sure I—"

Suddenly there was knocking at the door to the closet. Both Joe and Dottie became suddenly quiet and held their breath.

"Who is it?" Heather said as she looked back and forth between Joe and Dottie, then whispered at them, "Fraidy-cats!"

"Dottie, you in there?" Called Murray.

"It's Murray," she whispered for an unknown reason to Heather and Joe. Then she called, "Be out in a minute Murr!"

"Go, you crazy kids!" Heather blew them a kiss. "Oh, and Joe, sell your place!"

"Thanks, Heather," he said giving her a funny smirk and then hung up.

Dottie gave Joe a look asking if he was ready to leave their safe spot. This time it was he that shrugged.

"Well, no time like the present," she sighed and opened the door. Joe turned off the light as they walked out into the hall of the museum.

"Hey, Murray, what's happening?"

"Well, I should probably head home. The wife is getting... tired," Murray shrugged.

"Oh, I didn't even see Angela! She's here?" Dottie looked around.

"She's out in the car already. We were just about to leave, and I was turning the key in the ignition, and this popped out of my jacket," he said looking down at the opened envelope in his hand. It was face down and was carefully opened with a letter opener. It was a legal envelope that showed a little bit of the blue through the white that obscured the inner contents. "You see," he continued, "I got to thinking about this place after that dreadful meeting earlier in the month where the board decided to close you down," he shook his head. "Your family has been so wonderful to us over the years, and then with your father taking ill. Then you give up your dreams, for this place..."

Dottie waited patiently for him to continue. Joe wasn't so patient, and started to reach for the envelope, "Murray, do you mind if I..."

"Oh, no. Please!" Murray said, shaken from his reverie and handed the envelope to Joe.

"Well, with this place needing so many repairs, Frank and I were trying to help, but we knew you wouldn't just let us. And then that gal offered to pay for the roof—whoops!"

"You knew it was Heather?" Dottie asked. "I thought you said you didn't know who the mysterious benefactor was."

"Well, I... I guess now it's no harm letting the cat out of the bag," Murray shrugged.

"It's alright, Murray," Joe put his hand on Murray's shoulder, reassuringly. "She just told us," Joe laughed.

"Yes, well... I always knew this place was special... but I thought maybe there was a way to make sure that it couldn't get harmed again. So, I applied, and it was approved—"

"Dottie," Joe said quietly excited, "Murray got this house, this museum approved as an historical landmark."

"What?" Dottie asked putting her hand on Joe's wrist to move the paper closer so she could see it. Then she turned back to Murray, "You... you did this? For me?"

"Didn't take much, plus they already had to do the appraisal for the roof anyhow. So, I just sent in the paperwork, and I have a friend over in the records department. He called his friend at the registry, and... well, Bob's your uncle, you're registered."

Dottie jumped into Murray's arm's and hugged him tightly. "Now, now. Not too tight, Angela may be in the car, but there are others watching, and we don't want to start more rumors now, do we?" he joked and winked at Joe.

"Murray, this is the best Christmas present..."

"Well, you're welcome," Murray said and nervously looked toward the front door. "I'd better go, we can speak more another day about it. There are several things you need to still, but I'll help with the paperwork. I need to get to the car before Angela decides to drive herself home," Murray teased.

"Merry Christmas!" Dottie hollered after him. "Merry Christmas," he answered back over his shoulder as he walked out of the museum.

Dottie looked at Joe. "I…" she started to talk.

"I know. We can sort it all out tomorrow. But for now, we have one last dance before the end of the night," he asked hearing the music drift in from the ballroom.

"Sure," Dottie said as she took his hand and they walked together.

Just as they were entering the ballroom, she heard her name. It was Hetty. She pulled on Joe's hand and they stopped just under the doorway into the ballroom.

"Dottie, I just wanted to catch you before we head out. Did Murray find you? He was looking—"

"Yes! He got the museum landmarked!"

"He did? That old coot! Between the two of them, they're getting good at keeping secrets," Hetty winked.

"Speaking of," Dottie divulged, "you'll never guess who was the mysterious donor of the roof?"

"Who?" Hetty asked wide eyed.

"Heather," Joe said.

"Well, Merry Christmas," she kissed Joe on the cheek. Then she kissed Dottie on the cheek.

"Dottie, you're not a kisser… what's up?" Dottie queried.

Hetty laughed and looked up. Joe and Dottie were standing under a big ball of mistletoe. Joe turned Dottie in his arms and wrapped his arms around his waist. "Well, shall we?" he asked.

"Why, not?" Dottie smiled, "Everything else that happened unexpectedly today turned out really well, so I'll chance it," she joked.

Joe caressed Dottie's face with his thumb. He

looked into her eyes and he sparkled with happiness. Taking his time, as he now had the rest of their lives, he looked her face over memorizing it. He took a deep breath as she sighed. They had finally made it to where they were meant to be. Together. Joe leaned in and kissed Dottie.

"At last!' Hetty shouted, "My Christmas wish came true!"

ACKNOWLEDGEMENTS

Sometimes the muses and the fates just step in and tap you on the shoulder. Or shake you until you realize the direction they are pointing. In 2017 I was given the wonderful opportunity to work in beautiful Essex, Connecticut for the winter holiday season where a magical Christmas Train takes children to see Santa. The Nevins family adopted me and helped me heal from a deep trauma with good food and watching many a holiday themed romantic movie.

Performing is a funny life, as you not only become the character in your show, you become a family with your fellow performers. Then at the end of your contract, you move on. If you're lucky one or two of those relationships follow you for a while. However, I was given two lifelong friendships by Santa that year. Jessica and her family were one.

My friend Erin, the other.

In the winter of 2018, Erin and I were watching the same movie, she in East Haddam, Connecticut and me back in New York City. She texted that she wanted to play the best friend in one of these movies one day, and I needed to write it. To this day I don't know if she was joking or not. However, it sparked an idea, and two days later I started outlining. And five weeks later I was editing my finished book.

Those first, drawn out thank you's that seem barely

enough for the gifts I've been given go to Erin for the idea for this novel and Jess for giving me a warm place to land when I need it.

Next to my fantastic crew of support Alex, Grace, Michael, Rebecca, Renee, MommySuan, Lecinda, Dad (who actually does love model trains!), Audrey and especially to Derrick who didn't mind that I was an editing fiend on our vacation were more than once we chased pages down the beach that got swept away by the wind.

Thank you to my NPE family (Say Hooray!) thank you for our magical seasons together, and Ira for bringing me into this group which truly has changed my life. Also, thanks to my crazy Nutmegger friends Jill, Greg, LaLa, Christopher, and Sergeant King who are NPE adjacent.

I know this is cheating, but to those of you who are my support but don't find your name listed here: you ARE important, and I appreciate the love! If at any time you have ever asked me in person, via email or text or on social media about my writing, please know that it means a lot to me that you remembered and asked.

To those of you who tell me you're inspired by me or ask for me to chat about writing: please KEEP telling me and asking me. I love talking about creative process and inspiration! And I love inspiring others to follow their muses!

To all of my readers who came back, thank you, too! It's kind of that tree-falling-in-the forest phenomenon: you can write a book but, if no one reads it does it really exist?

ABOUT THE AUTHOR

Clare Solly is an actress and writer in New York City. She has severe cravings for seltzer and coffee. While not writing or performing Clare makes various appearances at office jobs, plans weddings, and ushers on Broadway. And has a master's degree in Psychology. She also is the apprentice director of The Bechdel Group, a theater company in New York that workshops new scripts that focus on roles for women and other under written about groups. A baseball fan since she was a child, Clare is a hopeless romantic growing up watching and rooting for the Cubs and the Padres. Clare sings, tap dances and pretends to go to cycling class. Her first novel *The Time Turner* is in paperback and eBook.

Made in the USA
Middletown, DE
05 December 2025

22753994R00166